His touch was everything she had ever imagined about love—tender, suggestive, thrilling. She stopped thinking and started feeling. For a moment she stood perfectly still within his arms, savoring the tantalizing warmth that was spreading over her, mixing up her thoughts. She felt his mouth on hers again in a soft kiss while his hands stroked her hair gently. She let out such a long, deep sigh that he pulled back and looked down at her, a question on his raised eyebrows.

"What's wrong?" he asked, his voice full of concern.

For a moment she couldn't respond. She opened her mouth to speak and nothing came out. She could swear she'd heard the tinkle of bells during their kiss and she knew that she definitely tingled inside! *How ridiculous! I'm not ready for this. I'm really losing it.*

Indigo Sensuous Love Stories

are published by

Genesis Press, Inc.
315 Third Avenue North
Columbus, MS 39701

Love Doesn't Come Easy

First Edition

Love Doesn't Come Easy

by

Charlyne Dickerson

Genesis Press, Inc

PROLOGUE

Gasping for breath, Jennifer Johnson struggled to awaken from the nightmare that had periodically plagued her sleep most of her life. Her body was moist from sweat, even though the San Francisco night air wafting through her half-raised bedroom window was cool enough to sleep under a blanket.

She struggled against the clamminess of the tangled sheet that had an inescapable hold on her. Groggily disentangling herself, she rolled over to the side of her bed. She slowly drew the back of her hand across her forehead, still feeling the insecurity, the loneliness, the isolation, the hopelessness she always experienced during the nightmare.

In her dream she sits on some metal steps of a large building with a blanket thrown around her. She sees dim lights in the windows above her, but it's pitch black where she is. Her fear of the dark increases and she draws the blanket closer. She hears the wail of sirens near her but cannot see the vehicles. Her sniffles increase as she waits for her mother to come back for her. Then she hears footsteps in the dark and calls out. A deep voice asks what she is doing out there by herself, but she is too frightened to give him an answer and her crying grows louder. He pulls her into his arms and tries to calm her while carrying her to a room with a lot of bright lights and people rushing round.

Then someone starts asking her name and her mother's name and father's name and where she lives. She tells the stranger her name is Jennifer and her mother's name is Mommy. Still sniffling, she begs the people to take her home but she doesn't know where home is. She begins to sob silently, and as the tears flow down her cheeks, she begins to tremble and can't control the sounds she doesn't recognize as her own pleas for her mother. A few minutes later she sees a stranger in white with a long needle in her hand standing above her and she begins to scream...

The screams in her nightmare always awakened her from a troubled sleep. Now just thinking about the bad dream made her shiver, and she blew out a puff of air, hoping to stop the tremors that threatened to take over.

Why did that particular nightmare continue to haunt her? She had asked herself that unanswerable question most of her adult life. When she was a child she had been sure the recurring nightmare was the result of her viewing some weird television program that had embedded itself into her subconscious. In later years she began to associate the nightmare with something that had actually occurred in her childhood, and became more disturbed when she couldn't put the pieces together.

She had never told her adoptive parents about her nightmares. She hadn't the foggiest idea why. Maybe because they had always been so loving to her and so protective of her. Maybe she didn't want to worry them. Maybe...

Knowing she wouldn't be able to get back to sleep right away, she rose from the side of the bed and padded across the soft blue carpeting to the mirrored bathroom with only the dim rays of the moon lighting her way. She gazed into the mirror and saw the terror of the dream reflected in wide-eyed expressio of her coffee-colored complexion was paler than usual. She splashed her face with cool tap water and held her wrists under cold water a few moments. As her fear slowly subsided, the nightmare gradually faded from her conscious mind.

On her way back to bed, she picked up a half-read novel from her chaise longue, switched on the bedside lamp, plumped up the pillows on her bed, and became engrossed in the mystery. She read a couple chapters before the book slid from her hands. Sighing, she turned over to sleep peacefully until the bright morning sun streaming through half-closed drapes awakened her.

CHAPTER 1

Pacing the floor of her spacious office, Jennifer Johnson stopped long enough to toss a folder onto her desk. She slowly ran her slender hand across her coffee-colored forehead as if that would free her mind of the disturbing thoughts running through it. Finding her birth parents had become an obsession. She desperately needed something to validate who she really was. Something to make her feel whole, to take away the feelings of inferiority and insecurity that being adopted had created in her. She frequently asked herself the same questions: Why didn't my family want me? Will I ever fill this emptiness in my life?

She turned back to her desk and sank into her soft leather chair, determined to keep her mind on the work piled in neat stacks. Finally managing to concentrate on reviewing an audit report from one of her staff, she masked her frustration when her long-time friend, Sherry Brown, marched into her office, firmly closing the door behind her.

Confronting Jennifer, Sherry got right to the point. "You must be in one of your funky moods again, Jennifer. I called you over the weekend and left messages, but did you return any of my calls? No! So what's going on with you, girlfriend?"

Jennifer exhaled slowly and laid aside the report. *Sometimes that woman gets on my last nerve!* "I'm in no mood to discuss me, Sherry, so what else is on your mind...besides meddling in my business?"

"I just want to know what's gotten into you, and—"

"Oh, cool it, Sherry. I'm okay...just having one of my moments, I guess."

"You wouldn't have 'moments,' as you call them, if you'd get off your butt and spend some time with people—especially men—instead of burying your head in all those books you're always reading."

"Been there, done that, as you well know, and what has it gotten me? Absolutely nothing except reinforcing my ideas about men, especially black men."

Sherry examined her nails. "So what about Greg? You go places with him in tow."

Jennifer thought for a moment. "I guess Greg and I are what you call platonic friends. He's about the only interesting man I've met out here. And for your information, he has no romantic interest in me."

Sherry hid the smile beginning to form. Her friend didn't have a clue that Greg thought he was in love with her. She took another tact. "Maybe it's your so-called biological clock sending you a message. But with your attitude about black men, you'll probably ignore the hint."

Jennifer ran her hand through her long relaxed hair. *Let her think that's my problem. No need to get into what's really bothering me—not knowing where I come from, who my birth parents are, whether I have brothers and sisters...* "I don't care what you say, Sherry, I'm entitled to my own 'attitude' as you call it. Whether it's black men or white men, they just don't think about love the same way women do. Men are brain dead when it comes to romance, the kind of romance most women dream about. I just don't get it." Jennifer's big black-velvet eyes snapped at her friend standing on the other side of her desk.

Sherry cast her eyes heavenward.

Sighing heavily, Jennifer shuffled the work piled high on her desk, hoping that would convince Sherry she was not in the mood for a long conversation. All she wanted at the moment was to get her friend out of her office. "I'm sick and tired of hearing you defend black men as if they were God's gift to women. Huh!"

Sherry again rolled her large brown eyes toward the ceiling, ignoring the hints of her friend. She wasn't the least bit offended, having heard Jennifer's opinionated comments many times during their long friendship. Unconsciously she reached up and pulled her long braids behind her ears, a habit she had developed after she got her weave. *Jennifer still doesn't get it,* she decided as she listened to her friend's emotional tirade.

Glancing up from her papers, Jennifer saw that Sherry had not budged from her spot. *That woman always thinks she has all the answers when it comes to dealing with black men.* She tried another approach. "If you know so much about black men, Sherry, why don't you have a man of your own?"

A sly smile on her face, Sherry responded immediately. "I'm working real hard on the one I'm seeing. I think I'll reel him in any day now."

Jennifer raised her eyebrows. "That's the first time I've heard you're that serious about Hal. You sure can be secretive about your own business, so why are you always in mine?"

Sherry sashayed back to Jennifer's desk. Her voice was low and soft. "The trouble with you, Jennifer, is that you expect too much of men, expect them to be everything you want them to be. That's really messed-up thinking." She stopped for a moment. "You always manage to find something wrong with every guy you go out with. Nobody's perfect, girl, you need to lighten up. Work on making a man think he's the greatest you've ever met if you expect to have a relationship that goes somewhere. Just think of all the men you've dated and—"

Incensed, Jennifer interrupted. "And not one of them that I was interested in had the decency to even mention making a commitment to anything before wanting to jump in bed with me! So what am I supposed to think? All most men think about is satisfying themselves...except Greg, of course."

For several moments Jennifer glared at Sherry.

Sherry returned the glare. "Humph. With your attitude you might as well be in a nunnery. You just haven't met the right black man. When you do, I bet you'll change your attitude mighty fast!"

"You could be right, but I'll deal with that when and if it happens. I'm surely not going to lose any sleep waiting for him to come along."

Sherry sucked her teeth and again rolled her dark eyes to the ceiling, a frown on her dark brown face. "Damn, you really are in a funky mood. One of these days you're going to meet a brother who'll make you swallow your words in a New York minute. And I'll be right there to say 'I told you so.'"

Jennifer threw her a dirty look. "That would make you sooo happy, wouldn't it?"

Sherry shrugged her shoulders, knowing what Jennifer said was right on target. Nothing pleased her more than proving her opinionated friend wrong every once in a while. Tossing her head, she turned to leave

Love Doesn't Come Easy

and then turned and faced Jennifer again, not wanting to leave on an unpleasant note. "I'm having lunch in today, Jennifer. Want to send out for something and bring it to my office?"

Jennifer shook her head. "I...I think I'll go out for lunch today, might even do a little shopping."

"Hope you feel better when you get back," Sherry threw over her shoulder as she bounced out the door swinging her long braids, swaying her ample hips, and leaving behind the scent of her overpowering perfume.

"Whatever," Jennifer tossed after her.

Rubbing her forehead, Jennifer felt sorry she had been rather harsh with Sherry and announced to the empty office, "Sometimes that woman pushes my buttons too hard." Because they were bonded by a long, close friendship, she knew Sherry would not hold her outbreak against her. It wasn't the first time they'd disagreed and it wouldn't be the last. Maybe she would pick up some little do-dad for her friend while she was out. Some fun thing for her long braids.

Instead of returning to her work, she leaned back in her chair and closed her eyes, reflecting on her long-time friendship with Sherry. Both had grown up in comfortable middle-class homes in the Midwest. While Sherry came from a family of five sisters and brothers, she had been reared by loving foster parents who took her in as a very young child, then later adopted her and treated her as if she were their own offspring. She loved her adoptive parents, but deep inside she envied children reared by birth parents. Her adoption was a secret she kept locked in her heart from everyone except Sherry, who couldn't have cared less. Jennifer recognized that being adopted had made her vulnerable and inhibited. She knew it also prevented her from becoming too close to others, particularly men.

She suddenly shook her head to clear it. Reminiscing always left her in a restless mood. She rose from her chair and wandered to the window of her office high up in the TransAmerica Pyramid Building in the center of San Francisco's financial district.

Staring out the window at the late morning sun that warmed the glass, she imagined she could feel the light summer breeze that moved scraps of paper around in the street below her. The fog had burned off and she could see Alcatraz across the San Francisco Bay. For several minutes she watched the sailboats plying the choppy water and wished she were on one of them. The scene in front of her usually calmed her ruffled feelings. Not so today.

Her conversation with Sherry had affected her more than she wanted to admit. She knew deep inside she was concerned that her biological clock was ticking away too fast, but her main problem was finding her roots. Until that was settled, her hope of having a family of her own was on the back burner. Unconsciously, she twisted a strand of her relaxed hair when one of her adoptive mother's favorite sayings ran through her mind: Be careful what you wish for, Jennifer, you just might get it!

Smiling, her mind drifted to thoughts of the woman who had reared her, the handsome, ebony-skinned middle-aged woman who had loved and cared for her as if she had been her own biological child. She had grown up a happy child, and with the help of her adoptive parents had attained most of the things she thought she wanted in life.

So why did life recently seem to be the pits?

She swung around from the window and returned to the large beige chair behind her desk, glancing around her well-appointed office done in soft earth tones—her proof that her hard work and dedication had paid off. She had a challenging and fulfilling career, and she liked the power and the perks that came with it. Even all the traveling she was required to do for the firm appealed to her.

Yet here she was in an extremely despondent mood—feeling lonely, sad, miserable. It had happened before, and she usually could shrug it away. Not so today. Her feelings threatened to overwhelm her. She had to get out of the office. Opening her desk drawer, she grabbed her purse and dug around in it until she found her compact. Quickly checking her mirror, she applied a touch of tangerine lipstick to her lower lip. She drew out a vial of perfume and applied a drop behind each ear and on the inside of her wrists. She would have a quick lunch and then do a little shopping. Buying something was supposed to raise one's spirits...and her spirits surely needed raising today!

Exiting her building, she made her way down the street through the tourists and shoppers who always crowded the area at that time of the day. She took her time walking along the street, stopping to look into several shop windows.

She headed for a restaurant a couple of blocks away, a popular one for corporate diners who usually took a long lunch. After a five-minute wait she was seated at a small table and quickly selected a crab soufflé and a glass of white wine. She devoured her lunch as soon as it arrived and rose to leave.

On her way out of the restaurant she spied one of the most handsome men she had seen in a long time. She noticed he was sitting alone, evidently having just finished his lunch from the looks of his table. She stared at the dark mahogany-complexioned man, the epitome of one of Ebony Magazine's most eligible bachelors! In just one long glance she took in his deep-set black eyes with crinkles at the corners, giving him a slightly mischievous look. And humor seemed to lurk in the smile lines at the corners of his full-lipped mouth beneath a neatly-trimmed, thin mustache. His obviously expensive suit outlined broad shoulders, reminding her of her favorite San Francisco '49er football player.

Nearing his table, she became aware he was also staring at her. Evidently knowing he had her attention, he raised his glass to her. Smiling up at her as she passed, he held his glass high. "You really got it goin' on!"

For a moment she felt as if she were drowning in the depths of his twinkling dark eyes. Hearing his low husky voice, she tensed but managed a smile, determined to maintain her cool equilibrium even though her heart was racing. Slightly embarrassed, she managed to speak. "Thanks," she said softly and hurried toward the door.

That brother certainly has it goin' on, too, she thought, wondering who he was. Sherry would probably call him a hunk. Just another one on the make! But then brothers can be so pushy. Probably thinks he"s the answer to all women's prayers. Also more than likely married as well, she decided. Married men are always more forward than single men. She tossed her head, hoping to get his image out of her mind, thinking she would probably never see him again anyway. She headed for her favorite boutique.

Even while shopping she couldn't get the handsome stranger out of her mind. She finally pigeon-holed him as one of the many corporate types she had met in the past, the type so interested in their own advancement that they had little time for a woman, except to go to bed with. And she had no time for any more men like that!

Although she wasn't entirely happy with her own life at the moment, she certainly didn't want to become bogged down in a relationship that probably would turn out to be another one-sided affair like her last relationship with Kevin, something she tried hard not to think about, still not over the pain that relationship had caused her.

She glanced at her watch, amazed it was time to get back to her office. Frustrated that she had walked past the shops and was almost to her building, she blamed it all on her thinking about the good-looking stranger. And she hadn't picked up anything for Sherry. What in the world is the matter with me? she wondered as she hurried into her building. When she got out of the elevator and turned toward her office, she caught a glimpse of Sherry in the hallway. She tried to duck into her office without Sherry seeing her. She failed.

"Jennifer, Jennifer, wait up," Sherry called.

Jennifer swallowed a groan when she heard her friend's voice.

"You still haven't told me whether you want Hal and me to pick you up for Greg Dixon's get-together tonight."

Jennifer hit her forehead with the palm of her hand. She had forgotten all about Greg's party; he would never forgive her if she didn't show up. No way could she do that to Greg. To her, he was a co-worker who had turned out to be a very good friend that she sometimes confided in when they were out together. Why she wasn't attracted to Greg in a romantic way, she didn't know. Physically, he certainly was her type: a tall, brown-skinned athletic guy with short cropped hair and smiling dark eyes above his wide, full mouth and white, even teeth. Most of the single women in their firm hit on him, but, as far as she knew, Greg didn't give any of them any play outside of the office.

"It really slipped my mind, but, yes, I'm going and, no, you don't need to pick me up. I'll probably not stay too long. Thanks, though, Sherry. I'll see you two there," she added before heading into her own office, determined to leave early since she had a couple of stops to make before dressing for Greg's party.

CHAPTER 2

Jennifer arrived late for Greg's party. She glanced around at the well-dressed African Americans: men posturing in expensive suits framing their broad shoulders and women sashaying in designer dresses of various colors and lengths. Expensive perfume wafted through the room. She ran her hands down the under-stated silk tangerine dress, satisfied she had selected the perfect dress for the affair.

Before joining the crowd, she was drawn to the mouth-watering odors of food on a long table. Greg really got this together, she thought as she surveyed the beautiful display. Flanked by tall crystal candlesticks and vases of flowers, two large crystal bowls were filled with an assortment of cut-up fruit. Glass platters were heaped with a variety of hors d'oeuvres and canapés. Other platters held jumbo shrimp, cold cuts, buffalo wings, and assorted cheeses and crackers.

She surveyed the table a few moments before deciding which delicacy to tackle first. While filling a small plate, she greeted several acquaintances who passed near her. Nibbling a canapé, she made her way through the crowd until she found Greg, who was busy refilling a champagne punch bowl.

Spotting Jennifer, Greg put down the crystal pitcher and threw his arms around her shoulders, giving her a quick peck on the cheek before releasing her. "Where've you been, Jennifer? I was just thinking about you!" he exclaimed, a big smile spreading over his face. "You know I can't have a party without you."

"Oh, Greg, you're always exaggerating." She patted his cheek. "I'm sure the single gals here have been falling all over you, as usual. Probably some of the married ones as well," she added, a sly smile on her lips.

"But I've been waiting for only you," he said teasingly, although in his heart he knew it was one of the truths of his life. He also knew he would scare her away if he even hinted at his secret longing for her.

She let his comment go right over her head since he always said things like that to her. Taking the champagne flute Greg filled, she wandered into the next room, casually greeting couples she passed. Looks like every gal here is attached to a guy, she thought, which only increased her feeling of loneliness.

Making her way through the crowd, she suddenly stopped dead in her tracks. Her drink splashed over the rim of her glass but luckily did not spill on her. Across the room was the hunk she had seen at lunch earlier in the day! Surrounded by several people, he was doing most of the talking. She stood rooted to that spot, her legs suddenly feeling like over-cooked spaghetti.

The man in her view turned and did a double take when he saw her standing alone. He immediately excused himself from the group and headed toward her.

Heat rushed to her cheeks as she watched him saunter across the room toward her. Still incapable of moving one foot in front of the other, she prayed the warm flush she felt inside wasn't showing on her face.

He stopped in front of her, his eyebrows raised. "Didn't I see you in the restaurant at noon today?" His deep, vibrant baritone voice matched his tall compelling figure. Not waiting for a reply, he continued talking, ignoring the flush spreading across her face. "You're even prettier tonight." He extended his large manicured hand. "Michael Maxwell."

For a few seconds Jennifer's voice stuck in her throat while she stared up into his handsome face, totally enthralled by the compelling masculinity exuding from him. Finally coming to her senses, she accepted his firm yet gentle handshake, noticing the slightly appraising smile on his dark mahogany face as he looked into her eyes. She quickly withdrew her hand. She was positive she felt sparks flying between them. "Jennifer Johnson," she managed to squeak out. What in the world is wrong with me, she wondered when she heard her own strained voice. This is probably just another brother on the make, she reminded herself, even though she felt drawn to him. Why, she didn't know. She immediately became more self-conscious at the thought of being attracted to him.

"Well, Jennifer Johnson, how about walking out on the deck with me for a few minutes? I'd like to know more about you." Michael did not miss her ringless finger holding the champagne flute. Not waiting for her answer, he took charge of the situation, placing his hand on her elbow.

He really has his nerve, Jennifer thought, a bit put off by his taking for granted that she would wanted to go with him. He was also looking at her in the way a man gazes at a woman he finds very attractive, and she found his stare exceedingly upsetting.

Almost in a trance, she permitted him to guide her through the crowd and dropped down onto the first lounge chair she saw when they reached the deck. He drew up a chair close to her, his nearness making her temperature rise, the power of his masculinity really getting to her.

Get a grip, girl, she told herself and drew in a couple of deep breaths. Exhaling slowly, she held the stem of her glass so tightly she was afraid it would snap. Totally shaken up by his presence, she nervously raised her glass to her lips and took a long sip of champagne.

He was silent for a moment. "Do you work near the restaurant we were in today, Jennifer?"

"Yes...uh...I'm with a CPA firm on Bush Street," she stammered. "I'm manager of its auditing department." Unconsciously, her lilting voice conveyed her pride in her position.

This did not escape him.

His eyebrows rose slightly. "Oh, we're almost neighbors then. I'm with a law firm in the same area."

She suddenly felt as tongue-tied as a teenager on her first date, and she looked away from his unsettling stare. "Is San Francisco your home?" she finally got out.

"Oh, no. I moved here from Atlanta a few months ago. My firm had an opening here, and I jumped at the opportunity without giving it a second thought. It's beautiful here...but very expensive compared to Atlanta. Even the fog, which some people complain about, fascinates me." He smiled crookedly as if he thought she might think that was an absurd idea.

She was captivated by his deep, resonant voice; several times she had to consciously try to keep her mind on what he was saying.

Looking out over the city, he was silent for a moment. "My one regret at the moment, though, is that I haven't had the time to really get to know San Francisco, not to mention many of the interesting places in other parts of the Bay Area."

"You're really a newcomer, then. I moved here directly out of college several years ago. San Francisco really lives up to its reputation for being the city of romance and adventure. And there're so many places to go I'm afraid I haven't taken the time to explore as much as I'd like to either." She hoped she didn't sound as if she were suggesting that they explore together. But that's exactly what ran through her mind.

"Did your family move out with you?" she asked innocently, as if she were merely making conversation. What she really wanted to know was whether or not he was married. His not wearing a wedding band meant nothing, she decided, since nowadays many married men did not wear their bands.

"I'm not married." He seemed to emphasize that fact by the tone of his voice and the bluntness of his words.

"Well, that must make all of the single women here have some hope." Her voice carried a flippant note, but inside she was very serious, hoping his reply would tell her more about him.

Blushing slightly, his comeback surprised her. "There really are a lot of single women around...most of the ones I've met are very candid about their looking for husbands. I'm just not interested in that role at the moment. My priority right now is keeping on top of the work in my office, so I've had a rather limited social life since I've been here."

They chatted about other inconsequential topics for

a few moments. She found his nearness and his frequent appraising glances toward her extremely disconcerting. His effect on her was frustrating since the last thing she wanted at the moment was a man invading her well-ordered life. She breathed a sigh of relief when Greg stepped out onto the deck looking for her.

Putting his hand on her shoulder, Greg bent down near her. "I missed you inside, Jennifer, and wondered where you had disappeared to...but I see you've evidently been in good company." He nodded toward Michael. "Michael is usually surrounded by women. Where's your entourage tonight, Michael?" he asked, a bit of asperity in his voice.

Greg's demeanor did not go unnoticed by Michael. "I found this lovely person walking around and decided I wanted to spend some time with her. No objection, I hope," he added, noting the tense expression on Greg's face.

"No...uh...no objection," Greg finally got out, all the while wanting to punch him out. "Well, I've got to get back in there to look after my guests." He stared at Jennifer before he walked away, as if he needed to protect her from Michael. Of all the women in San Francisco, why did that jerk zero in on Jennifer? Greg asked himself as he wandered back indoors, leaving Jennifer and Michael on the deck.

She wondered why Greg seemed upset as he left.

He wondered whether Jennifer was involved with

Love Doesn't Come Easy

Greg.

By the end of their conversation, Michael was so captivated by her that he knew he could not let her get away without getting her phone number. "May I call you? I'd like to see you again."

She hesitated a few seconds since men had sometimes asked for her number and then never called; yet she was unable to deny his request.

He withdrew a silver case from the inside pocket of his suit jacket and extracted a card. He wrote her phone number on the back and returned it to the case. He removed another and offered it to her. She dropped his card into her purse without glancing at it.

Letting out a loud sigh, he announced, "I suppose we better go back inside... though I'd rather spend the rest of the evening out here with you."

She blushed, feeling the same way, but what could she say? She was certain he had brought a date with him.

He reached for her hand, pulling her up from the deck chair.

She was positive electricity really did spark as they touched. Walking back inside with him, she noticed several heads turning as they passed through the crowd.

A tall, brown-skinned woman, who walked and looked like a high-paid model, met them and claimed Michael's arm. She stared at Jennifer. "Hello, Jennifer. Where's your escort?"

Jennifer tried desperately to keep her cool. She

20

merely answered, "Hello, Tawana."

Jennifer took in Tawana's flawless make-up which accentuated her classic features. Her lavender jersey designer dress clung to her shapely body like a second skin. Her insincere smile, however, negated her other good features, Jennifer decided.

Mystified by the vibes swirling around them, Michael looked from Jennifer to Tawana. "I take it you two know each other."

"I've seen her around," Tawana replied, pulling on Michael's arm. "It's almost time for the party to break up, Michael, and you've practically neglected me since we got here."

"Sorry, Tawana. I guess I haven't kept track of the time." Michael turned a placating smile in Tawana's direction. "I'm ready to go any time you are."

Throwing an arrogant look in Jennifer's direction, Tawana drew Michael away. The two disappeared into the crowd, Tawana's hand firmly clutching his arm.

Just another brother with a line, Jennifer decided as she watched Michael and Tawana make their way through the crowd. She was sorry she'd given him her phone number. Walking through the room to find Greg, she ran into a breathless Sherry.

"Jennifer, come out on the deck with me...I've got to talk to you."

The two friends made their way outside, Jennifer wondering what in heaven's name had now happened to

Sherry, knowing she was always getting into some kind of predicament.

As soon as they reached the deck, Sherry turned and faced Jennifer. "I just saw you and that gorgeous hunk come from out here, Jennifer. Don't you know he's the heartthrob of the city? What did he say? Are you going to see him again?"

Jennifer's face showed her surprise. "Girl, you really do get into everybody's business, don't you? I just met the guy. No big deal."

Sherry put her hands on her ample hips. "You mean to stand there and say 'no big deal' when half the women in San Francisco have been after that brother ever since he landed here? Don't tell me you weren't impressed!"

Jennifer shrugged her shoulders. "Why should I be 'impressed' as you put it? He's just another good-looking black guy, and he evidently has already hooked up with Tawana," she answered nonchalantly. "The women will have no competition from me. Is that all you wanted with me, Sherry? I thought something had happened to you. You're always getting involved in something or other."

"Me?" Sherry cried. "From the look on your face I think something happened to you, whether you want to admit it or not."

Jennifer refused to respond to Sherry's allegation. "I've got to find Greg before I leave, Sherry. See you tomorrow—maybe." She left Sherry on the deck, her hands still on her ample hips.

Sherry stood outside for a few moments, shaking her head from side to side as she watched Jennifer edge her way around the room. "There's no hope for that woman," she said into the dark night and went inside to look for her friend Hal.

Jennifer found Greg huddled with a group. She nudged his shoulder and he immediately turned aside to face her.

"I had a great time, Greg, but I'm going to call it a night."

"Can't you stay a while longer?"

"I'd really like to, Greg, but I'm kinda bushed. It's been a long week, and I need to hit the sack." She didn't add that any reason to remain had just walked out of the door.

Greg's face mirrored his disappointment, but he gallantly walked her to the door and gave her a light kiss on her cheek before returning to his guests.

On her way home, Jennifer thought about Michael and the way sparks had flown between them during their introduction and the way her heart had acted up during their conversation. She shook her head to get him out of her thoughts and consciously turned her mind to the upcoming busy week when she had to check on one of her auditing teams out in the field. Thinking about her work was always her excuse for not thinking about the absence of love in her life. Sometimes that worked, sometimes it didn't.

If Jennifer had known what was going on in Michael's mind, she would have had cause to be more excited about her future.

৵৵ ৵৵ ৵৵

After dropping off Tawana at her apartment, Michael refused her invitation to have a nightcap and drove home slowly, deep in thought. He tried to recapture the effect Jennifer had had on him. In his mind he could clearly see the reddish highlights in her shiny, dark hair which framed a face the color of lightly-creamed coffee. Her large intelligent eyes which reminded him of soft black velvet were slightly upturned at the corners beneath naturally well-shaped eyebrows. Her rather classic high cheekbones accented sensual full lips that seemed vulnerable and yet smiled so easily. Faint make-up gave her skin a soft glow. And her long, shapely legs had to be the envy of most women. He thought she exuded pride and confidence and independence, as if she were sure of her future. Yet while he talked with her, he thought he had detected a forlorn look in her eyes and wondered who or what put it there. He guessed she was probably in her late twenties or early thirties and wondered about the man—or men—in her life. Unconsciously, he felt a twinge of jealously for no particular reason when he thought of another man being interested in her.

Despite some misgivings, he knew he was very attracted to her, against his better judgment. Damn. He needed no complications in his life at the moment. There were too many loose ends he needed to tie up before he became seriously involved with any woman. The added responsibility of his new position as a partner in the law firm was about all he could handle right now.

At thirty-five, he was just about where he wanted to be with his career. The occasional casual dates he'd had the last few months were okay since he set the limits of any relationship from the beginning, letting his partners know that their dates were just that—casual—and that he wasn't interested in getting seriously involved. Most of the women he dated accepted his terms and when the relationship ended, neither was too affected.

His instincts warned him that with Jennifer it would be different. Something about her drew him to her, but she seemed so standoffish she probably needed no one in her life on a permanent basis. And if he were sensible, he wouldn't even think of getting entangled in a serious relationship with her. Yet...she intrigued him.

She was intermittently in his thoughts most of the weekend. Her face would appear in his mind at the most inopportune times, regardless of what he was doing.

Love Doesn't Come Easy

Then he would stare into space until his conscious mind told him to continue whatever he was doing. What really bothered him was not knowing where Greg fit into the picture. Was Greg more than a casual friend?

CHAPTER 3

Late Sunday afternoon, Michael glanced at the clock and threw aside the work he'd brought home. He was not looking forward to an obligation he had later on, a formal affair he'd promised Tawana he would take her to, but, there was no way to get out of it. A friend of one of his associates, Tawana had been between men friends when he first met her, and she had more or less attached herself to him, inviting him to various affairs where he'd met people who were now his friends. He usually enjoyed going out with Tawana as she was one of the few people he'd met who was a native of San Francisco; she was also fairly well acquainted with many of the people whose names were known in the community. Even though from the beginning he'd told her he wanted no serious involvement with anyone, he suspected Tawana was more attracted to him than he was to her. He knew that he definitely didn't want to have an affair with her, no matter how physically attractive or popular she was. She just wasn't the kind of woman he could ever get serious about.

Showering and shaving quickly, he dressed in record time, except for the black bow tie which took him ten minutes to get just right. He pulled on his tuxedo jacket and glanced quickly in the floor-to-ceiling mirror. Much to his chagrin, he found himself thinking about Jennifer again and wishing it were she he was on his way to pick up. He shook his head to clear Jennifer out of his thoughts, knowing that Tawana would demand his full attention the rest of the evening.

ॐ ॐ ॐ

While Michael was getting dressed Sunday evening to go out with Tawana, Jennifer heard her doorbell chime. She left her bedroom and walked through the foyer to the peephole. Even before she looked out, she suspected the caller was Sherry wanting to talk about "that hunk." She opened the door reluctantly, not really in the mood to discuss Michael. She couldn't care less if she never laid eyes on him again. Why would such a successful man want a woman who knew nothing about her background, had no roots, so to speak. Let Tawana and all those other women make a fool of themselves over him—not her!

Sherry greeted Jennifer and followed her into the kitchen, plopping down on a chair at the table in the breakfast nook. She glanced at the plants filling the window sill.

"Coffee, Sherry? I just finished my dinner and there's still plenty in the pot."

"That sounds good, girlfriend, but go light on the sugar. I'm trying to cut down—my hips are getting bigger by the day."

Jennifer hid a smile. Sherry needs to cut down on more than sugar in her coffee, Jennifer mused as she glanced at Sherry's well-rounded hips accented by her tight-fitting skirt.

Sherry leaned over to look closely at the plants. "I don't know how you do it, girl, but your plants seem to have grown inches every time I see them. Your plants in the living room are so green they look artificial. Mine just sit there and eventually wilt, regardless of what I do to them. Then, after a couple of months, I have to throw them out and get some more. Maybe I just don't have a green thumb."

"Did you ever try talking to your plants? That is, after you water them regularly, of course."

Sherry glanced sideways at Jennifer as if she were slightly off her rocker. "Talk to my plants? Girl, you sure have some weird ideas. What...what do you say to yours?"

Love Doesn't Come Easy

"Oh, Sherry, you're hopeless. Just say whatever comes into your mind. That shouldn't be a problem for you. You don't have any trouble talking to men," Jennifer added snippily.

The mention of men was all Sherry needed. "So, girlfriend, speaking of men, tell me more about Michael Maxwell. Has he called you yet?"

Jennifer sighed. "That's really why you came up here, isn't it? You don't fool me for a minute. Well...I hate to disappoint you, but I just wasn't that impressed with your hunk. And, no, he hasn't called me. Michael's really handsome and he's got a great voice, but he's probably like all the other corporate types I've met out here— too interested in promoting themselves to think about getting seriously involved with women." She took a sip of her coffee and sighed again. "I guess they just don't make men like they used to, men who want to marry for all the right reasons, like having a home, a family, and all that kind of stuff. The ones I meet are just too self-centered to even try to find out what some black woman are all about. And especially the black women who have managed to get good positions and make good money. We have a hard time finding someone interested in having a meaningful relationship...and then we never know whether the guy's sincere. Most black men consider us a threat—a threat to what I don't know. A lot of those same men now go for white women who they think will treat them like kings."

"Oh, girl, they're not all like that. You know, you really should try to do something about this thing you have against black men. Talk about prejudices!"

"Okay, okay, but how many eligible black men do you know right here in San Francisco that aren't married, or aren't with white women, or aren't homosexuals?"

"There're many eligible black men who don't fit into those slots—you just don't go to the right places to meet them, Jennifer."

"I think I've met my share in the years we've been out here, Sherry. And they turn me off. The rest are either too stupid, too old, too possessive, too ugly, too irresponsible, and a lot of other things I won't take the time to mention at the moment."

Sherry sipped her coffee slowly, looking at Jennifer over the rim of her cup for a few moments. "Just what are you looking for in a man, Jennifer? You've gone out with several I would gladly have snapped up, yet none of them stayed around too long. Except Kevin, that is, and I still think you two could have made it if you hadn't been so darn stubborn. So what do you want in a relationship?"

Jennifer slowly moved her cup around in her saucer, not looking at her friend. Hmmm...just what do I want?

Sherry sipped her coffee and waited, knowing Jennifer would eventually give her some kind of an answer.

Jennifer lifted her head and looked at her friend. "I

guess I want what most women want—someone who is truly a friend. Someone who's sensitive, kind, considerate, understanding, attentive. Someone with whom I can be myself with no pretense, who lets me have my own space when I need it. Who loves me as much as I love him. Someone who wouldn't see me as a threat if I make as much money or more than he does. And he has to want children as much as I'd like to have them." Jennifer's eyes lit up as she thought about her last statement, then the gleam dimmed. Her eyes were sad as she looked toward her friend. "I guess, most of all, he'd have to be comfortable with the fact that I was adopted and know nothing about any real relatives. You know how many people are hung up on family background—or 'roots' as it's called since Alex Haley's book came out years ago."

"Whoa, girlfriend!" Sherry interrupted. "How about sex? You haven't even mentioned that little thing!"

Jennifer shrugged. "Are you crazy? Of course I'd want a good lover—that's a given." Her eyes had a faraway look. "I've never met anyone that I dreamed about at night, or made me stare into space during the day, or—" She stopped for a moment. "I want someone who makes me hear music and tingle inside when he kisses me, and who—"

"You really believe in asking for the stars as well as the moon, don't you?" Sherry interrupted with an exasperated sound and rose to pour another cup of coffee.

Settling down in her chair again, she surveyed Jennifer with half-closed eyes. "You're actually a hopeless romantic, girl. So how're you going to find someone like that? You're always so fast to find faults—or imagined ones—in the men you meet that you don't give a relationship enough time to even get off the ground." She took another sip of her coffee. "My mama always said you can't tell a book by its cover, so maybe you need to really get to know a person before you jump to hasty conclusions about him." Sherry was silent for a moment before she said softly, "I know you have a lot going on which is important to you, but girl, when you don't have love in your life, those other things sometimes become meaningless. I read somewhere that if you want the rainbow, you've got to put up with a little rain."

Jennifer squirmed in her chair. She knew most of what Sherry said over and over was true, but the bottom line was that she just didn't need a man in her space at the moment. Maybe later. Maybe when she could spend more time thinking about a man and less about her career or finding her biological parents. Maybe she would eventually meet a brother she could fall in love with. Someone who understood what her career meant and wouldn't care about her being adopted. Someone who wouldn't think she was as sexless as cold mashed potatoes, the description Kevin had thrown in her face when their relationship went sour. But she wouldn't hold her breath until the man of her dreams came along.

Love Doesn't Come Easy

The two friends gossiped about Greg's party and a couple of their mutual friends for a while before Sherry announced that she needed to get back down to her apartment. She squeezed Jennifer's hand as she walked out the door. "Hang in there, girlfriend, I have the feeling you might get your soul mate sooner than you think."

After Sherry left, Jennifer thought about her present situation while getting ready to go to bed early so she could get back to her novel. Reading before she went to sleep was as much a part of her life as brushing her teeth.

While undressing, she heard the beginning of a discussion about a woman's biological clock on TV and immediately switched to another station. That was the last thing she wanted to hear about! Maybe that was another thing that had been bothering her recently. She thought she had gotten over her disappointment in not meeting a man who could offer her all the things she really wanted in a husband. Maybe she had waited too long and now was getting too picky.

The last guy she'd dated seriously—Kevin—had made it clear that he wanted a wife who would be the proverbial little housewife, a full-time mother to raise the children he wanted. She wanted children, too, but she also wanted her career. Yet Kevin had insisted that the two couldn't possibly be compatible and refused to even consider what her career meant to her. For him, women had only one biological purpose: to satisfy a man's sexual desires. They could reach no compromises, so she and Kevin had gone their separate ways. Kevin taught her

34

that love has the power to hurt. Even though Kevin had left a void in her life, she never regretted the decision she made to stop seeing him.

CHAPTER 4

Jennifer hurried to her office early Monday morning to get a head start on the work facing her, since she was due in Los Angeles the next day to check on two of her auditing teams working in that area. Plunging into the paperwork piled on her desk, she worked without noticing the time. It was past her usual lunch hour when Greg peeked into her office.

"Nose to the grindstone as usual," Greg observed. "I was hoping I could get you out of the office for a late lunch."

"Oh, come on in, Greg. Wish I could join you but I'm leaving early today. Have to get my hair done before I go to Los Angeles. I swear, I think hair is the black woman's curse—it's so hard to keep it looking good. A little bit of moisture in the air makes my hair so frizzy I could scream." Jennifer patted the back of her hair. "Sometimes I wish I had the nerve to have it all cut off!" A half smile crossed her face. "How do you think I'd look if I did that?"

"Bald." Greg laughed at his own quip.

Jennifer sighed and threw him a dirty look.

"You look a little under the weather. Bad day, babe?" Greg looked at her curiously as he walked over to flop down on the chair beside her desk.

"Oh, I don't know what's wrong with me, Greg. I'm not ill, if that's what you're thinking. It's just that...that sometimes I feel so at odds with myself...maybe with the world. It's such a stupid feeling. Maybe I need a change of scenery. Maybe I should go home for a few days, but I don't know whether I could take all my mother's pampering at the moment; I might not want to come back." She smiled self-consciously.

Greg stared at Jennifer. She usually did not open up to anyone, so he was now surprised at her confession. "That's probably a good idea, Jen. You've been putting in some long hours since your promotion. The last few weeks I haven't been able to even get you out for lunch, not to mention dinner. Maybe we can get together when you get back from L.A."

Greg stood up and was halfway to the door before he stopped, turning back to Jennifer. "By the way, I hope you remember you promised to go with me to the famous or infamous Ingalls' party next week."

"Of course I remember, Greg. In fact, I have a great dress I'm dying to wear." Jennifer felt a twinge of guilt; she really had neglected her friend. "And we'll do lunch next week."

Shortly afterward Jennifer closed her briefcase, put on her suit jacket, and hurried to the elevator, determined not to be late for her hair appointment. She made it to the hair salon located on the other side of the city with minutes to spare. She approached the attractive black receptionist who immediately consulted her appointment book to check Jennifer in. "It'll be a few minutes before your stylist is ready for you," she informed Jennifer with a smile.

Jennifer took one of the two vacant leather armchairs and looked around the comfortably furnished waiting room. Three other smartly-dressed black women were seated on a long leather sofa, leafing through hair magazines and commenting on some of the outrageous hair styles. Several women were in the large room facing her, all in various stages of having their hair styled. Some were being shampooed at the back of the room while others sat on another side of the room, their heads wrapped in towels.

All of the stylists were busy at their stations with clientele and took part in the lively gossip floating around the big room. *Less talk and more work would make waiting a little less irksome,* she decided. She hated to waste time waiting for anything and having to wait in the hair salon was her least favorite thing to do.

She leafed through a couple of magazines before the receptionist called her name and took her back to the row of sinks for her shampoo, which left her refreshed by the time the young girl finished washing her hair. Her head wrapped in a large towel, she took another seat to wait until her stylist was ready for her.

Halfway through another magazine, she suddenly heard some women discussing Tawana Coleman, who was well-known in the black community. Perking up when she heard Tawana's name, she forgot her magazine. She saw Tawana sometimes at various affairs around San Francisco but was only on speaking terms with her. Tawana wasn't the type she wanted as a friend. She knew Tawana was frequently described as a man-chaser, which turned her off.

Still, listening to the women diss Tawana, Jennifer remembered how Tawana had acted toward her at Greg's party, how she attached herself to Michael when she was ready to leave.

She peered around at the woman who was doing most of the talking. "...And Tawana's determined to snag Michael Maxwell one way or the other. You all know her reputation. He probably won't know what hit him when she gets her claws in him. That woman doesn't let anything or anyone stand in her way when she goes after something. You can put your money on that!" To add emphasis, the woman threw her magazine down to the

Love Doesn't Come Easy

floor.

"You got that right," another voice added. "That woman's a real pushy bitch and she does get what she wants one way or other, if you know what I mean," another voice added. "Personally, I can't stand her. I don't know what men see in her, though I've got to admit she's really got it goin' on, always impeccably dressed and made up like a movie star."

A third voice chimed in. "Maybe they're not looking for style." Her words evoked a chorus of raucous laughter around the large room.

Even though the conversation was like a splash of cold water on her face, Jennifer continued to listen intently as the women bashed Tawana and her pursuit of Michael.

Shaking her head from side to side, she leaned back and sighed. "I knew Michael was just like all the others!" she said under her breath, even though she felt a funny little flutter in her chest thinking about him. Her heart and her mind were at war, and she didn't know what to do about it. She turned her attention back to her magazine, leafing through it until her stylist was ready for her.

By the time she got home, it was way past dinner time and she was in no mood to cook a decent meal. She quickly made a grilled cheese sandwich and threw together a salad, taking her food into the living room to watch the news while she ate. Her phone rang as she swallowed the last bite of her sandwich. Sliding to the end of the couch, she picked up the receiver.

Before she could say hello, a deep, husky voice inquired, "May I speak to Jennifer Johnson? This is Michael Maxwell."

She held the receiver out and stared at it, hardly believing her ears. Michael was really on the other end! She swallowed a couple of times before she found her voice. "This is Jennifer," she finally got out in a squeaky voice.

After inquiring about her day and other mundane things, he asked, "Are you free Wednesday evening? I'd like to take you to dinner."

Flabbergasted, she almost dropped the phone. *He is asking me for a date? What about Tawana?*

She finally collected her wits enough to answer him. "Oh, I'm sorry I can't, Michael. I'm leaving for Los Angeles in the morning for a few days."

She could almost hear the disappointment in his voice. "Just my luck! I really want to see you again...maybe we could get together when you return. When will you be back?"

"Late Thursday night or early Friday morning if everything goes as planned."

"How about having dinner Saturday evening?" he suggested.

She hesitated. She really wasn't ready for this. Then she remembered her last conversation with Sherry. Why not go out with the guy? Why should she worry about

Tawana being in the picture? What did she have to lose?

She finally answered, "I'd like that. What time?"

"Around seven thirty? Is that okay with you?"

"That's fine. I'll be ready."

"See you then." Running the back of his hand across his forehead, he sighed audibly as he hung up the phone.

Hearing the click at the other end, she sat very still for a few moments staring at the phone after she heard the buzz of the disconnection, not quite believing she had agreed to go out with him. Her heart had started beating faster the moment he asked her, and it still hadn't slowed down. What in the world was she thinking about? She must be losing her cotton-pickin' mind!

Shaking her head, she rose and carried her plate and glass to the kitchen. Quickly rinsing them both and stacking them into the dishwasher, she looked around the kitchen to check that everything was in place before she hurried to her bedroom. She had to decide what she needed to pack for the next few days. Between deciding what clothes to take and thinking about Michael's call, she didn't finish packing until almost midnight.

ॐ ॐ ॐ

"What have I really gotten myself into?" she asked herself several times during her week in Los Angeles whenever she thought of her upcoming Saturday evening date with Michael. *Why am I doing this? It's really stupid to get involved with someone like him regardless of the vibes I feel when I'm near him. I must be going bonkers!* The more she argued with herself, the more confused she became. She couldn't get her mind and her heart on the same wavelength.

The conversation she'd overheard in the hair salon about Tawana and Michael raised more questions in the back of her mind. Was that just gossip she heard, or could it be true that he was more involved with Tawana than she thought? Or was he just another brother with a macho mentality who thought he was irresistible to women and enjoyed playing the field? She got no answers.

ᔓᖬ ᔓᖬ ᔓᖬ

By the time Saturday evening rolled around, Jennifer was still as confused as she had been all week. She dressed with special care, selecting one of her favorite black after-five dresses with very simple lines that looked very understated until she slipped it on, then became sensual. But definitely not sexy, she decided, looking in the long mirror on the closet door. She found her favorite black satin pumps and rummaged in a drawer for a small matching bag. After applying the sparse makeup she used, she dabbed her favorite scent, Estee Super Perfume, behind her ears, on her wrists, and behind her knees. The fragrance permeated the room by the time she finished dressing.

While transferring her lipstick, comb, tissues and some money into her small bag, her doorbell chimed. Her heart beat furiously as she walked through the foyer to open her door. Her legs suddenly felt rubbery when she saw him standing there, a big smile on his face.

She drew in her breath as she took in his dark expensive suit fitting his broad shoulders as if he had been poured into it. She wanted to reach up and touch the printed silk tie that set off the snowy white shirt against his dark skin. He exuded masculinity from the top of his close-cut curly black hair to the tips of his highly polished black shoes. Almost miraculously her frustrations about their date flew out of the open door.

He greeted her when he walked into the foyer, and the appreciative look in his eyes as he surveyed her from head to foot made her know her choice of dress had been the right one.

You're more beautiful than I remembered," he said huskily as he closed the door. "All week I've been looking forward to this evening."

She felt the blood rush to her cheeks, and she floated back to her bedroom to get her purse and matching coat, turning out the lights on her way back to the door.

They smiled shyly at each other as the elevator descended to the lobby of her apartment complex. Reaching over, he took her hand while they walked out to his sleek silver Mercedes.

Turning to him as he pulled away from the curb, Jennifer asked, "So where are we having dinner?"

"I'm in charge tonight, so just sit back and look beautiful until we get there." He reached across and patted her hand, as if to reassure her.

So he's "in charge"—that's my kind of man! she decided.

Little was said on the short drive to their destination, and she was ecstatic when he turned into the circular drive of the famous Mark IV Hotel on Nob Hill and released his car to the valet.

They entered the elevator for the Top of the Mark and were seated immediately on their arrival at a window table with a breathtaking view overlooking San Francisco's financial district. Even though the city was wrapped in a soft blanket of fog, they could make out the car lights on the streets below and the lights on the tall buildings around the city. A few blocks away they saw the TransAmerica Pyramid Building with its top penetrating the fog-shrouded city. She let out a soft sigh as she looked out across the city. That magnificent view never failed to thrill her and tonight it was doubly so.

He looked at her with raised eyebrows. "You also like this place, I take it," he said softly and was rewarded by her wide smile.

Neither was aware of the subdued voices around them nor the clink of ice as glasses were raised to the lips of the other guests. They were happy just being together and had eyes for no one else except each other.

Relaxed in their chairs, they listened to the soft, romantic music of the 1950s playing in the background.

He turned his attention to the wine list handed to him by the white-coated waiter. Studying the wine choices, he finally ordered a bottle of Cabernet Sauvignon. The waiter returned almost immediately and held up the bottle for Michael to read the label.

She silently watched the waiter's ritual of opening and decanting the wine.

"Excellent," Michael informed him, and the waiter solemnly filled their crystal glasses. When the waiter left the table, Michael raised his glass to her. "To a beautiful evening, Jennifer."

She smiled and nodded to him over her raised glass, her eyes as sparkling as the glass she held. Setting down her glass, she asked flippantly, "Do you usually take your women to such fabulous places, Michael?"

"All of them," he answered just as flippantly and smiled as he claimed her hand lying on the table. An unimaginable thrill went through her as she felt the pressure of his hand on hers. Her hand would never be the same!

Their waiter approached with long embossed menus, and Michael removed his hand. They studied the menu a few moments. He looked at her expectantly.

"Why don't you order for both of us?" she asked softly.

"You trust me, I take it."

"As long as you don't order escargot."

"Don't worry—that's not my favorite thing either." Michael again looked at the menu several moments before he gave their order to the waiter.

Leaning back in his chair, he said, "Since we work near each other, I wonder why we haven't run into each other before this. Do you ever stop at any of the happy hour places after work?"

"No, I usually go straight to my exercise class or go home in the evenings," Jennifer said in a small voice as if apologizing for her uneventful existence. She was glad the small band returned from their break and started playing one of her favorite numbers.

"I love their music," she commented, glancing at the band.

"Let's take advantage of it." He rose and led her to a small spot where another couple was swaying to the soft music in the background. She inhaled a subtle, spicy fragrance when he pulled her into his arms and held her tightly as they circled the small dance space. The music was as romantic as the surrounding elegant atmosphere, and they moved in perfect harmony. Dancing in companionable silence through several numbers, they returned to their table when they noticed the waiter arrive with their entrees.

Both devoted their attention to eating for a few moments, each feeling an undercurrent of attraction that neither wanted to acknowledge was there. They glanced covertly at each other several times while enjoying their dinner.

She laid down her fork after a few moments. "Ummm," she murmured. "The poached salmon is delicious. I'm glad you also like seafood."

"Even if I didn't, I'd eat it for you, but I really prefer it...although sometimes I actually crave a big hamburger with cheese and pickle and a thick slice of Bermuda onion."

"Ugh! Now the truth comes out." She smiled over at him. "What other bad habits do you have?"

He laid down his fork, feigning a serious look. "Sometimes I leave my clothes wherever I take them off. I'm not the neatest person, even though my mother made me keep my room neat as long as I lived there."

"Oh, come on, you must have some habits that are worse than that!"

"Probably...but I'm not going to tell you. What about you?" he asked.

"I'm afraid I'm a neat freak. I have to have a place for everything and everything has to be kept in its own place."

"Hmm...I'll remember that. There are worse habits to have, I guess."

Looking at each other, they burst out laughing, and people at nearby tables smiled when they heard the infectious laughter of the handsome couple.

They sipped their wine and held hands while listening to the piano player who seemed to be playing his romantic music just for them. He finally broke their comfortable silence. "Ready to go?"

She nodded and he rose to pull out her chair. He reached for her chiffon scarf, caressing her shoulders as he draped it around her.

Suppressing a sigh when his hands touched her, she prayed her face did not betray the warmth and the tingle she felt deep inside.

Holding hands, they made their way to the elevator and out to his waiting car. The evening was cool with fog surrounding them and they could barely see the moon through the car windows as he drove the short distance to her place. Finding a parking space near the entrance to her building, he walked around and helped her from the car, still holding her hand as they walked through the lobby to the elevator.

Reaching her apartment, he took her keys to open the door. Once inside the foyer, she turned to thank him for a lovely evening, but before she could speak, he leaned down and kissed her lightly on the forehead. "I'll call you," he announced before making his way back to the elevator.

She closed the door and softly rubbed the warm spot he'd left on her forehead.

ॐ ॐ ॐ

Feeling too restless to go to bed, Jennifer tried Sherry's phone number, not really expecting her to be home, but she was in luck. Before she could tell Sherry about her date with Michael, Sherry asked, "So did Michael call you?"

Jennifer stared at the phone. Sherry had a habit of getting right to the point.

"We had dinner this evening, Sherry."

"Isn't Michael a hunk like I said? Women actually swoon when he comes around. How did you two hit it off?" Sherry always wanted to know every detail.

"We had a great time. Dinner and dancing at the Top of the Mark, no less. Michael has a great sense of humor and we laughed a lot. He's also a smooth dancer. Unlike some men, he really seemed to be interested in what I said rather than just pretending to."

Sherry was properly impressed. "So you had a good time, but what do you really think about him, girlfriend? I haven't heard anything negative yet. You usually find some kind of fault with your dates."

Jennifer thought for a moment. "I...I really don't know how I feel about him. Michael's okay, I guess. I have to admit he's the first man I've felt comfortable with in a long time."

She certainly wasn't going to commit to anything more definite than that until she knew whether Michael was serious about seeing her again. She was going to take it slow with this one.

Nor was she going to share all her feelings with Sherry. Jennifer knew from experience that the problem with confiding everything to a friend—even a close one—was that too much could be said which would be regretted later if circumstances changed. So she switched the conversation to topics more impersonal, and shortly after hung up her receiver.

She had some thinking to do.

CHAPTER 5

The fragrance of roses greeted Jennifer when she opened the door of her office. Hurrying to her desk, she removed the card from a tall vase holding twenty-four beautiful red roses. She read its short message: I want to know you better! No signature. Nothing else, just those simple words. Her heart suddenly beat faster and her body felt warmer as she placed the card among the flowers. She pulled one of the long stemmed roses out of the water and inhaled its fragrance several moments. "That man really knows how to get to me," she said aloud as she replaced the rose.

Slipping off her jacket before starting on the stack of papers in front of her, she unconsciously hummed softly while she sorted through her day's work. Everything was suddenly brighter in her world, and even though she had interruptions, the day moved along smoothly. Late in the afternoon her secretary announced that Michael was on the line.

Taking a deep breath before picking up the receiver, she said softly, "The roses are gorgeous, Michael."

"Roses?" he feigned surprise.

"Oh, stop teasing, Michael. Who else would send such a message?"

"Maybe one of your secret lovers," he answered rather matter-of-factly.

"Is that what you want me to believe?" A broad smile crossed her face.

"You better not even think it!" he retorted. More seriously, he added, "You've been interrupting my work most of the day, Jennifer. I can't seem to get you out of my mind." He waited for a moment before announcing, "Incidentally, my firm, along with several other black-owned businesses, is having a community recognition affair Wednesday evening. I hadn't planned to go, but if you'll go with me I might consider it. I know this is short notice but—"

She cut him off. "A friend and I already plan to be there. But I'd love to go with you."

"What about your friend? Won't he be disappoint-ed?" His voice suddenly changed.

She gave a short chuckle. "You just automatically assume my 'friend' is a man. But you're wrong. Sherry Brown—you met her—and I plan to go together, but we can meet her there and sit at the same table."

"Hey, that sounds good! I'll pick you up around seven o'clock." His voice was now enthusiastic.

She assured him she would be ready and was hanging up her receiver when she heard him calling her name.

"Jennifer, Jennifer!"

"Yes, Michael?"

"I'm glad you're going with me," he said softly before the phone went dead in her ear.

She was happy inside the rest of the day.

ॐ ॐ ॐ

Jennifer and Michael walked into the ballroom of the St. Francis Hotel and looked around for Sherry.

"Sherry is usually on time," she said, her eyes roaming around the room. She finally spotted Sherry talking to a group on the other side of the ballroom. "There's Sherry over there, Michael," she said, pointing across the room.

He smiled. "Oh, yes. She's really one put-together sister. I'll go get her. We better claim a table before the groups start breaking up."

She was watching him walk across the ballroom to get Sherry when she felt an arm on her shoulder. She turned and faced Kevin, her former lover.

"Hey, Jennifer. You're sure looking good tonight," Kevin greeted her.

She automatically stiffened and moved out of his reach. "Hello, Kevin. Nice to see you again," she said evenly as she glanced at him. Same old Kevin. Full of the charm that had once captivated her.

"How about having dinner tomorrow evening? Kinda talk over old times," Kevin suggested.

"Sorry, Kevin, I'm not interested."

"How about Friday. Busy then?"

She stared at him. *He just doesn't get it,* she thought. *He can't accept the fact that his charm is now wasted on me.* "As far as you're concerned, Kevin, I'll always be too busy," she answered softly and turned away.

A smirk on his face, Kevin started to reply but stopped when a beautiful young woman resembling Vanessa Williams walked up and took his arm. Kevin leaned down and kissed her hair. "Come on, sugar, we've got better things to do."

Michael and Sherry walked up as Kevin and his friend were leaving.

"Was that Kevin, Jennifer?" Sherry asked and immediately knew she had blown it when she saw a disgusted expression cross Jennifer's face.

"Yes, that was Kevin," Jennifer answered shortly. "We better look for a table."

Michael followed the two women, a quizzical expression on his face. They found a table near the dais and joined two couples already seated. While introductions were made at their table, the master of ceremonies introduced the dignitaries seated on the dais.

Immediately a squadron of waiters and waitresses descended on the tables, serving the usual banquet fare— stuffed chicken breast, mashed potatoes and gravy, green beans, and a tossed salad. The noise level decreased to a minimum the moment food was served at the tables.

She noticed Michael giving her quizzical looks throughout the dinner while she chatted with others at the table.

While dessert was being served, the master of ceremonies started the awards program. Although they knew some of the recipients of the community awards, they soon became as bored with the long, drawn-out program as many others around them seemed to be.

Near the end of the program Michael whispered, "Let's get out of here, Jennifer." She readily agreed and they excused themselves and made their way to his car. It was a short ride to her apartment and little was said on the way.

While he was parking, she asked, "Would you like to come in for a nightcap, Michael?"

He brightened at her words, and his step was much lighter as he accompanied her through the lobby to the elevator. Reaching her apartment, he took her key and opened the door.

"How about a mimosa?" she asked.

"That sounds good," he answered on his way to the living room. He glanced around the room while waiting for her. He admired the African artifacts scattered around the room. Several small figures from Ghana that adorned the mantle caught his eye, and he walked over to examine them more closely.

She walked in while he was looking at the statuettes. "A friend of mine spent several months in Ghana and brought those back for me," she said, depositing a tray of chips and salsa along with the mimosas on the glass-topped coffee table.

He joined her on the sofa, and they sipped their drinks in silence for a few moments.

"So...do you have any brothers or sisters, Jennifer?" he asked, starting the conversation.

A pained expression crossed her face.

He saw the confusion and thought, *Why is she upset about a question like that?*

She swallowed hard before answering. "No, I...uh...I grew up an only child. How about you?"

"I have two of each—two younger brothers and two older sisters. And it was really a trip being in the middle like that. That and growing up with a zillion cousins. My mother is big on family. Mom is from one of those old southern families where you are judged by not only who your mother is but who your grandmother and her mother were. You know how some black folks are. Ever since Alex Haley's book came out more people are hunting for their roots as they call it. Naturally Mom got more involved in tracing our ancestors. A person's heritage is a real big thing with her. She still spends a lot of time filling in our family tree when she learns about some distant cousin or other relatives from years..." Noticing a peculiar look crossing Jennifer's face, he stopped talking for a moment. He finally asked, "Is something wrong, Jennifer? Do you feel okay?"

His question startled her. "Oh...I'm...fine," she answered haltingly. *No way could she tell him what was going through her mind.*

He twirled his glass a few moments before he continued. "Mom puts a lot of stock in where people came from. Her favorite saying is 'An acorn never falls too far from the tree,' which we heard many, many times while growing up. When we were young and first started dating, she always told each of us to check on the kind of family our dates came from. And she told us boys never to mess around with a girl we wouldn't marry." He smiled when he remembered that admonition. "Even now we have to stop her from grilling people about their family background when they come to her house. Sometimes it's downright embarrassing, but that doesn't stop Mom. She still manages to ask them about their family one way or another."

He took another sip of his drink. "I guess I have a lot of my mother in me. Another thing I remember is that Mom always said that problems in childhood are often manifested in later life. Her exact words were 'A troubled childhood makes a troubled adult.' When I meet people who fall into that category, I realize it really is important to know about a person's family."

Hearing that long discourse on his family, Jennifer shrank further into the sofa, a sinking feeling in the pit of her stomach. She felt her self-esteem slowly slipping away the more he talked and cringed at the thought of not having roots of her own. Not only did she not know who her birth parents were or whether they were alive or dead, she also had no idea whether she had any aunts, uncles, cousins, or whatever. More than ever the reality of being adopted really bummed her out and her hands began to sweat. She also felt a twinge of envy as she listened to Michael talk about his family. How great it must have been growing up in such a large, tightly-knit family where everyone was kin. Maybe in time she might be able to relate to a man without always having doubts and inhibitions about being adopted, but when would that day come? Her thoughts caused a chill to ripple across her skin.

He was puzzled by the pained expression so evident on her face. "Why so serious all of a sudden, Jennifer?"

She shook her head as if that would clear it and managed a weak smile. "I was just thinking about my family." She offered no further information. Although still puzzled by her reaction, he didn't press her, thinking she probably didn't want to talk about her family at the moment.

They sipped their drinks in silence for a few

moments before he abruptly set down his drink. "Do you have a man in your life, Jennifer?"

She almost dropped her drink but quickly regained her composure. "I'm not in a relationship, but I go out occasionally with Greg."

"Are you serious about him?"

"Not in a romantic way. Greg's someone I've known since I've been out here...just a platonic thing." Thinking for a moment, she decided to be as blunt as Michael. "Do you have what they call a 'significant other,' Michael?"

He squirmed uneasily. "I guess I've been seeing Tawana Coleman more than anyone else. We go out occasionally, as you know. Tawana seems to know almost everyone in San Francisco, and she's quite the proverbial social butterfly. I've met a lot of people through her. But being with Tawana is hardly what you would call having a relationship. From the way she acts sometimes, I'm sure she would like it to be otherwise, but I've let her know several times I'm not interested in making any commitments."

She remembered that Tawana's father owned one of the most prestigious realty firms in the Bay Area, and Tawana was one of his best agents. Oh yes, she knew quite a bit about Tawana. No man was safe around her.

She started inspecting her nails. "I guess I haven't devoted much of my time to social affairs. I travel a lot, checking on my audit teams working with firms in various regions."

He was intrigued. "How long are you usually gone? Where do you have to go?"

She laughed. "Slow down, Michael. How can I answer when you ask two or three questions at the same time?"

Realizing what he'd said, he smiled. "Okay, okay, I'll take the answers one at a time."

"Well, some of my auditing staff are out every week across the country. One of my main responsibilities is helping the teams out in the field. I love to go to the East Coast, especially New York, when I have teams there. I can leave time to pamper myself, like seeing the latest plays and window shopping for all the fads that will later reach California." She thought she noticed a hint of amazement in his eyes when she finished explaining.

"How many do you have on your staff?"

She was aware he really seemed interested as he listened to her, and she warmed up to the subject that was important to her.

"There're about sixty auditors in the department which I manage, but then there are other levels of supervisors who handle the day-to-day activities. But I like to have first-hand knowledge about what's going on in the firms we have under contract, so I drop in on the out-of-town audits as frequently as I can."

"You must like what you do, it shows on your face when you talk about it," he observed, noticing the sudden sparkle in her eyes. "That's heavy. Aren't you a little young for that kind of responsibility?"

"If you're fishing for my age, I'm thirty-two." She smiled when his eyebrows went up. "This is the only firm I've ever worked for, and I went with it right out of college. Luckily, I had someone who took me under his wing. Sounds easy, but it hasn't been. I've fought for every step in one way or another, and I still have to fight sometimes to maintain my present position. Not everyone is happy to have an African American for a boss, much less a woman."

He noticed the confidence in her voice as she talked, as if she took her strengths for granted, that what she had attained was no more than her just rewards. She sounded very sure of herself and he rather admired her ability to get and keep what she wanted. It was also a little frightening, he thought, and wondered if there could be a permanent place for anything or anyone else in her life. She seemed to have everything going for her. Had the world by the tail, so to speak.

"But don't you ever want more out of life than just having a high-powered job?" he asked, rather bluntly.

His question didn't daunt her. "I see no reason why I can't have my career and a family as well when I decide to go that route. And I wouldn't marry a man who didn't appreciate my ability as well as my body!" Her voice grew a bit softer as her eyes searched his face.

"But how realistic is it to want a career that demands

so much travel and raise a family at the same time? You can only be so successful in having it both ways, you know. Wouldn't you have to make some choices?"

She twisted her hair for a moment. "I don't quite understand what you're saying, Michael. Many women are successful in having a career as well as a family. If I were a man, I'd want a woman who knows what is going on in the world, who's out there making a place for herself, one who can talk about something other than what kind of baby food is best when he comes home in the evening."

"Maybe I just don't get it, Jennifer. Or perhaps I'm a bit old-fashioned, but I certainly can't see my wife running around the country every two or three weeks just to satisfy the demands of her career. There're more important considerations it seems to me if a woman has a family."

She gazed down at her drink for a moment. *I knew he was too good to be true. Why can't men accept the idea that women's careers can be just as important as their own? Or that women can handle more than one responsibility at the same time?*

While he waited for her to respond, all kinds of thoughts ran through his mind. *I hope she's not one of those women who thinks her career is the be-all and end-all in life and that a man is only necessary to have a family. What are women thinking about now-a-days?* He blamed it on women's lib. As far as he was concerned that movement was for the birds in some ways, even though he acknowledged it had its merits in other ways. But basically he thought women's lib was responsible for most men not knowing how to relate to women nowadays.

Having heard enough of his views, she changed the subject. "So what do you want out of life, Michael?"

He was silent for a few seconds. Then he reached over and placed his hand over hers. "I've probably been in the same space as you until very recently, Jennifer. That is, totally involved in my work. I didn't really concern myself about the future. But I'm thirty-five now, and since I've been out here, I've had some gnawing doubts every once in a while that I'm missing out on something." He stopped talking and looked down at their clasped hands.

"Missing out on something?" she repeated quietly, loving the warmth of his hand.

He shifted uneasily, not sure he was ready to share his innermost longings with anyone.

She was aware of his hesitation. "What do you really want, Michael?" she persisted.

"What I really want, I guess, is to find someone I can love totally. Someone who loves me as much as I love her. Someone I like as a friend as well as a lover. Someone who needs me as I need her and—" He stopped and looked at her, wanting to see how she was taking his sudden twist into sentimentality. "Haven't you ever...felt you...needed someone?"

"Yes," she said in a low voice. "I know what you mean."

Both lapsed into silence for a few moments.

"I'm curious, Michael. Tell me more about yourself. What you like to do, what you like to eat, the kind of music you like, things like that."

He dropped his eyes to his glass. He didn't like to talk about himself, and he felt doubly shy with her. "Oh, I'm just your average guy, I guess. I like sports, especially football and basketball. I like to listen to music, mostly light classical and jazz." She smiled at the combination as he continued. "I like to read, especially the who-done-it books. I even like to cook every blue moon; omelets and grilled cheese sandwiches are my specialty. And I like to lounge in front of an open fire and stare into the flames, especially if I have my favorite person next to me." He grinned at her lasciviously, causing her to blush. "So what about you, Jennifer? What do you like?"

"Some of the same things you like, I think, especially football games and open fireplaces. And I read every night before I go to sleep. I like quiet moments...having time to myself occasionally and—" She stopped for a moment. "I don't like crowds, loud voices, brash people, or hard rock. And that current fad—rap music—sends me up a wall!" She smiled as he looked askance at her.

"You don't like rap music? How can you be so out of it?" he asked, a sly grin on his face.

"You mean you go for that stuff?" she asked incredulously.

"No, not really," he assured her. "But some of the rap messages I've heard are pretty much right on target for what's happening in the world today."

She acquiesced somewhat. "I suppose you have a point, except I can never understand the lyrics of most of them... maybe it's an age thing."

The rest of the time they spent sharing stories about escapades of their youth, their prejudices, their political preferences. They even got into some of their personal philosophies and discovered they were in agreement about a lot of things.

"Life is weird, isn't it?" he finally said. "Just think, if we both hadn't gone to Greg's party, we might never have met."

She glanced over at him. "Maybe it was fate," she suggested.

"Perhaps," he continued, "but then it's up to us to ignore fate or to make the most of it, don't you think?"

"I...suppose so," she answered, rather reluctantly.

Shortly afterward he got up to leave. She walked to the door with him. Before opening it, he gently lifted her face and bent down, kissing her softly on each cheek, then crushing his lips to hers. He finally withdrew his lips, looking intensely into her eyes a couple of moments before saying he would be in touch. He slowly turned away from her and headed for the elevator.

She closed the door softly and padded back into the living room to turn off the lights for the night. She continued through the room to the wide front window and looked out into the bright moonlight for several moments, thinking about the physical signals her body had sent during their long kiss. Could he possibly have known how much she wanted to respond to him? Her face grew warm, remembering the way his full lips felt against hers. She shook her head, knowing she was not ready to even think about him that way.

It had been a long time since she had felt so drawn to a man, but she didn't trust her judgment enough to hope they had a future. From past experiences she knew how quickly things could go wrong in a relationship. Sometimes just little things could turn off one person or the other, and both would go their separate ways.

Then her mind turned to Michael's description of his mother and her emphasis on family background. *Michael will probably drop me like a hot potato when he finds out I'm adopted. No way can I keep that a secret. I've got to tell him. Maybe the next time I see him. And then that thing he has about having a career and a family. No way am I giving up what I've worked so hard to get. Maybe it's better to let him go now and forget about how he makes me feel.*

Still staring out the window she wondered why everyone couldn't be herself or himself and the other accept the person for what she or he was? She decided that was the trouble with the world today—everyone had to fit into a preconceived niche in life. Some things could never be solved; perhaps it would be best to let her own life take its course without too much complaining. Philosophizing about it certainly would change nothing.

She drew back from the window and turned off a small lamp as she passed through the living room, continuing on to her bedroom, her favorite room. She had spent hours before deciding on furniture for the large mauve and white room which had a small alcove she used as a dressing room. Her long chaise longue, which she plopped down on many evenings after a long day, had been recovered to match the room when she couldn't find the kind she wanted. She drew back the purple satin spread and crisp sheets on her king-size bed and rearranged the pillows, throwing the small round ones, which matched her spread, onto the chaise longue. She plumped up her down pillows and arranged them for comfortable reading.

Undressing slowly, she hung up each piece before going to the bathroom. Studying her face in the mirror, she saw a happy countenance which was new to her. Her dark eyes shone like stars and her mouth was curved in a half smile. She removed her makeup and creamed her face with the moisturizer that was a daily part of her toilette.

She stopped brushing her teeth and leaned closer to the mirror, looking for the sign of any wrinkles. "Who knows what happens after thirty?" she said aloud to the mirror. Seeing no visible changes in her skin, she padded back to the bedroom, a satisfied smile on her face.

Picking up her novel on the way, she climbed in between cool sheets, hoping her book would put her to sleep. She read only a few pages before her thoughts again turned to Michael's remarks on his family's obsession with people's background. Her concern about her own adoption crept into her mind again. She certainly couldn't invent a family. How could she possibly fit into a family like his? Her mind wandered to her affair with Kevin and the reasons for it ending. Would she ever find a soul mate?

CHAPTER 6

The rest of the week sped by for Jennifer. She worked long hours getting caught up with the paperwork that had accumulated the last couple of weeks. Greg stopped by to remind her she had promised to go with him to the Ingalls' party on Friday.

She talked with Michael a couple of times and agreed—against her better judgment—to have dinner with him Saturday evening.

By the time Friday arrived, she rushed home, excited about getting ready for the Ingalls' party. Everyone who was anyone in San Francisco would be there. Also, being with Greg would be fun as he always seemed to know exactly what to do and what to say regardless of the situation. There wasn't even a spark of romance between them as far as she was concerned and she sometimes felt guilty in taking up his time, even though he always insisted on taking her places when she didn't have a date.

Jennifer rushed into her apartment and arranged her weekly purchase of cut flowers and sprigs of baby's breath in her favorite crystal vases, placing one vase in the foyer and the other on her coffee table in the living room before going into the bedroom to get ready for the evening.

Looking through her closet and pulling out several outfits, she finally settled on a white low-cut silk top and a long black silk skirt that molded to her body, a long slit up the left side. She held the combination up to her body and looked at it for several moments, deciding it really was a good choice. A bit on the sexy side, but what the heck...she needed that kind of look for a change.

Glancing at the clock, she saw that she still had time to indulge in a long luxurious soak in the bathtub, hoping to get rid of the frustrations of the day. When something bothered her, she found that soaking in a tub of hot bubbly water was the best place to relax. She turned the hot water on full force and dumped in a handful of perfumed bath crystals, slowly inhaling the aroma as it filled the bathroom. Slipping into the water slowly, she let the water run until it almost reached the top of the tub. She breathed in deeply as the hot scented water swirled around her, and she lay in the tub for several minutes before soaping her sponge to complete her bath.

She stepped out to dry herself with a long fluffy

towel, glancing into the full-length mirror now covered with steam. Wiping it clear with one end of her towel, she gazed at the reflection of her nude body, looking at it as if she were really seeing herself for the first time. She was satisfied with the overall image in the mirror—high firm breasts over a slim waist which curved out to meet the supple line of her hips and long smooth legs. Not bad for an over-thirty broad, she decided. Tossing her towel across the rack, she hurried to her bedroom to get dressed and apply the sparse makeup she used.

Shortly after nine o'clock she opened the door for Greg. Giving her the once-over, he let out a long, soft whistle. "Whoa, girl! You've really got something goin' on in that dress! I'll probably have to beat off the men with a stick when we get to the party."

She smiled widely, pleased with his compliments, and in a voice mimicking the innocence of a southern belle exclaimed, "Why, Greg, how you do go on!"

"I just haven't seen you look like this in a long time!" he exclaimed with raised eyebrows.

"I feel like painting the town tonight," she answered, a bit giddily. "And you know the other women who'll be at the party will all look like fashion models—each one trying to outdo all the others."

He agreed. "If it's the usual crowd, you're probably right. The hair salons probably made a mint this week, not to mention Nordstrom's and Saks Fifth Avenue."

The mere fact that he had noticed her outfit boosted

her confidence. She suddenly felt as glamorous as he thought she was. "Let's get the show on the road...I'll get my wrap off the bed."

While they were in the elevator and later in the car, she could feel his surreptitious glances toward her when he thought she wasn't looking, and her confidence level rose to its peak. Driving up the circular drive of the Ingalls' complex, he let her out at the door, and she went into the lobby to wait until he parked.

She greeted several fabulously-dressed African American couples also on their way to the penthouse elevator. Eager for the evening to begin, she waited impatiently for Greg to return. He finally walked across the lobby and claimed her arm on their way to the elevator, which stopped only at the penthouse level. Exiting the elevator, they heard talk and laughter, and they joined the noisy crowd in the long, lavishly decorated living room.

White-coated waiters circulated among the guests, bearing trays with crystal flutes of champagne. Taking the stemmed glasses, they joined a group, and he immediately became involved in a conversation about a current litigation that television and the daily papers were playing up.

While he talked, she surveyed the handsome group of men and women professionals, some doctors, some lawyers, some well-known business executives. Some were married; others were still looking for that blissful state. The brothers looked handsome in their elegant Armani suits and hundred dollar ties, and the sisters gorgeous in designer gowns, many of which she would give her eyeteeth for. After a few minutes she felt Greg's hand on her elbow, and they moved on to greet others as they circulated through the living room to an adjoining room.

She suddenly froze in her steps, causing Greg to bump into her from behind. At the other end of the room she recognized Michael's profile. He was smiling at a woman standing close to him. Jennifer recognized Tawana Coleman when the woman turned around. She couldn't help noticing that Tawana was holding on to Michael's arm rather possessively and looking up at him very seductively.

Jennifer turned abruptly to face Greg, and he bumped into her a second time. "What's wrong, Jennifer? Are you all right?"

"I think...uh...I think I need to find the bathroom," she stammered, not knowing what else to say to explain her reaction to the scene in front of her.

"Oh...okay. I'll wait here for you."

She rushed from the room in search of a place to compose herself, furious at the way she was reacting at seeing Michael with Tawana. *Why am I acting like this?* she asked herself. *Why should Michael's being with Tawana upset me since I already knew he was seeing her? But why didn't he ask me to go to the party with him?*

74

Frustrated, she got in line for the bathroom and, once inside, ran cold water over her wrists and checked her makeup. Taking several deep breaths to compose herself, she returned to the room to find Greg in the same spot she had left him.

She smiled up at him. "Sorry, Greg. I'm okay now, just a little emergency." Marshaling all the nerve she could call on, she proposed, "Let's go over and say hello to Michael and Tawana."

Putting her arm through his, Greg led her through the crowd to where Michael and Tawana were standing.

Michael didn't see Jennifer until Tawana smiled slyly and greeted her. "Why, Jennifer Johnson, imagine seeing you again so soon."

Michael swung around and faced Jennifer and Greg. He suddenly looked dumbstruck. Jennifer noticed the surprised expression on his face and wanted to tell him to close his mouth.

While the four exchanged greetings and commented on the crowd, neither Tawana nor Greg missed the pained expression flitting across Michael's face while they were talking. Both could also feel the tension in the air as Jennifer and Michael gazed at each other.

"Well, where has our top executive been keeping herself?" Tawana snidely asked.

"Here and there," Jennifer answered, not wasting her words since she knew Tawana couldn't have cared less where she had been.

Michael and Greg exchanged a few words before Jennifer moved closer to Greg. "Greg and I have some other people to see. Enjoy the party." With that, she took Greg's arm, leaving Michael looking almost as dumbstruck as he had been when he first saw her.

For the next couple of hours Jennifer noticed that Michael's eyes seemed to stare at her from wherever he was, but he turned away each time she caught him looking at her. In one way his attention boosted her confidence; in another way she became a little nervous, wondering what he was thinking.

For Michael, those two hours were pure torture. He felt like a raging fire had started in his gut, and he didn't know how to extinguish it. Watching Jennifer and Greg dancing, Michael's palms began to sweat, and he excused himself to Tawana and walked out onto the wide deck where the cool air wafted around him for several minutes, somewhat assuaging the emotions he was having trouble dealing with.

When Michael returned to Tawana, she stared up at him. "You look awful, Michael! Don't you feel well? Have you had too much champagne?"

Unknowingly, Tawana had supplied Michael with an excuse to leave the party. "I don't know what it is...I don't feel well and I probably should go home." He hesitated when he noticed a peculiar expression on Tawana's face. "I'm...I'm sorry to spoil your evening, Tawana. Would you like to stay? I'll leave you my car and take a taxi." He reached into his pocket for his car keys.

"Oh, I think I'll just go along with you. It's almost midnight and I've had a chance to talk to almost everyone. I'm closing a rather complicated real estate deal tomorrow morning and really shouldn't stay too much longer either. Let's just slip out as unobstrusively as possible after we say good night to the Ingalls. You look rather washed out and don't need people asking whether something is wrong."

Michael thought Tawana sounded a bit put out, but he wasn't that concerned about how she felt at the moment—he just had to get out of there, and he could have kissed Tawana for that last suggestion. He took Tawana's arm and they skirted the long room. Just as they reached the front door, he turned and saw Jennifer staring at him from across the room. Not knowing how to interpret her look, he frowned slightly and followed Tawana.

Jennifer's eyes followed Michael and Tawana as they circled the room, speaking to their hosts before heading toward the front door. She saw Tawana tuck her arm into Michael's and smile up at him. *So Michael really is tight with Tawana,* she thought as she remembered the gossip she'd overheard at the beauty shop. She flinched...a band seemed to have settled around her heart.

Shortly after Michael and Tawana left, Jennifer mentioned to Greg she wanted to leave. Always the gentleman, Greg said he was also ready to go and insisted on her waiting in the lobby while he got the car. On the drive home he noticed she was unusually quiet, responding to his comments in monosyllables. He remembered the tense looks that had passed between Jennifer and Michael.

Finally he asked, "What's the Michael deal all about, Jennifer? Are you two friends or enemies? Sparks were certainly flying between you two for some reason or other. His eyes followed you most of the night. I could tell Tawana also noticed...it was that obvious."

"Oh, Greg, I'm sure you're exaggerating. Michael seemed rather attracted to Tawana. Once a brother's in the claws of a sister like Tawana, he has a hard time shaking her loose."

"Maybe Michael doesn't want to be shaken loose," Greg suggested, turning to see how Jennifer reacted to that statement.

She didn't bother to comment...her mind was too busy. How could Michael be interested in a sister like Tawana? That thought bothered her the rest of the way home. Her silence perplexed Greg, and he wondered what had suddenly come over her.

Breaking their silence, he asked, "Have you known Michael long?"

She heaved a long, loud sigh before turning to Greg. "I met Michael at your get-together, remember? We've had a couple of dates...that's the extent of our relationship," she answered in a rather terse voice. How could she tell Greg that Michael had just confirmed what she thought about brothers in general—they just couldn't be trusted.

Greg gave her a long, hard look, guessing that there was more to the story than she was willing to tell, but he didn't press her. Her whole demeanor told him that something was not quite right with her, but he didn't know what he could do to make her feel better. She would probably tell him more when she was ready to talk...he could wait.

As they neared her apartment she was sorry that all of her earlier enthusiasm had suddenly dissipated, and she now felt like a deflated balloon. When they exited the elevator on her floor, it took all of her energy to ask him in for a drink. She at least owed him that. "Would you like to come in for a nightcap, Greg?"

Out of his concern for her, Greg declined and left her at the door of her apartment, depositing a light kiss on her hair. "Have a good night, Jen," he said before turning down the hall to the elevator, a worried expression on his face. The last thing he wanted was to have her hurt, and he was afraid Michael would do just that. And he could do nothing about it.

Jennifer slowly closed the door and locked it, threw her wrap on the nearest chair in the living room and wearily made her way to her bedroom. What had started out to be a fun evening had turned into a fiasco as far as she was concerned. She took a long time undressing, hanging up each piece carefully as she shed it. She didn't want to admit why she was in such a down mood, and she wasn't looking forward to the rest of the night. How could she possibly keep her date with Michael tomorrow night and act as if nothing had happened? She supposed she'd just have to get through it somehow, but it would be the last date with him she would ever agree to, even if he begged her! Which, of course, was unlikely!

Michael thought of Jennifer's stare as he escorted Tawana to his car. He only half-listened to Tawana while she chatted about how great Jennifer looked and what a great couple she and Greg made. He cringed when she mentioned Jennifer and Greg—he didn't want to even think of the two of them together. Now all he wanted was to head home, and he breathed a sigh of relief when they finally reached Tawana's apartment. Outwardly he looked calm but inside he was in turmoil.

"Sure you don't want to spend the night again?" Tawana asked when he stepped into her foyer.

He shook his head, remembering the one night he'd spent with Tawana a few weeks earlier after he'd had too much to drink and she drove his car to her apartment. He had been in no shape to know where he was until he awakened in her bed the next morning, not knowing how he got there until she told him.

"Well, go on home and get a good night's sleep then—I'm sure you'll feel better tomorrow," Tawana advised, knowing when to give up.

He patted her cheek, saying that was exactly what he had in mind and hurried back to his car to drive the short distance to his own apartment.

ॐ ॐ ॐ

In his own place at last, Michael slowly removed his clothes and hung them in the closet. His shoes he placed on a rack. He carefully folded the comforter back to the foot of the bed. As he turned back the blanket and sheet, he wondered how he could turn off his thoughts of Jennifer so he could get some sleep. He couldn't get out of his mind the image of Greg holding Jennifer close while dancing, for at least an hour or so. He turned off his bedside lamp and lay staring into the darkness for a long time. Never having felt this way about any woman, he didn't know how to deal with his present feelings.

Finally giving up all hope of sleep, he reached for the television remote and clicked through several channels before he found a spy movie that had just started. He didn't know how long he watched it—a bright sun was shining through the half-closed shades when he awakened late Saturday morning. His first thought was his dinner date with Jennifer that evening, and he let out a loud groan, wondering how she would react after last night's fiasco.

Love Doesn't Come Easy

Michael would have felt better had he known that Jennifer was just as confused and frustrated as he was.

CHAPTER 7

The peal of her doorbell awakened Jennifer early Saturday morning. Glancing at the clock on her nightstand, she grumbled, "Who in the world has the nerve to ring my bell at this hour of the morning?" The doorbell chimed again. "I'm coming! I'm coming!" she called as she struggled to get fully awake. She threw on her robe and rushed through the living room, a deep frown on her face when she peeked through the peephole.

Flinging the door open, she practically shouted, "Sherry, what are you doing up here at this god-awful hour? Don't you know what time it is?"

"Cool it, girlfriend, and let's make some coffee before you bust a gut." Sherry sashayed into the room, leaving a scent of her heavy cologne behind her. "I just got out of the shower and hurried up here. You might want to hear some gossip right from the horse's mouth."

"Better be something damn important," Jennifer informed her tersely as they made their way to the kitchen. "I suppose you also expect me to offer you breakfast."

"I could use something besides coffee." Sherry was not in the least put off by her friend's attitude.

Jennifer groaned while putting some bran muffins in a pan to warm in the oven while she made the coffee. In no time they had steaming cups of coffee and hot muffins in front of them. "I suppose you want your usual sugar fix for the day," Jennifer quipped as she got up for the sugar bowl and grimaced as Sherry put two heaping spoons of sugar into her cup before adding more than a dash of cream.

Sherry glanced impishly over to Jennifer. "I like coffee with my cream and sugar," she announced, reaching for the hot muffin.

A scowl still on her face, Jennifer stared at Sherry silently devouring her muffin. "So what earth-shattering news brought you up here at the crack of dawn, Sherry?"

"Oh, just cool it, girlfriend, and I'll tell you." Sherry took another sip of her coffee before answering, totally enjoying the suspense she was creating. "You didn't tell me you were going to the Ingalls' party last—"

"What has that got to do with anything?" Jennifer demanded, for the first time wondering why Sherry hadn't been there.

Sherry smiled. "Well, seems like you created quite a ruckus at the Ingalls last night when you came in with Greg. My spies tell me Michael was really shook up that you were there with Greg, and that Michael insisted on leaving early, saying he didn't feel well. Of course Tawana left with him."

Sherry shifted around in her chair and watched her friend, waiting for Jennifer's reaction to her news.

Her mouth hanging open, Jennifer returned Sherry's stare. "How do you know all that? You weren't even there!"

Looking smug, Sherry settled back, knowing she had Jennifer's full attention now. "Well, it seems Tawana called her friend Barbara—who is also a friend of mine— and Barbara called me late last night." She stopped and walked across the kitchen to get another hot muffin.

"Will you please just get on with your story, Sherry? I'm not interested in all the little details!"

"Okay, I'm getting to the point. Barbara told me that Tawana said if Michael even thinks he's going to drop her for you, he's got another think coming. Seems Tawana was really pissed off over the way Michael's eyes followed you everywhere last night."

Jennifer set down her coffee cup with a clatter. "That's about the most asinine thing I've heard in a long time! It's ridiculous! In the first place, I've been out with Michael a couple of times, which certainly can't count as his being serious about me!" She took a deep breath and another sip of coffee. "And in the second place, I'm not sure I even like the guy, not to mention thinking of getting serious about him." She rose to get another muffin from the oven and stopped in the middle of the kitchen on her way back to the table, waving her muffin in the air. "And another thing, why in hell does Tawana think Michael is interested in me?" she demanded.

Sherry shrugged. "I haven't a clue, girlfriend...I'm just telling you what I heard. Seems that for some reason Tawana thinks he's quite taken with you." Sherry rose to refill her coffee cup and then sauntered back to the table, looking at her friend with raised eyebrows. "For whatever it's worth, I think you'd be crazy not to at least give Michael a chance if he's interested. What a hunk!"

Jennifer bristled. "If I hear you say another word about what a hunk Michael is, I think I'll throw up. There's much more to being a man than looking like Denzel Washington...or whoever the current hunk is." She took a vicious bite out of her muffin.

Sherry chuckled silently inside. In some ways she always enjoyed seeing Jennifer in a snit instead of that cool, calm composure she usually had, a facade which also irritated her no end at times.

The two friends sipped their coffee for a few moments, eyeing each other cautiously. Sherry finally got up enough nerve to ask, "So are you going to see

Michael again?"

"You're something else, Sherry. It's really none of your business but I'll tell you anyway. I have a dinner date with Michael this evening."

Sherry's cup clattered on the saucer and her eyes got bigger than normal. "Girl, you've got to be kidding! Oh, how I'd like to be around when Tawana gets a whiff of that!"

Jennifer leaned back in her chair, feeling more human after her second cup of coffee. "Look, Sherry, I think you're trying to make a mountain out of a molehill. It's no big thing. Who knows whether I'll ever see Michael again after tonight. You know how these San Francisco men operate. Here today, gone tomorrow seems to be their modus operandi."

Sherry thought for a moment. "You may be right, but I kinda hope that this works out for you. For some reason, I can't explain why, you two seem so right for each other." She carried her dishes to the sink, glancing sideways at Jennifer's scowl. "I've got a lot to do today, so I better get my butt outta here."

Jennifer followed her to the door. "I suppose I should thank you, but I believe you're whistling in the dark. I just don't think Michael is any different from any of the other men I've met."

"Keep the faith, girlfriend," was Sherry's parting shot as she opened the front door. "You just never know what's around the corner, so to speak."

Love Doesn't Come Easy

Closing the door behind her friend, Jennifer's mood plunged. All of a sudden she felt at loose ends. She wandered into her bedroom, made the bed and straightened up the cosmetics on her dresser. When she opened her drapes, bright rays of sun streamed through the shutters. She looked out at the beginning of a beautiful day. There wasn't even a hint of fog over the Golden Gate Bridge. She suddenly knew what she wanted to do and quickly changed into her jogging suit and shoes. Grabbing her purse, she headed for the garage.

By the time Jennifer unlocked her car door and climbed in, she knew she had made the right choice of getting out of her apartment for a while. She sat for a few minutes deciding where to drive to—she wanted some place peaceful and serene. The beach below the Cliff House on the Great Highway which ran along the Pacific Ocean would be the perfect place she decided and headed in that direction.

As usual that area was crowded with tourists, and she was lucky to find a place to park. She scrambled out of her car and started jogging toward an almost deserted part of Ocean Beach, a slender ribbon of sand more suitable for sweaters than swimsuits. She drew her collar up around her neck even though it was a sunny day. The breeze from the ocean was always chilly. Looking out over the ocean she saw a couple of tankers on the horizon making their way to the Golden Gate Bridge. Nearer the shore, she watched a couple of surfers riding

the huge waves, cringed when one of them lost his surf-
board, and then sighed in relief when he recovered it.
She jogged on toward Cliff House where the tourists
became more numerous.

She suddenly became more depressed as she merged
with the crowd; everyone she saw was part of a couple.
It's just like Noah's Ark, she thought, and felt tears gathering behind her lids. Feeling sorry for herself was something she seldom did, and she didn't know how to handle the emotions almost suffocating her.

She veered off the beach and climbed the short distance to the sidewalk leading to the Cliff House restaurant. The closer she got to the building, the hungrier she
became and could almost taste one of the omelets the
restaurant was famous for. While waiting in line for a
table, she again noticed that no one else seemed to be
alone. By the time she was finally shown to a table near
a window, her appetite had somewhat waned, but the
omelet still appealed to her. Waiting for her food, she
marveled at the scene below her. Waves crashed against
Seal Rock, sending foam into the sky. Some sea lions
were frisking around while others were merely basking in
the sun on the jagged rocks. Shore birds dove in and out
above the sea lions, some diving down on the rocks looking for food when debris washed up.

Finishing her meal, she noticed it was still early
afternoon and decided to take in a movie before going
home, thinking that would help her while away the next

few hours. Maybe she could shake her depressing thoughts by becoming involved with what was happening on the screen. She passed a couple of theaters on her way and finally chose a comedy she had read was the hit of the season, if the critics were to be believed. Luckily the next feature was starting in a matter of minutes and she hurried to find a parking spot on Sacramento Street.

Hunting for a seat, she again noticed everyone seemed to be in couples. She found a seat near the front of the theater; she didn't want to look at the coziness of couples with hands around shoulders. The movie lived up to its advertisements, and a couple of hours later she was in a much better mood when she exited the theater and headed home.

By the time she reached her apartment, she discovered she had only a short time to get ready for her date with Michael. She already knew exactly what she was going to wear and after a quick shower, she donned her clothes and was just putting the finishing touches on her makeup when Michael rang her bell.

She opened the door, and both felt the tension surrounding them, each having different thoughts about the past night. After a brief greeting, she hurriedly picked up a short coat and her bag and they made their way down the hall to the elevator, looking surreptitiously at each other several times. Both were unconsciously holding their breaths, not knowing how the other was going to react.

During the ride down to the lobby, conscious of the silence that surrounded them, she inquired, "Where are we having dinner, Michael?"

"I made reservations at Sinbad's." He quickly added, "I hope you like that restaurant."

"I really do...I love eating near the water."

Very little else was said on the short ride to Sinbad's, and both were aware that neither knew just what to say. He pulled into the valet parking lot and turned his car over to the attendant after helping her from the car. Their table was ready for them, and they were seated almost immediately at a window table overlooking the bay. They could hear the waves slapping against the building as they sat down. It had been a perfect day for sailing, and they watched a few sailboats still plying their way between the Bay Bridge and the Golden Gate Bridge. Neither spoke for a while, enjoying the scenery before them. In truth, neither knew what to say to the other.

He finally broke the silence. "I really like this place. I've been here a couple of times during the week with some guys from the office, but we didn't get a table with a view like this."

She nodded and continued to look out over the water.

A waiter approached, much to their relief, and they ordered an appetizer of fried clams. "We seem to like the same kind of food," he observed as he dipped a piece of

Love Doesn't Come Easy

clam into the sauce. "I haven't had fried clams anywhere else that I like better. In fact, I could really pig out on just fried clams!"

She smiled but did not comment. She was too busy trying to think of something to say. And for the life of her she couldn't keep Tawana out of her mind. Why she was even concerned about that woman she had no idea. Maybe she should just chill out. After all, it really was his choice to date anyone he wished to go out with.

They devoured their fried clams in record time, and, thankfully, just as they finished, the waiter appeared with their menus.

"What would you like, Jennifer?" he asked as he studied the menu. "I'll go along with whatever you select."

Without giving the menu a second glance, she suggested, "Let's have the prawns stuffed with crabmeat, a Caesar salad and a glass of white wine."

"Perfect! I really like your choice."

Waiting for their dinner, they managed to make small talk, filling in each other about their work week. But in the back of both of their minds was the business of the Ingalls' party. Both welcomed the arrival of their dinner which would occupy them for a few minutes, and they attacked it with gusto.

While having coffee, he started fiddling with his fork, moving it around in circles. He was silent for a few more moments. Finally lifting his head and looking

92

rather embarrassed, he glanced over at her. "Jennifer," he began, "about Friday night...I should have told you Thursday when we talked that I had promised some time ago to go to the party with Tawana, but at the time I'd actually forgotten I'd promised to take her until she called to remind me...I didn't think about mentioning it to you, and then I—"

She held up her hand to stop his babbling. "You don't have to explain anything to me, Michael." Her voice was low and soft.

"That's...that's not really all I want to talk about, Jennifer. What I mean is..." He stopped, as if he were confused about what he really wanted to say.

"Just what *do* you mean, Michael?" she prodded, holding her breath while waiting for his answer.

Looking slightly embarrassed, he blurted out, "Do you go out often with Greg? Are you having an affair with him?"

Oh, so that's what's bothering him, she thought. *Typical male jealously, that's all it is.* "Greg works in the same firm as I do—he's a tax lawyer. I've known him for quite some time, and we go out occasionally. I told you about him when we first met. And he's really a great guy, a lot of fun to be with."

He was not too happy to hear what a great guy Greg was. "But are you having...what I mean is—"

She stopped him again. "No, Michael, we do not have a sexual relationship, if that's what you're trying to ask me. Greg's just a good friend who happens to be a man."

He visibly brightened. "Yeah, I guess that's what was really bothering me."

Oblivious to others in the restaurant, he leaned over and kissed her forehead, but pulled back quickly when he noticed the waiter approaching their table. Both broke out laughing and even the waiter chuckled when he placed the check in front of Michael. Shortly afterward they made their way out of the now crowded restaurant and headed for his car.

"It's still early. Want to check out the Wharf?" he asked. "Or maybe a movie?"

Jennifer hesitated. Where would she be more comfortable with him? She decided to choose a stroll along the Embarcadero. "It's so nice out, why don't we settle for the Wharf."

They walked out to the parking lot and waited for his car. When it arrived, he helped her with her seat belt and headed down the Embarcadero. "Everybody and his brother must be down here tonight," he observed as he moved slowly with the traffic. He pulled into the first parking lot that showed a vacancy sign. Going around to her side of the car, he helped her out and took her hand and they proceeded to join the hundreds of tourists that lined the street. She hardly noticed the tourists—her hand in his warm hand was almost too much.

"Believe it or not," he said, "this is only the second or

third time I've been down in this section of the Wharf since I arrived in San Francisco. There's something about this street that fascinates me, but for the life of me I can't tell you what it is."

She smiled. "I think most people feel the same way. I'll bet there are very few tourists that don't make this their first spot to see when they arrive in the city. Which, of course, makes the Chamber of Commerce members very happy."

He held onto her hand as they pushed their way through the throngs of people on both sides of the street. For the next couple of hours they browsed in several of the souvenir shops and stopped to watch some of the street entertainers before crossing the street and heading back to the parking lot.

On their way to her apartment he asked, "How'd you like to go over to Alcatraz tomorrow? I haven't made it over there yet, and I keep promising myself to go. Will you go with me?" He held his breath, hoping like sin that she would agree.

She was silent for a few seconds, thinking of her resolve not to see him again after tonight, but her heart overruled her head.

When she didn't answer immediately, he continued. "We could go around noon and catch the four o'clock ferry back. That would give us enough time, wouldn't it?"

Finally she turned to him, her voice very controlled

even though her heart was out of control. "I haven't planned on doing much of anything tomorrow, so I guess I could manage that."

He'd really hoped for a more enthusiastic reply, but at the moment he would take whatever he could get, his pulse suddenly doing double-time.

They arrived at her apartment shortly afterward and he left her at her door after planting a kiss on her forehead, saying he would pick her up at noon the next day. He'd turned to leave when he had another idea. "Why don't we have brunch on the Wharf before catching the ferry? About ten-thirty?"

"You've got it," she agreed before closing the door softly behind him.

"Slow down, girl," she admonished herself as she made her way to her bedroom. "That guy's really my type, but with all his talk about family background I probably don't stand a chance of having a future with him." She threw off her clothes and climbed into bed, determined to put him out of her thoughts.

She had been asleep only a short time when her nightmare began again, the first time in several weeks. She struggled, twisting and turning, trying to escape from the horror of her dream. As usual, she awakened at the sound of shrill screams. Throwing back the tangled cover and sheet, she sat up on the side of the bed, her head buried in her hands. Would she ever be free of that periodic and devastating interruption of her sleep?

She rose wearily and made her way to the bathroom, not bothering to turn on the light beside her bed. She turned on the cold water tap and held her face cloth under it. After wringing out the excess water, she held the cold cloth to her face for a few seconds, then repeated the process several times until she felt the heat leave her face. She was wide awake when she padded back to bed, still shaken by the nightmare. As she turned her thoughts to spending the next day at Alcatraz with Michael, the dream slowly subsided.

CHAPTER 8

Glancing out her window, Jennifer could see no fog over the bay, rather unreal for such an early hour. Happy it was going to be a great day to take the ferry across the bay to Alcatraz, she padded to the kitchen to start her coffeemaker.

Since they were having an early brunch, she decided to forego the rest of her breakfast. She showered while the coffee was brewing and threw on a short robe. Getting the morning paper from her hallway, she took it and a cup of coffee out onto her balcony.

Sipping her hot coffee slowly, she enjoyed the quiet of an early Sunday morning. A couple walking their dog across the street waved to her. No cars had passed since she'd come out and she relished the peacefulness of the morning. Looking out over the bay she saw only one small sailboat out in the water, while on the marina, several people were on their docked boats, evidently readying their crafts for an early sail. For several minutes she became engrossed in the scene in front of her before she opened her paper to catch up on the news.

Her coffee was cold when she noticed the sun was much higher in the sky. Checking her watch, she was amazed at the time and jumped up, gathered her paper and cup, and hurried into her bedroom to get dressed, determined to be ready to step out the door when Michael arrived.

After applying a little makeup, she went to her closet for a pair of burgundy gabardine pants and a long-sleeved, pale pink blouse. She rifled through her sweater shelf until she found a burgundy sweater to match her pants. Satisfied with her choice, she drew on some taupe sandals to complete her outfit. The doorbell sounded as she tied the ropes of her sandals.

Her heart flip-flopped when she opened the door to Michael's smiling face. Dressed in a pair of khakis topped by a light blue Calvin Klein polo shirt, a dark blue cardigan thrown around his shoulders, and dark brown Gucci loafers, he looked like he had just stepped out of an advertisement for sportswear in the popular *Ebony Man Magazine*.

He greeted her with a low whistle. "You look great!"

"You look pretty snazzy yourself," she responded, her heart beating faster than usual as she picked up her purse and sweater. Still smiling at each other, they hurried out to his car to start their day.

Since it was still early, he had little trouble finding a parking spot on the Embarcadero near the restaurant where they were having brunch. They hurried in and were served champagne shortly after they were seated. Getting in the buffet line, they returned to their table with heaping plates. They made small talk until they finished their meal and then made their way back to the car, eager to get to the ferry to pick up their tickets.

Rows of tourists were already lined up by the time they drove the short distance to the pier and parked. They ran to get into the long line of noisy people purchasing tickets for the tour.

The short trip across the bay to Alcatraz Island was over before she had time to complain about the choppy waves, and they followed the crowd off the ferry when it docked. Passing some tables where literature was displayed, they stopped and took several minutes selecting information about the island before starting up the hill to the buildings.

"Listen to this, Jennifer," he said, leafing through one of his brochures. "A Spanish explorer named this 'The Island of the Pelicans' way back in 1775, long before California became a state.

She listened attentively while he talked and then became engrossed in the pamphlets she'd picked up. "Did you know the Island was the Army's Pacific Branch

Military Prison in 1907? The soldiers who were shipped out here were sentenced to hard labor chipping rock, building roadways and erecting buildings. By 1912 it was the largest reinforced concrete structure in the world. And then in 1933 the Army transferred Alcatraz to the Federal Bureau of Prisons, which redesigned it as a maximum security facility to house incorrigible civilian inmates from other federal institutions. It was nicknamed 'The Rock' by the inmates who were surrounded by barbed wire, guard towers and double-barred windows as well as the natural isolation of the cold waters of the San Francisco Bay."

As they read they hurried up the hill to catch up with their guide, who was explaining the building they faced. They learned that Cellhouse, which originally could accommodate six hundred men, had housed an average population of about two hundred sixty men during the federal prison era. Most of the time there was one guard for every three inmates.

Walking down the central corridor nicknamed "Broadway," they looked into the individual five-feet by nine-feet cells where men spent sixteen to twenty-three hours a day with armed guards in the caged walkways at either end of the corridor.

"Can you imagine being locked up in one of those small places for years on end?" she asked, a frown on her face.

"Unbelievable," he replied.

Their next stop was at D Block, also known as Segregation or the Treatment Unit, according to their guide. They faced heavy steel doors and a three-tiered gun gallery they learned was reserved for inmates who broke Alcatraz regulations. Their guide explained that men were usually kept in these cells twenty-four hours a day, seven days a week, and left their cells once a week for a ten-minute shower.

All of the tourists were quiet, listening and looking, many shaking their heads at the horrors some of the inmates faced.

Fascinated by the history of the island, Michael had a question on his mind. "I remember reading about a group of Native Americans being on the island. What about that?"

Their guide stopped the group and told the story. "In 1969 a group of Native Americans, citing an 1868 treaty, claimed and occupied Alcatraz. They wanted to establish a cultural, spiritual and educational center here. Although they never reached their goal, their occupation of the island became a symbol of resistance and hope to the Indian movement and focused national attention on the problems and concerns of the American Indian."

"So who is responsible for Alcatraz now?" Jennifer asked.

"The island was made part of the Golden Gate National Recreation Area. The National Park Service is responsible for maintaining and restoring the historic buildings for public enjoyment." Their guide looked at his watch. "We better be getting back down the hill. The ferry will be here shortly."

In the distance, they spotted the ferry in the middle of the Bay, returning to Alcatraz. They hurried down the hill to join others in the long line, not wanting to wait two hours for another ferry.

The sun was rapidly moving toward the west as they drove across the city to her apartment. "Want to come up for some coffee or dessert?" she asked after he parked the car.

Having hoped she would ask, he sucked in his breath before he responded to her invitation. "I'd like both."

Going up in the elevator, neither touched the other. Both were aware of the distance between them but were afraid to close it. When they reached her floor, he took her keys and unlocked the door.

"I'll make the coffee and get some banana pudding out of the refrigerator. I hope you like it," she called, hurrying toward the kitchen.

Following her, he assured her that banana pudding was one of his favorite desserts. He leaned against the sink watching her get the pudding from the refrigerator, his stomach feeling as if he had just swallowed a dozen butterflies. When she came back to the sink and accidentally brushed him as she got the coffee can , something inside him snapped. Without a word, he pulled her into his arms. A moan escaped from his throat as he crushed his mouth against hers.

The feel of his lips electrified her, sending shivers down her spine. Against her will, she became powerless in his arms when she felt his tongue probing inside her mouth, caressing her lips and her teeth. His hands moving up and down her sides left a brand on every spot he touched.

His touch was everything she had ever imagined about love—tender, suggestive, thrilling. She stopped thinking and started feeling. For a moment she stood perfectly still within his arms, savoring the tantalizing warmth that was spreading over her, mixing up her thoughts. She felt his mouth on hers again in a soft, almost impersonal kiss while his hands stroked her hair gently. She let out such a long, deep sigh that he pulled back and looked down at her, a question on his raised eyebrows.

"What's wrong?" he asked, his voice full of concern.

For a moment she couldn't respond. She opened her mouth to speak and nothing came out. She could swear she'd heard the tinkle of bells during their kiss and she knew that she definitely tingled inside! *How ridiculous! I'm not ready for this. I'm really losing it.*

Smiling smugly, she murmured, "I'll tell you some other time."

He pulled her closer still and in a voice husky with emotion whispered, "I don't know about you but I think we've got something going for us."

Charlyne Dickerson

His words were like music to her ears as she unconsciously snuggled closer, close enough to feel the crush of
his chest against her breasts. She could hardly deal with
the slow burning urgency building up within her. She
tightened her arms around his shoulders as he stroked
her hair. Raising her head, she gave him her lips. He
softly explored her mouth intimately, his tongue probing,
touching hers erotically in a way no one else had claimed
her mouth.

"Just hold me tight, Michael," she whispered as she
drew back when he started to unbutton her blouse.

Regardless of the passion he aroused in her, she still
had doubts about giving herself to him completely. For
reasons she couldn't explain even to herself, she held back
even though she knew she wanted him as much as he
wanted her.

He realized she didn't want him to go any further.
Pulling her tightly against his chest, he held her for several moments before she pushed away from him and
turned back to the counter to finish gathering the cups,
the coffee and banana pudding. Letting out a heavy sigh,
he helped her put everything on a tray and carried it into
the living room.

While having their dessert, he steered the conversation toward more mundane things for the next hour or so
and rose to leave shortly afterward.

"Thank you for going to Alcatraz with me. I'll call
you," he said softly.

She nodded mutely before slowly closing the door behind him, desperately hoping he would keep his word about calling.

She spent some time analyzing her growing feelings for Michael. Why was he so frequently on her mind when they weren't together? It wasn't like her to become so involved with a man. What had he done to her that she would now spend so many of her waking moments thinking about him?

She suddenly felt very lonely and thought how nice it would be to have someone to share the same space, breathe the same air, say good night every night. Living alone had its advantages and compensations, but it could be lonely as well, even for such an independent soul as she. Then she remembered some of her married friends and the problems they were always complaining about. She sighed deeply. Maybe she was better off than she thought. Her independence allowed her to come and go as she pleased, do what she wanted to do whenever she wanted. She answered to no one. If only she didn't have these increasingly frequent bouts of loneliness...

Finally deciding to go with the flow for the time being, she remembered she still hadn't mentioned her adoption to Michael. She hadn't a clue as to how he would react if or when she told him, since he made such a big deal out of knowing one's family background. On the other hand, her mind told her, maybe their dates were just a temporary thing and he'd be on to someone else as soon as he tired of her. In that case, her being adopted would never be an issue between them, nor would her obsession with her career be an obstacle.

CHAPTER 9

The insistent ringing of her phone awakened Jennifer early Monday morning. Still half-asleep, she rolled over to pick up the receiver but sat straight up when she heard Michael's voice.

"Sorry to awaken you, Jennifer, but I'm leaving for Atlanta in a few minutes and—"

"Atlanta? Something wrong, Michael?"

"Dad's in the hospital. His heart, I think. I'll call you when I find out how long I'll be there."

She heard the tension in his voice. "I hope it's not too serious, Michael. Try to calm down before you get there. You sound really uptight."

"Yeah, but I'll be okay as soon as I get out of here."

"I'll be thinking about you, Michael. Hope everything turns out well."

"Thanks, sweetheart. And I'll miss you every minute until I get back."

A few moments later she slowly put her phone down. Knowing there was no way she would be able to get back to sleep, she padded to the bathroom to get ready for the day.

ॐ ॐ ॐ

That evening Jennifer slipped into a loose robe, breathing a sigh of relief at being out of her office clothes. She had stopped for a quick sandwich when she left work, not being in the mood to cook when she got home. All she wanted was to have a quiet evening watching her favorite television programs and later on reading her book. While Michael was out of town for a few days, she intended to straighten out her feelings about him.

She found her remote control on the side of her bed and switched on the news. She threw back the satin comforter on her bed and piled the pillows against the headboard. She could hardly wait to fall back against them.

"That's pampering yourself, girl," she said aloud to the empty bedroom and climbed in on top of the blanket.

She was in the middle of her favorite news program when her phone rang. "Damn!" she said out loud as she reached for the receiver. She hoped it wasn't Sherry as she was in no mood for a gossip session.

"Hello, Jennifer, this is Tawana. I wonder if you could give me some information."

Jennifer glared at her receiver. Why in heaven's name was Tawana calling her?

"Information? What kind of information, Tawana?" she asked rather abruptly, thinking Tawana was up to no good. Jennifer's tone of voice did not deter Tawana. "I tried to get Michael all afternoon, and when I finally wormed some information out of his secretary she said he'd gone to Atlanta for a few days. She hinted you might know when he'll be back. Have you also been seeing Michael?"

Jennifer drew in her breath sharply. What did that woman mean by asking whether she was *also* seeing Michael? Red devils danced through her brain.

"Are you there, Jennifer?"

"I'm here. What do you really want to know, Tawana?" She knew she sounded like an overgrown idiot.

"I asked if you know when Michael will be back."

Jennifer hesitated. Why did Tawana want to know that? "Not really. He just left...his father is ill...and no, I don't know when he'll be back."

"But you *have* talked with him?"

"Well, yes...yes, he called me to say he was leaving." *That woman really has balls!* ran through Jennifer's mind.

110

"I see." Tawana paused for a couple of seconds before she dropped another bombshell. "Have you told Michael about Greg?"

Jennifer considered banging the receiver down. She saw red. Tawana was such a bitch! But she certainly wasn't going to let Tawana know how upset she was. She drew a deep breath and softly replied, "I have no idea why you're asking me that, Tawana."

"You've never seemed to hold a man more that a date or two before he loses interest, darling—except Greg, of course...I just wondered whether Michael was aware of your thing with Greg," Tawana purred.

"Maybe you better ask Michael when you see him," Jennifer countered, again ready to slam the receiver down, but her better manners took over.

"I'll do just that as soon as I talk to him." Tawana stopped for a few seconds before she zinged Jennifer again. "You see, Jennifer, I think you should know I rather fancy having Michael all to myself, maybe permanently. Just thought I'd better warn you so you won't get any ideas about having a future with him."

Jennifer bit back the words forming on the tip of her tongue. *Don't go there,* she cautioned herself. She would not let Tawana know she was getting on her last nerve. "Thanks, Tawana, for informing me you want Michael all to yourself as you put it, but it's Michael you need to tell that slop to, not me. Sorry to cut this conversation short, but I have better things to do."

She replaced the receiver and stared at it for several moments, her mind in a turmoil. Was there really something serious going on between Michael and Tawana as she had certainly suggested? Maybe what she heard in the hair salon was truer than she thought.

She turned her attention back to the news, but didn't hear a word the newscaster said.

☙ ☙ ☙

The next morning Jennifer called Sherry's office and asked her to do lunch, saying she wanted to talk about something that was really bothering her.

"So what's the problem, Jennifer?"

"I don't want to discuss it over the phone...I'll tell you when I see you, Sherry."

"Can't you even give me a hint?"

"I'll see you at the restaurant around twelve, Sherry." She smiled after hanging up the receiver. She knew Sherry would be on pins and needles until they met. She was too inquisitive for her own good. Jennifer turned back to the work on her desk, hoping to get most of it out of the way before lunch.

Hurrying from her office to meet Sherry, she ran into Greg headed in her direction.

"This must be my lucky week!" Greg exclaimed. "You going out for lunch for a change?"

She nodded. "I do occasionally have lunch out,

Greg."

His smile widened. "How about joining me for a real treat? A few days ago I was introduced to a small cafe not too far from here that's supposed to serve the best seafood in all of San Francisco."

"Now that is really tempting—you know I'm a sucker for seafood, especially fresh crab, but I'm on my way to meet Sherry. We have to discuss something or else I'd ask you to join us."

"A woman thing, huh?"

"Yes, Greg, a woman thing. But can't I have a rain check for that cafe you're raving about?"

"Of course, Jennifer, if you don't wait too long to cash it in. I just might give it away to one of my other women."

"Don't you dare!" she admonished him as they both headed for the elevator.

Greg suddenly felt very despondent. *Why do some men have all the luck?* he asked himself. *I'm a decent enough looking guy, I've got a great job, and I'm basically a good person. Why can't I even get to first base with that woman? Lord knows I've been in love with her from the time we first met, and she still insists on treating me like a big brother! But I guess I'd rather be a big brother to her if I can't be anything else. Who knows? Maybe someday she'll change her mind about me. And I sure haven't met any other sister who can hold a candle to her.*

Totally unaware of Greg's thoughts, she patted his

cheek on their way out of the building. "I'm sure they'd be happy to wait in line for the privilege of having lunch with you," she assured him as she said good-bye and hurried on to meet Sherry, who was already seated in a booth when Jennifer reached the restaurant.

"Sorry I'm a little late, Sherry, but I ran into Greg on the way out. He wanted to have lunch with us, but I discouraged him."

Sherry raised her eyebrows. "And that means it's a woman thing."

Jennifer stared at her. "That's exactly what Greg said."

The waiter approached their booth, and they ordered a Caesar salad, hot rolls, and a glass of white wine. As soon as the waiter departed, Sherry asked, "So what's on your mind, girlfriend?

Jennifer hedged. "Well...well, something has really been bothering me, and I'd appreciate your honest opinion."

Sherry took a sip of her water and waited for Jennifer to continue. "So, what is this world-shaking thing you want my opinion about, Jennifer?" she finally asked.

Abruptly, Jennifer plunged in. "How do you think most of the public feel about people who are adopted?" She stopped for a moment. "You know, people who don't know anything about their real background or haven't the foggiest idea whether they have any close family or relatives."

Sherry leaned forward, her eyebrows raised, thinking she hadn't heard Jennifer correctly. "Run that by me again, girl. Why are you asking me that?"

Jennifer hesitated, a soulful expression crossing her face, before saying softly, "I've never talked about this much, but remember one time I mentioned to you that I was adopted when I was very young."

Sherry thought for a moment. "So? I'd even forgotten you told me that. A lot of people are adopted. So what? The way the Johnsons brought you up one would never guess they aren't your birth parents. You certainly turned out okay." She stopped speaking for a moment when she saw Jennifer was very serious, in fact too much so to her way of thinking. "Why all of a sudden are you so concerned about being adopted, Jennifer?" A light bulb suddenly went off in Sherry's brain. "Oh! This must have something to do with Michael! Is that what this is all about?"

Jennifer twisted in her seat. "Well, in a way. What do you think he might say if he learned I'd been adopted?"

Sherry thought for a moment. "To be perfectly honest with you, Jennifer, I don't think it would matter a tinker's damn to him...or to anyone else, for that matter."

"There's more to this. Michael has often mentioned in one way or the other how important he thinks family background is. He also told me that his mother can trace their family back for four generations...and the way he said it, it seemed important to him that he knew all about his roots." Jennifer shuffled her silverware around for a few moments before she continued. "And in my case, I don't even know what my real last name is...not to mention who my relatives are, or even if I have any."

Sherry discerned that this adoption thing was really getting to Jennifer. And she had no answers to make her friend feel better. Finally, in a voice filled with emotion, she stated rather emphatically, "Oh, darn it all, Jennifer, haven't you seen that slogan pasted up in a lot of places that says something like it's not important where you came from, it's where you're going that counts? Well, in your case, think about where you are now and how your parents—adoptive or whatever—always helped you along the way..."

Sherry stopped speaking for a moment, not knowing exactly what else to say that would help her friend. Then she continued, "Now, I can't speak for Michael, of course, but I kinda think he might just agree with that slogan as far as you're concerned. He impresses me as being a very caring and fair person, so I think he might admire the way you've handled your life until now. I certainly do, if that's any consolation, and I know you pretty well."

Jennifer listened attentively to everything Sherry said and wished it were all true. She knew she had to discuss being adopted with Michael sooner or later. Maybe she'd feel better if she told him the next time she saw him. At least she wouldn't be as devastated now as she would be if she kept seeing him since she seemed to be getting in deeper and deeper as far as her emotions were concerned. She couldn't just dismiss what he'd said about family.

Sherry saw the conflicting emotions passing over Jennifer's face. "I'd like to give you a piece of advice, though," Sherry continued. "Since this is really bothering you, you should discuss it with Michael as soon as possible and find out what his true feelings are. You might be surprised that you're making a mountain out of a mole hill, worrying about something that doesn't mean a hill of beans to someone else."

"You really think so?" Jennifer asked plaintively. "Why did I have to meet a brother so concerned about his roots?"

"Didn't you tell me a lot of his relatives live in Atlanta? You know how most black southern families are, Jennifer. Remember when we were in college and had to listen to those southern gals brag about their family? They wanted to know everything about everybody, always asking everyone about their relatives. As if that makes them somebody important. Humph! I don't believe all that stuff! If you're a bum, what does it matter who your grandmother was? In my opinion—since you asked—everybody has to make his own life the best he can. Relatives aren't going to do it—even if they could."

Jennifer looked at her friend and thought about her

words. *Oh, I hope you're right,* she thought to herself.

Their lunch arrived and they both sank their forks into the crisp Caesar salad. They were almost finished with their food when Jennifer smiled. "You'll never guess who called me!"

Sherry looked over at Jennifer with raised eyebrows.

"Tawana!" Jennifer cried.

"What did that bitch want, Jennifer?" Sherry was not one to bite her tongue. She called a spade exactly what it was—a spade! Or in this case, a bitch.

"Tawana found out that Michael was out of town and wanted to know if I knew when he'd be back. Among other things she said in no uncertain terms that she wanted Michael and intended to get him."

"Well, I hope you told her that that was her problem! Did you?"

"I think I left her with that impression. We really didn't talk that long. In fact I kinda hung up on her."

Sherry smiled. "Good for you, Jennifer. Somebody needs to put that sister in her place." She was silent for a few moments before she asked, "By the way, how *are* you and Michael getting along, Jennifer?" She already knew some things Jennifer had told her about their dates.

Jennifer was quiet for a few moments. "I'm not quite sure. He acts like he likes me, but I'm not sure just how I feel about him at the moment. I don't want to get too involved only to find out he's appalled at my being adopted. And I'm surely not going to play second fiddle to

Tawana!"

"Go, girl!" Sherry said, eyeing the dessert trays. "I've got to have one of those cream puffs, but if you want another of my opinions—"

"I'm sure you're going to give it to me whether I want it or not," Jennifer cut her off.

Sherry glared at her. "Well, as I was about to say, I think you're making too much of nothing in both cases. I'm sure if Michael wanted Tawana he's had plenty of time to make his intentions clear. They've been paling around for some time now, and I think Tawana is certainly more interested in him than he is in her. He's probably on her wish list, but that doesn't mean her wish will come true."

Both young women were silent for several moments. Sherry broke their silence. She looked slyly at Jennifer. "By the way, girlfriend, it seems to me you might be changing your mind about black men. The last time we had a conversation you trashed men in general and black men in particular. Does meeting Michael have anything to do with your change of mind—or should I say change of heart?"

Jennifer fiddled with her silverware for a few seconds. She remembered their conversations very clearly. She suddenly acknowledged to herself that maybe she had been too hard on black men. Maybe she thought that way because she was too aware of the ticking away of her biological clock, thinking she might never have the joy of raising a family like most of her friends. Maybe she blamed others because she was unlucky in her choice of men. Maybe until now she just hadn't met the right black man. She knew that Michael certainly didn't fit any of the categories she had rattled off so glibly to Sherry. How could she have been so narrow-minded? She was an intelligent person, but what she often said to Sherry was really dumb, stupid.

Sherry watched the emotions flitting across Jennifer's face and wondered what she was thinking.

"So, girlfriend, do you still feel the same about black men?"

"I...uh...I...haven't had very good luck in meeting men...men whom I would consider spending time with much less have an affair with. None, that is, until Michael came along. With him, I..." her voice trailed off.

"Now you feel you'd like to know him better. That's the bottom line, isn't it, Jennifer?" she asked softly.

Jennifer looked over at Sherry and agreed. "Yeah, I think that's the bottom line, but now I'm not sure about anything."

"Welcome to the real world, girlfriend. All I say is go for it. Nothing ventured, nothing gained, as the saying goes." Sherry looked at her watch again. "I've got to get back to the office, Jennifer. There's a pile of work on my desk, and I'm sure not going to stay any longer than I have to today. See you later."

With that Sherry sauntered out of the restaurant

while Jennifer looked after her thoughtfully. She hadn't expected Sherry to have any answers, yet she felt so much better from just talking it over with her friend. Maybe she'd take off a few days from work later on and go home. Her mother might have some information about her adoption she hadn't shared with her. *Oh, how I wish I could find some information about my birth parents!* She sighed heavily and got some money out for the check. Never had she felt so anxious about not knowing who her real parents were.

CHAPTER 10

Jennifer's mind was on Michael's absence most of the day, knowing she would miss him more than she should. She stayed at the office later than usual and stopped in a deli for a sandwich before going home. To get her mind off Michael, she spent some time straightening up her apartment, putting magazines in order and throwing out some, and watering her plants. Still restless, she decided to jog for a few minutes before calling it an evening. Quickly changing into her sweats, she rushed out to start her run. The late evening traffic had thinned, and few pedestrians were on the street. In the distance she heard the screaming of a siren, an almost hourly occurrence. She stood for a moment and inhaled the crisp evening air while deciding which way to turn. She glanced across the street and noticed a man lounging against a mailbox, the same one she'd seen earlier looking up at her building. She was sure it was the same person—his hat slouched to one side gave him away. For some unknown reason, she shivered as she stared at him. What was he doing hanging around in that same spot? Why was he looking at her building? She wasn't easily frightened, but the stranger made her decide to forego her jogging.

She returned to her apartment, slightly unnerved, and rushed to the window, carefully peering out between the closed drapes. The man still stood in the same place, but now he seemed to be studying a piece of paper he held out to catch the light. She watched him a few moments, trying to make out his features but the dim light and his slouched hat prevented her from seeing his face.

She could not rationalize why the stranger frightened her. She pulled the drapes tighter and proceeded to the bathroom to remove her makeup. While applying cleanser to her face with tremulous hands, she could not get the stranger out of her thoughts. *Maybe he was a detective or something. Maybe he was checking the address for a client. Maybe...*

Her intuition clicked in and she couldn't resist checking the street again. Once more peeking out between the closed drapes, she breathed a sigh of relief. He had disappeared. Though she could think of no earthly reason why she should be afraid, she was. She changed into her night clothes, intending to watch an old movie with Bette Davis.

She was deeply engrossed in the movie and jumped when the telephone rang. Before she located the remote to turn down the television, her answering machine started recording a message. She heard an unfamiliar voice. "Hello, Jennifer. You don't know me, but I am your mother's friend. I have some information about your past you might want to know about. I know you're at home. Call me at this—"

She froze in her steps in the middle of the room. She listened to the number he repeated before he hung up. Her hands flew to her face. Instinctively she connected the voice to the stranger she'd seen across the street. *Am I becoming paranoid?* she asked herself.

She rubbed the back of her cold hand across her warm forehead as she sank to the side of her bed. Was she putting the two incidents together for no logical reason? What information could anyone have that would concern her? Where or how would the caller have gotten the information? Was someone playing a joke on her? She rubbed her clammy hands against her sides. Should she call the number he left on her machine?

She rose from the bed and slowly paced the floor for several moments, glancing at the telephone every few steps. She needed to clear up the mystery of the telephone call. She dialed the number with trembling hands and almost dropped the receiver when the same deep voice answered on the second ring.

She identified herself in what she hoped was a confident voice. "Hello, this is Jennifer Johnson. Are you the person who left a message on my answering machine?"

She noticed that the voice on the other end hesitated, and she almost hoped she'd reached the wrong number.

"Aren't you the Jennifer Johnson who used to live in Dayton, Ohio, with James and Elizabeth Johnson?"

Jennifer cleared her throat. "Yes," she replied amicably. "My parents still live there."

"You mean your adoptive parents, don't you?" he asked softly. "Didn't they tell you they adopted you?"

She gasped. How did he know that? She knew she was adopted while still very young; her mother had told her when she was old enough to understand. So she knew no other parents than the ones who had raised her with a lot of love and caring. They were the ones who had encouraged her to enter the college of her choice and who paid the bills while she was there, and then urged her to accept the position in San Francisco, even though her leaving left a big hole in their lives. They were the ones who occasionally flew out to California to spend their vacation with her.

"Of course I know I was adopted," she answered spiritedly. "But my birth mother is dead."

"So you really don't know the whole story. Your mother is alive and she's—"

She interrupted the caller in a voice an octave higher than usual. "She's...she's *alive*? Who are you? Why are you telling me this? How do you know about me and the Johnson's?"

"I guess I know more about you than you know about yourself, Jennifer."

She put her hand against her throat. After taking several deep breaths, she managed to speak. "You still haven't told me who you are."

"I'm Dave, a long-time friend of your mother and I live near the Johnsons in Dayton. I used to see you with the Johnsons occasionally when you were young. I'm out here to see about your mother and—"

She gasped again. "How do I know you're telling me the truth?" What right do you—"

The deep voice sighed through the receiver. "I mean you no harm, Jennifer. I hate to give you such bad news but your mother's very ill in a hospital across the Bay."

"You mean in Oakland?"

"She's been there about a week, I think. I want to tell you much more, Jennifer, but we need to talk face-to-face."

"Yes...yes, that would be better," she agreed even though she had a bit of trepidation in meeting him.

"I'm going to the hospital again tomorrow. Marian—that's your mother's name— made me promise not to contact you, because she doesn't want to interfere with your life after all these years. So far I haven't been able to persuade her that you should make that choice. When I get back, I can—"

"But I'm scheduled to go to New York for a few days."

"That's okay, Jennifer. I don't want to upset Marian in her condition by just springing you on her. It may take a while to get her to agree to see you, but I think I can handle it."

"I don't understand why my own mother doesn't want to see me." Her voice had risen an octave.

He tried to reassure her he knew what was best for the time being. "Trust me, Jennifer. Call me when you return."

Before she could reply, she heard a click and then the hum of the dial tone. Still holding the receiver in her hand, she sank slowly down onto her bed. She sat still for several minutes, inhaling and exhaling deeply, trying to think what she should do.

When her head began to clear, she realized her adoptive parents were the only ones who could tell her about Dave and her mother. *But why didn't they tell me more when they informed me about being adopted? How much did they really know?* She glanced at her watch. With the difference in the time zones, it would be after midnight in Ohio. No way would she awaken them now to ask questions. Besides, she should talk to them in person.

She felt as if problems of the world had suddenly descended on her shoulders, and she knew she was in for a long, sleepless night when she pulled back the comforter and sheet and crawled into bed. For the next couple of hours she struggled with questions she needed answers to: *Who is Dave and what's his connection with my mother? He'd said nothing about that. How did he know where I live and how to contact me? Why does he have to convince my mother to see me?* She felt she was losing control in a way she had never dreamed possible. In the end she knew that the first thing she had to do was to contact her adoptive parents. How to approach the subject of her adoption without alarming them was another matter she had to think through. It was nearly morning before she finally fell into an exhausted sleep.

ॐ ॐ ॐ

Dave hung up the receiver after talking with Jennifer. Thoughts of Marian Logan, his love for her, and the gypsy life she had led during the past years ran through his mind. He'd met Marian during a long singing engagement she had at clubs in Dayton, Ohio, and fell deeply in love with her. She told him her dream of becoming a concert singer was shattered when she became pregnant by her voice coach, who was married. Refusing to have an abortion, she had severed all ties with her deeply religious parents and traveled to another state, changing her name to Marian Logan, the one he knew her by. After the birth of her child, she got singing engagements in clubs wherever she could find them, traveling from city to city. While in Dayton, she decided she wanted a better life for her daughter and when her engagement ran out there, she left her young child on the steps of Miami Valley Hospital. He remembered begging her to marry him and settle down, but she had other ideas and moved on, ignoring his pleas.

Remembering the past years always made him feel melancholy. He was grateful Marian had always kept in touch with him regardless of where she went. Through the years he had helped her financially during her brief periods of unemployment, hoping she would eventually return to him. He recalled reading about a child being found and later adopted by a nurse who lived not too far from his home. After some investigation, he decided it had to be Marian's child, and throughout the years had kept up with the child he recognized as the spitting image of a younger Marian. Through mutual friends of his and the Johnsons, he eventually learned the child's name was Jennifer Johnson. During the next years, he saw her on the street on several occasions, knew when she left for college, and later moved to San Francisco. He photographed her when he could, sending photos to Marian whenever she contacted him.

Now he wanted to make Marian's last days as happy as he could under the circumstances. She was now near death, all because she'd neglected her health through the years. Two weeks ago she had collapsed while singing at a club and was taken to the hospital where the doctors diagnosed her problem as inoperable lung cancer. He had caught a plane as soon as the hospital called him in Dayton and now he intended to contact Jennifer, albeit against Marian's wishes. Before it was too late, he wanted Marian to know the terrific person she had once carried in her womb. All he needed to do now was to convince Marian that seeing Jennifer was the humane thing to do.

He had watched Jennifer enter her apartment complex a couple of times before he contacted her, and in his mind he thought she looked like a gentle, caring young woman who would want to know her birth mother.

ॐ ॐ ॐ

When her alarm sounded Thursday morning, Jennifer slowly rolled out of bed, a slow ache still at the back of her head. She was able to get through her day while worrying about the news Dave had laid on her, especially since she hadn't a clue what to do except to wait until he contacted her again as he'd promised.

As soon as she reached her apartment, she packed for her New York trip, having decided to leave early to spend the weekend with her parents before going on to New York. Perhaps she could get some information from them while she was there without their knowing about Dave's phone call.

In the middle of her packing, Michael called from

Atlanta, telling her his father was on the mend. He was getting a plane to San Francisco on Friday.

"Oh, Michael, I'm leaving for New York tomorrow and won't be back until the end of next week."

Michael tried to keep his disappointment out of his voice. "I've missed you like sin while I've been here, and now I'll have to wait another whole week before I see you. Can't you wait until Sunday to leave? That way we could at least have a couple days together."

Jennifer sighed. *I can't change my plans now. I have to ask Mom about my birth parents.* "I'm spending Saturday and Sunday with my folks, Michael. I haven't seen them in some time, and this is a perfect opportunity to spend a couple days with them."

"Well...we all have to do what we have to, I suppose, but I'll be unhappy every day you're away."

"Now I know you're exaggerating again, Michael, but thanks for trying to make me feel better."

After a few more exchanges, she replaced the receiver and returned to packing her bags since she was leaving for the airport from work.

CHAPTER 11

Waiting impatiently for her bags to be checked at San Francisco International Airport early Friday evening, Jennifer turned when she heard a familiar voice calling her name. Glancing toward the curb, she saw Greg Dixon getting out of a taxi. "Why, Greg, what are you doing here?"

Greg felt a rush of happiness in seeing her. "Don't you mean where am I going? I just got a last minute assignment to settle some legal problem they're having at our New York client's office. Where are you off to?"

"The same client, except I'm flying into Dayton from St. Louis to spend the weekend with my parents. I'll be in New York Sunday evening."

Jennifer waited until he checked his luggage, and then the two friends quickly walked to their gate, having only a few minutes to spare. Boarding the plane, they discovered several rows separated their seats.

"Maybe the plane won't be crowded, and we can sit together after take-off," he suggested.

"That would be nice," she replied while fervently hoping the flight would be filled to the last seat. She wanted some quiet time to think about the mysterious phone call and the matter of her adoption, as well as her growing relationship with Michael. As it turned out, she got her wish. All of the seats quickly filled. Shortly after the plane was air borne, she kicked off her shoes, pressed the button to recline her seat, and made herself comfortable with a pillow against the window.

Her thoughts turned to a conversation she'd had several weeks earlier with Sherry when she'd informed her friend that in general terms she had little interest in black men. Sherry, of course, had disagreed with her view and accused Jennifer of being extremely narrow-minded. Maybe Sherry did have a point. All black men couldn't be lumped together in the negative way she'd described to Sherry.

But at that time she was fed up to her eyebrows with men she had gone out with once or twice and then never heard from again. Could she be partly responsible for such actions? After all, she had to admit her usual haughty attitude toward men didn't invite the development of any kind of relationship. Maybe...but why bother with the past? She'd met someone who really made her head spin. How could she possibly lump him into the negative category she'd established for black men? No way! So what if she had to throw out some of her preconceived ideas? Michael was worth it. She'd give their budding relationship her best shot. Who knew what might happen?

Minutes later she dozed off and slept most of the way across the country. The plane was in its landing pattern at the airport in St. Louis when she awakened, hardly believing she'd had such a long, dreamless sleep.

Later, she was stirring in her seat when Greg stopped by her seat. "You had a really long nap, Jen. I walked by two or three times, and you were knocked out."

She resisted the urge to stretch. "I can't believe I slept most of the way. I must have been more bushed than I thought. I do feel better now. Where're you staying in New York?"

"At my brother's. He'll see that I get where I need to be while I'm there. Let me give you his number, and you can call me there when you get in. Maybe we can have dinner and see a couple of shows."

"Perhaps." She waited while Greg wrote down a number and gave her the slip of paper. She handed him the number of her hotel in New York.

"Don't forget to call me as soon as you get in." He heard the PA announcement about landing procedures and made his way back to his seat.

Entering the terminal, she learned that her connecting flight to Dayton, Ohio, had departed, and she had a wait of almost five hours for the next flight, putting her in Dayton early in the morning. Disappointment was in her voice when she phoned her parents of the change. Determined not let the change throw her into a down mood, she located a spot and settled down to review some of her notes for her auditors in New York.

ॐ ॐ ॐ

Very early Saturday morning James and Elizabeth Johnson rose from their seats and hurried to the gate as soon as Jennifer's plane was announced. Holding hands, they waited anxiously until they saw Jennifer hurrying through the passageway to greet them. Her father grabbed her in a great bear hug and caressed her hair before releasing her to her mother, who threw her arms around Jennifer's shoulders. The two women hugged and kissed warmly, holding each other tightly. A special bond had always existed between them and had only grown stronger as Jennifer grew older. In some ways they were more like sisters now than mother and daughter. Each considered the other her best friend.

Her father finally broke up their greeting. "Have a good flight, baby?"

"Except for that long layover in St. Louis, Dad. I could have done without that. I slept most of the way into St. Louis, so the flight must have been a smooth one. Have you been waiting long?" She smiled lovingly at her good-looking, dark-skinned father, her respect and adoration coming through in her eyes and voice.

Her stylishly-dressed mother smiled when her husband answered, "You know your mother. Elizabeth started getting ready hours before we had to leave home, and then she continually reminded me of the time every ten minutes or so until we got into the car. So, yes, we've been waiting longer than we should have been."

Elizabeth patted her husband's arm. "And who kept asking what the flight number was the minute he got up this morning, James?" She turned to Jennifer with a wink. "I could hardly get breakfast down him. He even helped me clear the dishes so we could be on our way and then fidgeted around in the kitchen until I put everything in the dishwasher."

Jennifer smiled tremulously at the two people who had always been her world. *I hope they never change,* she thought to herself. *I'd give my eye teeth to have a relationship like theirs. After all these years, they are still in love and everything they do reflects their love for each other.*

The three kept up a lively chatter all the way home, Jennifer asking about her school acquaintances, and her parents catching her up on the latest gossip.

As they approached the home she had grown up in, Jennifer took several deep breaths to hold in her sentimentality. What a happy place it had always been for her! They entered the driveway and she looked for the porch swing that had played a part in her high school romances. She noticed it had recently been painted and the cushions recovered in a floral print. She'd spent many late evenings in that swing with various boys when she was in high school, always knowing her parents were right inside the door supposedly watching television while hearing every single thing that went on out on the porch.

Her father gathered her bag and raincoat out of the trunk while she and her mother went on into the house, arms around each other's waist. He looked lovingly after them, happy to have his daughter home again, if only for a short time.

"I suppose you've had breakfast, baby. But would you like another cup of coffee?" her mother asked as they entered the sunny kitchen. "I'm sure James is ready for another one since he only half finished his at breakfast."

She smiled at the name they usually called her. It was easy to fall back into being their "baby" again.

"I sure would like another cup," her father announced as he came into the kitchen and sat down at his usual place at the table, smiling as his wife busied herself pouring coffee for the three of them. He took a long sip before he lowered his cup to its saucer and turned his attention to Jennifer.

Jennifer knew what was coming next. Her father never minced his words. He always wanted to know the bottom line of every situation.

Love Doesn't Come Easy

He looked over at her several seconds before he spoke. "So what's going on with you and that young man you talked about on the phone?" She knew he was very concerned about her, and that he really would make everything right for her if it were within his power to do so.

"Well...uh...it's because of him that I need some information," she hedged, moving her cup around in its saucer.

Facing the two people who'd been her world since childhood, she almost lost her nerve to ask about details surrounding her adoption. But she'd always talked over most of her problems with them, so she took a deep breath and plunged in. "Uh...I've been wondering about my birth parents and—" She stopped when she saw a guarded look pass between her mother and father.

James started to speak but Elizabeth held up her hand. Speaking haltingly, she asked, "What...what brought this on, baby?"

It was Jennifer's turn to stutter again. "Well...uh...I've been seeing a lot of—"

Her mother finished Jennifer's thought. "And you want to know about your roots—isn't that what they call it now? Everyone seems to be searching for their roots." She stopped for a moment. "I wonder if they're happy when they finally discover where they came from."

Jennifer blushed. Her mother was making it easier for her. "Sometimes when I was growing up I used to wonder about my birth parents, then for a while I'd for-get about them. I didn't have enough nerve to ask you two a lot of questions, because I didn't want you to think I was unhappy here, which was the farthest thing from the truth. I've always loved you both too much to cause you any unhappiness, so I pushed my questions to the back of my mind. But now...now I'm looking for some answers. Do you know who my natural parents are?"

Elizabeth turned to her husband, a question on her face.

James held up his hand as if he would take charge of the situation and settled back in his chair. "Your mother and I have often talked about what we could tell you when you asked us that question. It's been a long time coming. So now you think you're in love and you want some answers. What does your young man think about your being adopted?"

Jennifer moved her coffee cup around on its saucer several times again before she answered. "He—Michael is his name—has no clue that I was adopted. On occa-sion I've bragged about my wonderful parents and what a happy childhood I had, so I assume he thinks you're my real parents. I didn't tell him differently because—"

"So why are you now concerned about your birth parents?" Her father always asked the hardest questions, although she knew her mother would have asked the same, given the opportunity. Her mother, however, would have asked in a more gentle way, but the intent would have been the same.

She hedged again. "Michael and his whole family seem to put a lot of stock in family background, and he's talked at length about all of his grandparents, great grandparents, uncles, aunts, cousins or whoever. Seems to be a very large, tightly-knit family. So I suppose he would want to know something about my real family if he knew I was adopted. Naturally, I'd like to know also." She crossed her legs under the table and gripped her cup, hoping her nervousness didn't show. "Who were they? What kind of people did I come from?"

Neither parent answered her questions.

Elizabeth reached over and patted Jennifer's hand. "Has your young man talked of marriage, baby?" she asked softly.

Jennifer's eyes lit up and she smiled. "No, Michael hasn't asked me to marry him, but I think we're becoming very serious about each other. And if he does ask me, I'll probably..." Her voice trailed off. She suddenly found her hands very interesting.

Her parents exchanged meaningful glances which did not escape Jennifer. *They can read me like a book,* she thought. *They always could.*

A short silence followed.

Jennifer waited.

Her mother looked down at her hands, which slightly trembled.

Her father cleared his throat.

Jennifer reached up to twist a strand of her hair.

Her mother glanced over at her father.

Her father looked down at the table.

Jennifer waited.

"Baby," her mother finally spoke very softly, "I'd give everything I own to be able to tell you about your birth parents, but I never knew either of them." She took a deep breath before she continued. "You see, you were left on the fire escape steps in back of Miami Valley Hospital when I was head nurse there. A man found you and carried you to the waiting room. You had nothing with you but a blanket." She stopped for a moment, her eyes focused on her clinched hands in her lap. "It was finally discovered that you didn't belong to anyone in the waiting room. You must have been around two years old because all you could say when you were asked your name was something that sounded like Jennifer, not anything about where you lived or your parents' names except you said your mother's name was Mommy." Her voice had become lower as she spoke.

Jennifer straightened up in her chair and leaned over to hear her mother better.

Elizabeth looked sorrowfully over at her husband, knowing she had his support. He reached over and patted her hand, giving her courage to go on. Not looking directly at Jennifer, she continued softly. "I was on duty that night when someone on the nursing staff called the city's Children's Protective Services Agency, requesting that someone in that office come to the hospital to pick you up. While waiting for them to come for you, I took you into my office and got you some food, which you ate like you were starving."

Her voice got stronger as she thought about that night. "When you looked at me with your big black eyes, my heart melted. You were such a small, forlorn-looking little thing that I used all of my powers of persuasion with the social worker to talk her into letting me take you home with me for the night. It took her some time to decide I could take you with me, since it certainly was against their department's rules and regulations. But, thank goodness, I prevailed." Elizabeth stopped and took a deep breath. She looked appealingly at her husband.

James moved his chair closer to his wife's chair and reached over for her hand. "Let me tell Jennifer something we probably should have told her long ago, Elizabeth," he interjected, rubbing the back of his wife's hand with his well-manicured thumb. "You see, baby, we couldn't have children of our own. Some fluke of nature, I guess, except Elizabeth has always said we were just waiting for you to come along. I think she's right about that in many ways. You've always brought such joy into our lives that sometimes we ask ourselves whether we really deserve you." He looked lovingly at his wife. "So get on with your story, Elizabeth."

Elizabeth's eyes misted. "We both fell in love with

you that first night I took you home. We gave you a hot bath and tucked you in bed in what was then the guest room." She turned to her husband. "Remember how we put the dining room chairs by the bed so she wouldn't roll out, James?"

"Of course I remember, Elizabeth. Wasn't that my suggestion when you started worrying about her falling out of bed? I couldn't stand seeing you run into her room every thirty minutes or so to check on her. I had to do it to get some rest." His gruffness did not fool Jennifer. He'd probably been just as concerned as her mother.

While Jennifer always enjoyed the banter that went on between the two, she wished her mother would get on with her story. She got up to refill their cups when her mother was silent for a few moments. When Jennifer returned to the table, she looked at her expectantly.

"Well, to make a long story short," Elizabeth continued, "I used all of my influence for several months to keep you with us while the agency tried to locate your birth parents or any other relatives. They drew a blank at every turn and finally the court had to list your parents as 'unknown,' and that's what was listed on the birth certificate we finally got from the court. The lack of records made tracing any of your family impossible. That's when we applied to adopt you, and after almost a year and a lot of worry we were successful. So you see, we know nothing to tell you about your birth parents, except what I've just explained."

Elizabeth looked at Jennifer apologetically for having no other information.

Jennifer let out a soft sigh. So she still had nothing to connect her with her real family. *I've reached a dead end,* she thought as she continued to twist her hair.

Her father interrupted Jennifer's thoughts. "Have you ever remembered anyone or anything at all before you got to the hospital?" he asked.

Jennifer shook her head. She thought about telling them of the recurring nightmare she'd had since she was young, but decided against it. *What good would that do now, except to make them worry about me?* she silently asked herself.

Mr. Johnson studied his coffee cup.

Mrs. Johnson examined her nails.

Jennifer sipped her now cold coffee.

The three sat in silence for several moments.

Jennifer set her cup down slowly. "I can't remember any faces except yours when I was young. That bothers me. I should be able to remember someone or something that..." Her voice trailed off.

"You were too young to remember anything before we got you, I guess," her mother surmised. "And then maybe whatever happened to your parents before they left you at the hospital may have been too painful for you to remember. It could be that you've just blocked it out of your mind all these years."

Emotion overwhelmed Jennifer as her parents

talked. She wondered whether she deserved all their love and concern.

"Oh, Mom, Dad, how lucky can I be for you two to have chosen me! Nothing else is that important." She reached out her hands to each of her parents, and they smiled happily at her and at each other.

"I'll talk to Michael when I get back," Jennifer continued softly. "He has the right to know I was adopted, especially since he's so concerned about family background."

Her parents nodded their heads in agreement.

"If he loves you, Jennifer, and if he's the right kid of guy—which he probably is— your family background—or lack of it—won't matter a hill of beans," her father announced.

The rest of the weekend sped by too fast for the three, and when it was time for Jennifer to leave, they had a tearful parting at the airport.

"Let us know how Michael feels about your being adopted, won't you?" her mother asked as they parted.

Jennifer nodded her head.

༄ ༄ ༄

Michael arrived back in San Francisco on Friday, slightly disgruntled that Jennifer had left for New York. He was trying to deal with the loneliness he knew he would face the following week without her. He got some papers from his office to work on over the weekend. Passing one of his favorite cafes on his way to the parking lot, he remembered he had skipped lunch. Eating alone in his apartment had never appealed to him, and it had even less appeal this particular evening. Luckily, the dining area was not crowded and he was seated immediately. He was glancing over the menu when he heard a familiar voice calling his name. Inwardly he groaned. *How can I be so unlucky as to run into Tawana? I'm in no mood for her empty-headed chatter.*

Not waiting for an invitation to join him, Tawana seductively slid into the chair facing him. "Why, Michael, how nice to run into you just when I was feeling sorry for myself because I had to eat alone. Have you ordered dinner yet?"

He suppressed another groan. She was really pushing her luck, but there was no way he could refuse to have dinner with her. "Hi, Tawana. No, I haven't ordered. Would you like a glass of wine while we wait?"

"Of course. That would be great." She studied the menu he gave her. "What are you having?"

"Some kind of seafood, I guess. That's what I usually order," he answered with a noticeable lack of enthusiasm in his voice.

She cocked her head to one side and stared at him. "You seem rather out of sorts this evening. Miss your girlfriend?"

He was in no mood for games. "Girlfriend? Whom

146

are you talking about, Tawana?"

She was not one to easily take offense. "Why, Jennifer Johnson, of course. The grapevine has it that you're trying to cut out Greg Dixon. Everyone knows they've been lovers for a long time."

Tawana's bombshell hit Michael exactly where she intended—in the heart. *Jennifer told me she and Greg were just good friends. Tawana must be wrong!*

He knew his thoughts evidently showed on his face when she launched her second hit. "I do hope you didn't fall for that line that Jennifer tells everyone—that she and Greg only have a platonic friendship. Greg went to New York with Jennifer. Don't you know about that?" She chatted on and on with other gossip, but he only half heard her voice, shocked to hear Greg was also in New York. He didn't trust her and wondered whether she was telling the truth.

He could never remember what else he and Tawana talked about during their short dinner. All he could think of while eating was Jennifer in New York with Greg. He signaled the waiter for their check as soon as they finished their entree. "I don't think I'll stay for dessert, Tawana," he announced, eager to get away from her.

Her face mirrored her disappointment. "I thought we could make an evening of it, Michael. There's a great movie in the next block I'd like to see. Can't you spare a couple of hours, even if this is a spur-of-the-moment idea?"

He reached across for his briefcase. "No way, Tawana. I've got a lot of work to catch up on before Monday." He hoped the irritation he felt did not come through in his voice. Even though he was not looking forward to going home to an empty apartment, spending any more time with Tawana was even less appealing. He bid her a curt good evening when they walked out onto the street, and each went separate ways.

Michael breathed a sigh of relief as he headed for the parking lot to pick up his car.

Tawana called forth a string of ugly words under her breath before she reached the corner of the block, but then smiled as she remembered his face when he heard the lie about Jennifer and Greg. One way or another, she was determined to have Michael. She just needed to think of a plan that would work.

He soon reached his apartment and threw his briefcase onto a living room chair on his way to the bedroom to check his answering machine. No red light was flashing. He leaned down and looked at it closely, making certain that the answering machine had been on all day. It had. Maybe Jennifer would call later.

Feeling at odds with himself, he walked to the kitchen, hoping a cold drink would help. Pushing aside the beer and wine stashed in the refrigerator, he settled for a large glass of orange juice and took it to the living room. He settled on the sofa and picked up the remote and flipped through the channels until he found an old black and white John Wayne movie. Halfway through it, he dozed off and would have slept through the night had the phone not awakened him around midnight. Stumbling into the bedroom, he picked up the receiver only to find the caller had the wrong number. He slammed the receiver down. To assure himself that Jennifer had not called, he checked his answering machine again. The red light still was not on. Disappointed in not hearing from her, he felt like tossing the whole contraption out the window.

ॐ ॐ ॐ

Jennifer arrived in New York Sunday evening, almost as confused as she had been when she left San Francisco, even though she now understood more about her adoption. Yet Dave's phone call still plagued her. *Maybe I should have mentioned the call to my parents. But why worry them until I have something more definite to go on?*

Heaving a sigh of relief when she finally reached the solitude of her hotel room, Jennifer unpacked quickly and got into her night clothes, even though it was still early evening. She settled herself in the middle of her king-sized bed and dialed Michael's number, hoping he was in, considering the three-hour difference in time. On the third ring his familiar deep voice answered.

"Hello, Michael, I've missed you."

His chuckle come through her receiver. "And just who is this that's missed me?" he teased.

"Oh, Michael, be serious! I've even thought of leaving the audit team on its own and flying home!"

"Do you mean that, Jennifer? You really missed me that much?" he asked. The huskiness in his voice did not escape her.

"So what about you? Haven't you even thought about me? You haven't said so." She knew she was fishing for an answer.

His voice took on a serious note. "What have you done to me? It's been like...like a part of me is missing since you left."

"It's what we've done to each other that's the problem, I think." Her soft voice went right to his heart.

"When are you coming back?"

"Probably not until Friday, if the audit goes as planned."

"Not until then?" He sounded crushed and remained silent for a moment. "Well, call me when you can, sweetheart."

She got through the next couple of days by suppressing the excitement she felt whenever she thought of Michael. The audit was going as planned, but she found she didn't have as much free time as she had anticipated.

Greg was persistent in his calls after her arrival at the hotel. Pleading her workload in the evenings, she put off going out with him, but finally settled for meeting him at lunch on Wednesday. He was already seated at a table when she slipped into the seat opposite him.

He greeted her with a wide smile. "I was beginning to think I'd been stood up."

"I'm sorry, Greg," she apologized. "One of the auditors ran into a problem this morning, and I lost track of time for a while."

He took her hand. "You know I'd wait forever for you."

She retrieved her hand, ignoring his comment. "I can always count on you for flattery! So how is your legal problem going?"

"Very slow. Gets more complicated every day. I'd hoped to get home this weekend, but the way it looks now I'll be here for another week or so."

While she studied the menu, he studied her, wondering why she looked so...so different. *She has a kind of glow or something,* he decided. "New York must agree with you, babe, you look great!"

Feeling slightly flushed, she exclaimed, "Oh, you just haven't looked at me closely recently, Greg, or else your eyesight is failing."

The waiter arrived to take their order and both ordered a chef's salad.

"Wine?" he asked.

"Just some iced tea. I don't feel like having wine today." Looking rather wistful, she added, "I'll be glad to get back to San Francisco."

Love Doesn't Come Easy

"I'm sorry you said that, Jennifer—I'd hoped to persuade you to stay over for the weekend. You've often mentioned how much you always enjoy being in New York. We could take in a couple of plays or whatever you want to do."

"What a nice thought, Greg, but I really can't stay over. I have other plans."

The animation that suddenly showed on her face as she spoke puzzled him. "What's going on with you, Jennifer? There's something different about you that I can't put my finger on. Don't forget I've known you a long time, and you used to share a lot of things with me, remember?"

Feeling rather contrite, she'd started to answer when the waiter appeared with their lunch, and she thanked her lucky stars for the interruption. She found Greg still looking at her after the waiter departed, but she quickly unfolded her napkin and started in on her salad. Then noticing that he had folded his hands under his chin and was still looking at her, she laid down her fork. He knew her too well. "Remember I told you about Michael Maxwell?" she asked.

"I thought he was out of the picture now. At least that's the gossip I heard just before I left. Seems like Tawana has her hooks into Michael, or so she's telling her friends."

"I have a pretty good idea who might have started that rumor, Greg, but that's all it is—a rumor," she

152

declared. "I'm sure Michael would not be seeing me if what Tawana says is true."

He suddenly looked crushed.

"Why are you looking at me like that, Greg?"

He pushed aside his half-eaten salad and looked into her large dark eyes. "Don't you know that I've always hoped you would eventually feel something deeper for me than just being my friend, Jennifer?"

She dropped her eyes for a moment when she felt heat rise on her cheeks. "I...I don't know what to say, Greg. I...uh...I suppose I've just depended on your friendship without giving it much thought. Maybe...maybe I've been too self-centered to think about your feelings and took advantage of—"

"No, Jennifer, you didn't 'take advantage' of anything. We've enjoyed each other's company for so long, I suppose you just took our friendship for granted—which is okay. I'm the one who wanted it to be more than that. So don't start beating yourself up about something you had little to do with—except just being you."

"Oh, Greg, I'm truly flattered. Maybe if you had told me this months ago, I might have felt differently, but now—"

He interrupted. "Are you saying you're *really* serious about that guy?"

She hesitated a few seconds, then reached across the table and took his hand between both of hers. "I think so. I'm not sure where our relationship is going, Greg, I just know I have to take the chance that Michael might be the guy for me. Can you understand that?"

He shrugged. "Yes...I guess I know what you mean...but I could kick myself that I didn't at least give you more than a hint about my feelings a long time ago.." He hesitated for a few moments. "You see, I've been in love with you for a long time, but I couldn't risk our friendship by telling you."

Touched by his words, she hardly knew what to say. Several moments passed before she said softly, "You're a great guy, Greg. You'll meet someone someday who loves you and will give you everything you deserve. So can't we still be friends like we've always been?"

They stared at each other for several seconds before he gave her hand a squeeze. "I wish you the best if Michael is who you want. Just remember I'll be around in case you change your mind, and I'll always be your friend—count on it."

His words made her feel better inside. "And I'll always be your friend, Greg."

Picking up his fork, he attacked his salad, and she turned to her food. They ate in silence for the next few minutes, neither divulging the turmoil both felt.

Leaving the restaurant, he waited until she got a taxi. As it pulled over to the curb, he kissed her softly on the forehead before she climbed into the back seat. "Give me a call and let me know how things are going with you."

She patted his cheek gently. "I'll do that, Greg"

On her way back to the office, she remembered Greg's forlorn expression when he waved to her, and she felt a sense of guilt thinking about the part she'd played in the way he now felt. He had been her good friend for too long to lose his friendship now. She would take him to lunch when she got back to San Francisco. She was positive they could still be the same kind of friends they'd been for such a long time, once he got over his hurt. She was glad she had only a couple more days in New York.

CHAPTER 12

After her dinner with Michael on Friday, Tawana racked her brain for a scheme to make him her man and hers only. She was positive they would be a great couple once she got him to realize that he needed her as much as she wanted him. Over the weekend, a light bulb went off in her head. She knew exactly what she could do to snare Michael. And she also knew she'd better get things settled while Jennifer was in New York.

Early Monday afternoon she dialed Michael's office.

His gruff voice on the phone did not discourage her. "I'm up to my eyeballs in work, Tawana. My secretary said this call was urgent or I would have called you back later."

She was not easily rebuffed. "Michael, we have a

problem we need to talk about. Can you meet me for dinner tonight?"

"Problem, Tawana? Why didn't you mention whatever it is when I saw you last week?"

"I didn't know about it then." Her testiness came through in her voice.

He shifted some papers around on his desk, wondering why he'd ever gotten involved with Tawana. The last thing he wanted was to spend an evening with her; he'd rather be miserable by himself until Jennifer returned.

She waited a few moments. "I've changed my plans many evenings these last few months to fit your plans, Michael."

Her whining voice grated on his nerves. *Why is she trying to lay a guilt trip on me?* he wondered. "Tawana, you've known from the time we met that we were going to be only casual friends, and you've—"

"What I'm talking about can't be discussed over the phone, Michael. Trust me. You at least owe me the courtesy of hearing me out in a—"

"Okay, okay, Tawana," he relented, his exasperation clearly evident in his voice. Anything to get her off the line now and hopefully out of his life from now on. He was truly fed up with her and intended to let her know that over the dinner she proposed.

"Pick me up about seven. I'll make the reservations." She replaced the receiver, a triumphant grin on her face.

He hung up his phone feeling he had been trapped.

But trapped how? Into what? he asked himself. Leaving his office later in a very disgruntled mood, he dreaded meeting Tawana. All he wanted to think about was Jennifer, and he didn't want Tawana in the picture at all. Why hadn't he already told Tawana about his passion for Jennifer? Perhaps he at least owed Tawana that much consideration, he thought, as he took off his clothes and stepped under the shower head, hoping to wash away some of his weary feelings. It didn't take him long to dress, and in no time he was pulling up in front of Tawana's apartment building, eager to get the evening over and done with.

As soon as he stepped inside her apartment and saw her in a long slinky lounging robe, he had a premonition that the evening would not go well. And judging from the false smile on her face, he suspected she had her own agenda. He wished he knew what it was.

"Come in and sit down, sugar. Want a drink?"

He nodded and she disappeared into the kitchen. He heard the ice cubes falling from the tray. He felt as cold inside as the ice cubes must feel to her hands as she dropped them into their drinks.

Returning with two tall glasses in her hands, she handed one to him before dropping down on the opposite end of the sofa, smiling cunningly as she lifted her glass to her lips.

Oh, Lord, Michael thought, *what is going on in that woman's mind? She looks like the cat that swallowed the proverbial canary. Why isn't she dressed for going out?*

He finally asked, "What time are our reservations?"

She took a long sip from her glass. "Oh, I decided it would be better to have dinner here. It'll be ready shortly."

For the first time he noticed the cooking odors in the air. What was going on with her? Why were they having dinner here instead of a restaurant?

Setting down her drink, she moved closer to him. "I hate to lay this on you, Michael, but it seems we've got a bit of a situation. We may as well talk about it while dinner is finishing."

He turned abruptly on the couch to face her. "Situation? What kind of a situation?" Another problem was the last thing he needed at the moment.

"I'm pregnant!"

Pregnant? But what does that have to do with me? He let out a long breath, thoroughly confused.

She noticed the bewilderment crossing his face and moved a little closer to him. "I found out for certain this morning when my doctor confirmed my tests were positive."

"But...but...why are you telling *me* this?" His voice had risen. He was fast losing his cool.

She arched her eyebrows. "Why, Michael, you're the father! You have a right to know."

He set his glass down so quickly some of his drink sloshed out onto the coffee table. He quickly wiped up the liquid with a napkin. *What the hell does she mean?* He asked himself. *How could I be the father?*

"I...I don't understand—"

"Remember a night a couple or so months ago we'd been at a party and you spent the night here—you'd had a bit too much to drink and I drove home and—"

He tuned out her voice and hit his forehead hard with the heel of his hand. That night had never crossed his mind after it occurred. He'd appreciated the fact that she hadn't wanted him to drive when he was so loaded. All he remembered of that night was falling into her bed with his clothes still on and awakening naked the next morning.

"What the hell are you talking about, Tawana? I don't remember anything about that night with you! Nothing, except I was naked when I woke up!" He realized he was shouting.

She glanced over the rim of her glass. "Doesn't that tell you something?"

He shook his head in disgust. "Are you saying we had sex and I don't remember it? Impossible!"

"Nothing's impossible, sugar. And I'm afraid you'll have to accept what I'm telling you as fact." She glanced over at his angry face. "Believe me, I am just as surprised as you. My periods have always been very irregular and I'd lost track of the last one—I thought something else must have been wrong with me—and I had no symptoms of being pregnant and—"

160

"Stop that damn babbling, Tawana! The thing now is what to do about it."

She twisted in her seat and guilefully looked at him. "Do about it? Why, get married, of course, sugar! I don't intend to bring a little bastard into this world!"

His world crashed around him! Jennifer! How could he possibly marry Tawana? Unthinkable, yet...

"You certainly don't expect me to have an abortion, do you?" she asked petulantly.

He held up his hand in frustration. "Hold it. Just be quiet for a moment. I've got to think."

She sipped her drink and waited, glancing at him out of the corner of her eye.

After a few moments, he sullenly asked, "Why are you so certain this baby is mine? You've gone out with other men since I've known you. And our relationship has always been just a casual one—you know that."

"You're right...except for that one night—which, I take it, you seem to think was a mistake—"

"A great mistake, I see now...*if* what you say is true!" he exploded.

"Regardless of what you think, we *do* have this problem to deal with and I expect you—"

"I know what you 'expect'! It's just impossible!"

She slid over closer to him, putting her hand on his arm. "How can you say 'impossible,' Michael? We know each other pretty well. We can work things out."

He cringed at the purring sound in her voice and

161

moved away from her, several thoughts running around in his head. *She's a truly unbelievable person! How do I know the baby is mine? Aren't there ways to find out about such things? There had to be...no way can I even think of marrying her!*

He rose from the sofa as if he'd suddenly aged several years. His head began to pound. He felt a tightness in the pit of his stomach. He clinched and unclenched his hands. He had to get out of there before he did something totally insane!

She looked up at him standing above her, angry and stiff as a statue, hands clenched at his side.

"Where are you going, Michael? Surely you're not leaving—what about my dinner?" she cried, indignant at the thought that he was leaving.

He slowly rubbed the back of his hand across his forehead. "Sorry about the trouble you've gone to, Tawana, but I can't possibly eat anything after what you've just laid on me...I need some time to think about this mess you want me to believe is my responsibility."

Without another word or glance in her direction, he walked out of her apartment, not even taking the time to bid her goodnight.

She couldn't close her mouth as she watched Michael shut her door.

A few moments after he left, she stretched lazily and lay back on the sofa, a smirk on her face. She had set her plan in motion. *After all, many women have premature babies, don't they? And I can get pregnant as soon as we're married!* With that thought, she sauntered to the kitchen and made herself another drink. Suddenly she realized she was ravenous and filled her plate and carried both back to the living room. While eating, she thought about the progress she'd made in claiming Michael for her very own. He didn't know what had hit him.

ॐ ॐ ॐ

Michael tossed and turned in his king-sized bed a long time before he gave up on sleep and turned on the television set. Clicking the remote several times, he located a station showing an old movie, punched his pillows several times before putting them under his head and shoulders, then settled back to watch it. Two hours later he was still staring unseeing at the screen, his conversation with Tawana blocking out everything else. When fatigue put him to sleep around two o'clock in the morning, he was no closer to a decision about Tawana's situation than he had been earlier in the evening.

The next day his head felt fuzzy all day at work, and he had difficulty concentrating on the problems of his clients—his own problem looming in front of him as soon as he was alone. By the end of the day he had reached the only resolution he could think of. He would demand to see her doctor. There were tests to determine paternity, but could the tests be made before the child was born?

It was past eight o'clock when he rang Tawana's bell, thinking he probably should have called first. After several rings he decided she wasn't home and turned to leave when she opened the door, dressed in a thin, revealing robe.

She was so shocked when she faced Michael that she couldn't speak.

Not waiting to be asked in, he walked past her but suddenly stopped just inside the door of the foyer. A man was lounging on her sofa in the adjacent living room.

Turning back to Tawana, who was still holding the door open, he apologized for his behavior. "I'm sorry, Tawana, I didn't know you had company...I should have called before coming over."

She found her voice. "Oh, Tom was just leaving, Michael. Come on into the living room while I get his coat."

As if on cue, the man she referred to as Tom rose and put on his jacket when she handed it to him. He nodded to Michael as he passed and called out to Tawana, "I'll call you later, baby."

She turned to Michael, still standing in the foyer with a deep frown creasing his forehead. "Come on in and sit down, sugar. You don't look too comfortable standing there with your hands in your pockets."

I could easily strangle this woman, Michael thought as

he crossed the room to a chair by the window. "So was that one of your admirers?"

Unruffled, she shrugged. "Oh, he's a neighbor down the hall. He occasionally stops in to have a drink."

"How convenient," he threw at her sarcastically.

She dropped down on the sofa, not bothering to pull her robe over her long slender legs. "To what do I owe this visit?" she asked, a half smile on her face. "Have you finally come to your senses?"

He stared at her a few moments, swallowing hard to control his anger. "I'll make this brief, Tawana. At the moment I have to take your word that the baby you say you're carrying is mine, but—"

"*Say* it is? How can you doubt it? Of course it's yours. You're the only—"

"Okay, okay!" He held up his hand to stop the tirade he knew she was capable of. He turned around in his chair to stare out of the window for a few moments before turning back to face her. "I'm not the kind of guy to walk away from his responsibilities, but I've got to be sure they really are mine. Who is your doctor? I want to make an appointment to talk with him."

She glared at him as if he'd suddenly grown two heads. "Talk to him about what, Michael?"

"About a test to determine paternity, of course, as well as finding out the date the baby is due."

She tried another tact; she would not give up so easily. "What would be so wrong with me as your wife?

165

We've always gotten along fabulously, and I certainly can bring as much financially to the marriage as you—perhaps even more."

"You're probably right, Tawana, but the facts are that I don't love you, and you have no reason to think I ever have. I'm deeply in love with someone else," he informed her softly.

He saw a calculating expression cross her face as she stared at him for several moments.

"So who is this 'someone else'?" she finally asked.

"That is none of your business. I've already told you what we need to do as soon as possible, like tomorrow if that can be arranged. We'll see what happens after we check with your doctor."

Even though she knew he was not someone to be trifled with, she threw caution to the wind and plunged ahead.

"It's Jennifer you're so worried about, isn't it? No wonder she was so secretive when I talked to her."

"You...you talked to Jennifer? When?" he asked, aghast at Tawana's brashness.

"While you were away. Your secretary mentioned Jennifer might know when you would return and—" She suddenly stopped when she saw a murderous look on his face.

Finally he spoke slowly and distinctly, spacing his words. "What...did...you...tell Jennifer?"

She looked away. "I...I really don't remember. Ask

166

her if you're that interested," she hedged, a sly look now on her face.

He studied her for several moments. "You have a streak of evil in you, Tawana. I only wish I'd seen this side of you when we first met. I wouldn't have come within a mile of you."

His words infuriated her but she had gone too far to back down now. "Oh, I'm sure you can straighten this all out with Jennifer. If she loves you, she'll forgive you for this one little transgression."

He lowered his head between his two palms, pressing them against his temples. Then slowly lifting his head, he leveled his eyes at her and stood up, tightening his fists at his side, striving to control his temper. He didn't want to go ballistic on her. He shook his head before he spoke very softly. "I'm sorry I ever spent a moment of my time with you, Tawana. When you decide to give me the name of your doctor, call me."

He turned and headed for the door but stopped abruptly and looked back at her. "If you mention one word of this conversation to Jennifer before I see her, you'll have me to deal with. And that's not a threat, it's a promise!"

She watched him stride out the door and close it quietly behind him.

He did not see the ingenious smile on her face as she walked back to the living room.

Love Doesn't Come Easy
ৡ৵ ৡ৵ ৡ৵

Michael was not in the best of moods when his secretary informed him that Jennifer was on the line. He was still slightly peeved with her for being gone the whole week. But wasn't that a minor problem compared to his situation with Tawana? *Get your priorities straight, old boy,* he thought, as he picked up the receiver. "I just need to hear your voice, Jennifer. I've really missed you this week."

"I've missed you, too. So what have you been up to, Michael?"

She really doesn't want to know what's been going on here, he thought as he fiddled with the paperweight on the end of his desk, thinking of his latest conversation with Tawana. Now what was he going to do about Jennifer? Just when everything seemed to be falling into place for the two of them, when he'd made up my mind that he wanted more than anything else to marry her, then Tawana screws up everything!

Maybe Tawana would have a miscarriage, or maybe World War III would break out and he'd be drafted to help win it. Or maybe he'd just leave the country and start a new life. But he knew miracles don't happen. He'd have to make his own! And it would be a miracle if Jennifer didn't show him the door when he told her about Tawana. Lord, what a mess his life was in!

He brought his mind back to his phone conversation.

"What did you say, sweetheart?" he asked when he real-ized she'd been talking while his mind wandered.

"Is something wrong, Michael? You seem to be so distracted ...or something..." Her voice trailed off.

He hesitated. "Sorry, but my week's been the pits...and I guess I'm a bit out of it at the moment. I'll tell you about it later."

After a few more words, she slowly hung up the receiver, a frown on her forehead. He had never acted so...so distracted or something before. Something must have really gotten to him she decided before turning back to the work she brought back to her hotel room.

৵৵ ৵৵ ৵৵

Later that night Michael decided that Tawana was definitely giving him the run-around and resolved to call her the next day. After several phone calls early the next morning, he finally located her.

"Michael!" she exclaimed when she got on the line. "My secretary said you had tried to get me earlier. What's on your mind...have another problem?"

You! You are my problem! he wanted to shout at her.

"I want you to meet me for lunch today," he informed her in a matter-of-fact tone .

"That's a rather short notice, isn't it? Why couldn't we meet this evening?" she asked.

"This evening is not convenient for me, Tawana, and

I think you better meet me around twelve-thirty today. It's important for both of us." He waited for her reply.

She could tell from the tone of his voice that he was not to be trifled with at the moment. "Okay, then I'll meet you at the little restaurant in this block, close to my building. Is that convenient for you?"

"I'll be there." He sighed deeply as he replaced the receiver. He knew exactly the approach he would use with her and set about clearing his desk.

ॐ ॐ ॐ

She was already seated at a table when he entered the restaurant, and she stood up to let him know where she was seated. He looked at her keenly before she sat down and noticed her waistline seemed as small as it always had been. *Don't women gain weight when they're pregnant?* he asked himself. His anger deepened as he neared her table and saw the sly half-smile on her face.

"Well, Michael, this is a pleasantry I hadn't expected today. I took the liberty of ordering our lunch."

He stared at what he now knew was her deceitful saccharine smile, and he desperately wanted to wipe it from her face. Sliding into a chair facing her, he took a deep breath and waited a few seconds before he spoke. "What I have to say to you is far from being pleasant, Tawana, so you can stop your smirking right now."

"Do I detect some anger in your voice?" she asked,

looking over at him as if she really did have everything under control.

He was ashamed of his sudden desire to slap her and managed to speak in a normal tone of voice. "I'll get right to the point, Tawana. I don't want this meeting to last any longer than necessary so let's..." His voice trailed off as the waiter placed their food on the table.

She raised one eyebrow. "So what's on your mind?"

"You have ignored my asking for your doctor's name, so we'll pay a visit to my doctor. I've already made an appointment. He can tell me exactly when this baby is due, since you're so vague about that information."

She suddenly looked as if she had been physically assaulted. She started to fiddle with her silverware and looked down at the table rather than at him. But she said nothing.

"Surely that's a resonable request, Tawana."

She drew a deep breath. "My seeing your doctor is not necessary, Michael. Since you're not man enough to accept the consequences of your own actions without a lot of hoopla, I see that this is really my problem." She stared at him, venom in her eyes. "So you don't need to have any concern for me."

He leaned back in his chair. "What are you saying, Tawana? You're not making any kind of sense!"

"Whether or not I make sense is none of your business, Michael. I can take care of myself with or without you," she snapped.

He stared at her for several seconds, taking in her whole chic appearance. "Do you know that some of your friends are whispering that you're not even pregnant? You certainly wasted no time in telling everyone about your supposed condition. You must have spent most of your time on the telephone the last couple of days."

Her voice rose. "What do my friends know? What does anyone know except me?"

"That's what I'd like to clear up."

She shifted uneasily in her chair, giving him an angry, defiant look. "I suppose Jennifer put you up to this—well, you can go back and tell her that whether or not I'm pregnant is nobody's damn business but my own!"

"Jennifer knows nothing about this at the moment. So you will be at my doctor's office tomorrow?" he asked again.

She moved her untouched food around on her plate.

He waited without saying a word, just stared at her and tapped his nails on the table.

A few moments went by. She twisted in her chair, refusing to look at him. Finally, she almost shouted, "Will you please stop that damn tapping? And I'm not going to any doctor you pick out." She stared at him several moments with a look akin to hatred in her eyes.

Looking alarmed at her, he saw she was losing control. "Look here, Tawana—"

Without a word, she suddenly jumped up from their

table, picked up her purse, and rushed through the restaurant.

Flabbergasted, he watched her until she was out of his sight. Thoroughly frustrated by her actions, he suddenly was not hungry. He got up slowly and left some bills on the table.

Tawana had to be bluffing. But what kind of woman would lie about being pregnant? Could she possibly be telling the truth? What he needed most at the moment was to have a talk with Jennifer, but she was still in New York. He uttered a few unkind words under his breath about Tawana as he walked slowly back to his office. He'd hoped to bury himself in his work the rest of the afternoon, but Jennifer's face kept popping into his mind. What would she do when he laid this business with Tawana on her? A cold shiver went down his spine.

CHAPTER 13

Jennifer went directly to her office after landing in San Francisco at noon on Friday. Failing to reach Michael at his office to tell him she was back, she plunged into the work piled on her desk. Several messages were propped up by her telephone, and some papers marked "Immediate Attention" were stacked on the other end of her desk. After she read the department memos that needed her attention, she sifted through the phone messages, sorting out those she would take care of first. It was late afternoon before she got through to Michael.

"Jennifer, where are you?" his concerned voice boomed through the receiver.

Her heart beat faster when she heard the voice that affected every cell of her body. "I'm at the office and—"

"I'll be right over, sweetheart. I've got to see you."

"Hold on, Michael. My work is really piled up and there're some things I've got to take care of. Let's have dinner at my place this evening. I'll stop by on my way home and pick up a couple of lamb chops or—"

Michael cut her off. "I'll take care of dinner. I'll stop by the deli. I should get there around six or six-thirty. Is that okay?"

"Sounds good to me." Jennifer suddenly felt on top of the world. "I really missed you, Michael," she said softly, her hand cupped around the receiver.

"And I've nearly gone off my rocker thinking about you." Hanging up his receiver, he suddenly felt happier than he had in days.

Luckily, the afternoon passed quickly for both of them. She hurried out of her office before five o'clock and had time to shower, apply fresh makeup, and get into a long flowered caftan with time to spare before he arrived. Unable to sit still, she went into the kitchen to set the table in her breakfast nook. She had to stay busy. She didn't want to think about the problem of her adoption or how to deal with Dave's telephone call. She had almost finished with the table when she heard the doorbell chime. Her anxiety about her problems returned as she walked through the foyer to open the door.

Neither spoke when he entered, a large bag in each arm. He walked through to the kitchen to deposit the food from the deli. She followed close behind him. As soon as he put his packages down, he turned and took her in his arms, lifting her off the floor. As he let her slide back down, he claimed her lips in a long, crushing kiss. When he drew back, he saw the moisture in her eyes.

"Oh, Michael, I'm so glad to be back. Let's have dinner and then we'll talk."

He looked at her as if he couldn't bear for her to be out of his sight. "We'll both get it together," he informed her, letting her go long enough to remove his coat and tie, unbutton his shirt collar, and turn back the cuffs of his shirt.

She attacked the bags on the table, opening cartons and peeling back plastic wrappings. In a matter of minutes she filled their plates while he opened the wine and poured it into her crystal glasses.

Little was said during their dinner, he surreptitiously looking over at her, while she occasionally glanced up, wondering about the troubled frown he wasn't able to hide. When they finished, he helped her clear the table and stack the dishes in the dishwasher. Finally taking her hand, he led her to the living room.

"Let's light the logs," she suggested as she walked to the sofa and sat down, drawing her long legs under her.

He willingly obliged and soon had the logs burning. Walking over to the sofa, he gathered her to him, planting a light kiss on the top of her head before taking her face in his hands and asking, "So how was your trip?"

She told him, including her lunch with Greg. "And I couldn't wait to get back here," she finished.

He cringed upon hearing her confirm that Greg was also in New York.

Releasing her, he rose from the sofa and walked over to the fireplace and stared at the blazing logs.

An ominous silence filled the room for what seemed to her a long time. She watched him, her heart full. *What was bothering him?* she wondered. Though she would have to share the past week's events with him sooner or later, concern for him unconsciously pushed her own problems to the back of her mind. She thought he would never break the silence that swirled around them. What was he thinking? Had something happened that now threatened their budding relationship? She became tense waiting for him to turn his attention back to her. Unconsciously she began twisting a strand of hair around her finger.

He glanced over at her a couple of times before he spoke. "By the way, I saw Tawana and she asked about you and Greg."

Astonished, she leaned back. "Why would Tawana ask about Greg and me?" she demanded.

"Oh, Tawana seems to think you are having an affair with Greg."

"She told you that? Damn her! She's always making up some weird tale about someone. I guess she has nothing better to do! Fortunately all her so-called friends

177

know what she's like and usually don't put too much stock in what she says most of the time. Greg and I have been platonic friends for a long time. I told you that, remember?"

Relieved, he looked down into her flushed face and believed her. But that was not all he had to say about Tawana. He knew he had to tell Jennifer about the rest of his dealings with Tawana but couldn't get the words out.

Finally turning to face her, his face full of emotion, he sat down and motioned for her to join him on the rug before the fire. He put his arms around her shoulders and drew her close. "You're so independent; I guess I'll have to get used to not sharing everything in your life, but—"

Her mind tuned out his words. Could he read her mind? Did he suspect what was going on with her?

"Are you listening, sweetheart?" he asked, noticing a strange expression cross her face.

"Oh, I'm sorry. What were you saying?"

"I want to tell you how much I missed you. It was hell, not knowing what was happening, and you so far away." He found her mouth and explored it for several seconds before he released her.

They looked deeply into each other's eyes, both aware in the back of their minds that there was something each wanted to share with the other, yet neither had the nerve to start the conversation, afraid of the other's reaction. Both knew that harboring secrets could ruin a relationship, but at that moment their emotions got in the way. They drew closer together again, not wanting to spoil their romantic mood.

She felt his heart beating against her and breathed out a contented sigh.

He felt the slight trembling in her body. Touching her jarred his emotions.

Both had decided they could talk about serious things later.

He cradled her in his arms for several moments before putting his hand under her chin and raising her head to meet his lips. He kissed her slowly, teasingly, his tongue finding hers as eager as his. He lifted his head and she saw tenderness and passion flooding his face as he uttered her name deep in his throat, "Jennifer, Jennifer." Then his mouth was upon hers again.

She melted against him, a soft moan vibrating in her throat. Suddenly, more than anything she had ever wanted in life, she wanted him to make passionate love to her that very moment. She strained her hips against him as her hands clung tightly around his neck, and groaned softly as his hands cupped her breasts.

For a moment she stiffened. Was she doing the right thing in giving herself to him completely? Intimacy sometimes changed relationships. Would that happen to them? What would she do if his feelings toward her suddenly cooled? She'd survive, she had no doubt of that, but she shuddered at the thought that he might not take her surrender as seriously as she.

Her head battled with her body. Her body won out when she was swept away by another wave of desire, the likes of which were foreign to her. She pulled out of his embrace, stood up and took his hand. Together they headed for her bedroom.

The bright moonlight streaming through the partially-closed blinds sent light and shadows throughout her bedroom. He pulled her down to the side of the bed, tenderly kissing her for several moments. Pushing her gently from him, he reached into his back pocket for his billfold, extracting a small foil-wrapped packet and laying it on the nightstand beside the bed.

Her hands trembled as she tried to deal with the small buttons on her blouse, finally leaving some buttoned and pulling her blouse over her head.

He finished undressing before she got to her bra and panties. "Let me," he insisted, pulling down the straps of her bra and unhooking the snaps on the back before he reached down to remove her sheer panties. "You're as beautiful as I knew you would be," he murmured, surveying her nude body from head to foot. He had wanted her for weeks and now had difficulty maintaining control of his body. He drew a deep breath as he pressed his enormous erection against her thighs.

"I've dreamed about holding you like this since the first day I saw you," he murmured. He cupped her full breasts in his hands before lowering his mouth to her erect nipples.

The pleasure she felt was indescribable; her breath caught in her throat as his hands moved down her body, exploring every inch. The intensity of her need wiped out inhibitions she'd always had in intimate situations. She reached up, stroking his neck and then massaging his shoulders. She could not contain her passion for him. She clasped his head between her hands until their lips met and his tongue explored the inside of her mouth, sending hot jets of passion throughout her body. She swiveled her hips against him and felt the pulse of his desire against her stomach. Trembling, she moaned softly, barely able to withstand the emotion seeping through her.

He felt her trembling and his voice was a hoarse whisper as he called out her name over and over. He again struggled for control, wanting her more than he'd ever wanted any woman, yet not wanting to rush into the ultimate act. He moved down, kissing her breasts, her stomach, encircling her naval with his hot tongue. He raised his head. "I want to kiss every part of you." His voice was soft and unsteady.

She nodded, too overwhelmed to speak.

He slid farther down until his tongue found what he sought.

Moments later her body convulsed in spasms and she gasped as she cried out his name. "Oh please, Michael, please. I want to feel you inside me."

He reached over for the foil-wrapped packet before pulling her on top of him and holding her tightly while she struggled to contain her own emotions, feeling his arousal beneath her. She held his face tightly between her palms and placed her hot lips on his, kissing him with abandonment until neither could any longer control their passion for each other.

She wrapped her legs tightly around his hips, moving her hips instinctively while moaning deep within her throat. Oh, God! This was so unlike her; she could barely handle the fluttering of her heart.

Softly calling her name, he gently made them one. Again and again their bodies rode the tide, seeking to fulfill each other, murmuring words of passion.

Reluctantly, he finally tore his body from her and rolled over onto his side. She snuggled up to his chest, her arm circling his side while her breasts rubbed against him. He pulled her closer and they held each other in the moon lit room until their breathing was back to normal. Their ageless joining had been beyond belief. No words were necessary.

It was after midnight when he kissed her softly, saying he would let himself out. She smiled sleepily up at him as she drew the blanket up to her chin, watching him gather his clothes from several locations around her bedroom.

Fully dressed, he kissed her forehead, saying he

would see her Saturday evening. She was almost asleep when he tiptoed out of the room. Quietly locking the front door behind him, he made his way to the elevator, visions of Jennifer running around in his head.

৯৯ ৯৯ ৯৯

On her way to do some errands Saturday morning, Jennifer stopped by Sherry's apartment.

Sherry was on her second cup of coffee when she opened the door. "Well, girlfriend, it's about time you got your butt back here." Sherry smiled, happy to see her friend. "Sit down and have some coffee."

"I'm on my way out, but I guess I could use a cup." She followed Sherry into the kitchen, taking a seat at the small table.

"I see you've been to the plant store," Jennifer observed as she looked at the pot of African violets sitting in the middle of the table.

"I also got some for the windows in my bedroom." Sherry rolled her eyes to the ceiling. "The others just up and died," she explained as she handed Jennifer a steaming cup of coffee. "But is that all you've noticed?" She flung her left hand around in the air, then extended it to Jennifer's face.

"What the...?" Jennifer exclaimed, staring at the emerald-cut diamond flashing on Sherry's ring finger.

"That's right, girlfriend, I'm engaged," Sherry

183

declared, admiring her ring.

"To...to Hal?" Jennifer finally got out.

"Now who else would give me such a gorgeous diamond? Close your mouth, Jennifer, and I'll tell you all about it. Hal came by last night and actually got down on his knees to propose—"

"Get out of here! Hal really did that? Have you set a date?"

"Not yet." Sherry looked down at her cup. "His divorce won't be final for a few days, but Hal couldn't wait to give me the ring."

Jennifer felt she was coming unglued. *Some people have all the luck!* she thought as her mind turned to Michael. Why couldn't she be as lucky?

"...so I'm asking you now," Sherry ended.

Jennifer shook her head from side to side, realizing she had missed part of Sherry's conversation. "What were you saying?"

"What's wrong with you, girl? I just asked you to be my maid of honor," Sherry declared.

"Of course, Sherry, I'd be honored. Are you going to have a big wedding?"

"Oh, no! Hal and I discussed that last night and we both want only our families and very close friends. When I called Momma this morning I had a hard time convincing her I didn't want an elaborate affair. You know her! Well, naturally, she didn't agree but I finally persuaded her that we wanted to use our money for a

184

house. So I think she is going to give us a tidy little sum instead of throwing a big shindig."

Jennifer listened to her friend in awe. She didn't think of Sherry being practical, but she certainly sounded that way.

"So," Sherry continued, "it'll just be you as maid-of-honor and Hal's best man."

Jennifer set down her coffee cup and got up from her chair to embrace Sherry. "I'm so happy for you, girl. You hung in there for a long time and now it's paying off."

Jennifer told her friend all about New York, but didn't mention spending some time with her parents, deciding to do that later. *Sherry is too happy to be saddled with any of my problems,* she thought as she listened to more of Sherry's plans.

She finished her coffee and got up to leave. "I just stopped by to let you know I'm back. I've got to do some errands, so I'm outta here. Michael will be here this evening and I've got several things to do before then. I'll talk to you later."

Sherry looked thoughtful after her friend left. She didn't have the nerve to tell Jennifer that Michael was seen having dinner with Tawana while Jennifer was in New York, not to mention the fact that gossip had it that Tawana was saying she was pregnant with Michael's

Love Doesn't Come Easy

child. Not that she believed a word that Tawana uttered, but Jennifer was bound to hear about it one way or the other. She wondered how or how much she should tell Jennifer. Maybe she'd coerce Jennifer to have lunch with her early next week to clear up some things.

CHAPTER 14

Jennifer took several hours to complete her marketing, drop off her cleaning and make several other stops. It was early evening when she arrived back home. She hurriedly put away her purchases, wanting to have time for a long, relaxing bath before Michael arrived.

As soon as she cleared the kitchen counters, she hurried into the bathroom. Not wanting her chemically-straightened hair to get frizzy, she wrapped a towel tightly around her head before she turned on the hot-water tap full force, steaming up the room in a matter of minutes. She added enough cold water to bring it to a temperature she could tolerate. After pouring in a liberal amount of perfumed bath salts, she tested the water with her foot before gingerly sliding down into the tub.

Love Doesn't Come Easy

Letting out a soft sigh as her body was immersed up to her shoulders, she laid her head back against the rim of the tub, luxuriating in the hot, scented water for several minutes.

Her bath finished, she climbed out and pulled the towel from her hair and ran her fingers through it, satisfied that the steam had not gotten to it. After rubbing her body briskly with a long, fluffy towel, she reached to the shelf and selected a jar of Estee Lauder, her favorite body cream, to rub on from her neck to her toes. She inhaled the fragrance which filled the bathroom before padding to the bedroom, wondering what in the world she was going to put on for an evening at home. She still hadn't made up her mind after applying the sparse make-up she used. She located her small vial of Estee Lauder Super Perfume and applied several drops behind her ears, her wrists, and her knees.

Leaving a fragrance behind her as she moved around, she crossed to her lingerie drawer and rummaged through it until she found a black lacy bra and matching panties. After much shifting of hangers in her closet, she finally settled on a long silk jersey lounging robe in her favorite color, warm tangerine. She settled it over her head and went back to her dressing table to change the color of her lipstick to match the robe.

She fiddled with her hair several minutes, first piling it on top of her head, then pulling it back into a short ponytail. Neither style appealed to her and she brushed

188

it back to the flip she usually wore, pulling a few tendrils onto her forehead.

Satisfied she had done the best she could, she checked the clock on her bedside stand and saw she still had time to mix some martinis before Michael arrived. Finished with the martinis, she got out a tray and put the pitcher and two cocktail glasses on a tray, adding napkins and a dish of party mix she had picked up earlier in the day before taking it to the living room.

Looking around her comfortable and colorful room, she knew some soft music and crackling logs in the fireplace were the finishing touches in creating a romantic atmosphere. The fire had been burning briskly for several minutes by the time she heard the chimes of her doorbell. Rushing through the foyer to admit Michael, she stopped in her tracks when she opened the door and saw him standing in front of her. *My God*, she thought, *he really is one of the most handsome men I've ever seen.* The blood rushed to her face as she looked at him.

"Aren't you going to ask me in?" he asked, a broad smile on his face.

"Oh...oh, yes, come in," she finally got out, and moved aside for him to enter the foyer.

The second the door closed, he pulled her into his arms and planted a deep kiss on her lips. "I've waited all day to do that," he informed her as he followed her into the living room.

She took several deep breaths before she reached the

sofa and sat down on one end, drawing her legs up under her. Following her motion for him to sit, he plopped down in the middle of the sofa in front of the tray on the long glass-topped coffee table.

"Would you like a martini now?" she asked in a slightly tremulous voice.

He nodded his head, and she slid over to pour for both of them. They took several sips before either said a word.

Unable to resist the temptation, she leaned over and kissed him gently on the lips. "So how's everything with you tonight?"

He shifted his body a couple of times but didn't immediately answer her question.

She watched his body movements and the fleeting expressions crossing his face. She thought he suddenly seemed confused, worried, uncertain. She thought about their phone conversation while she was still in New York when he'd sounded rather strange. *What's going on with him?* she wondered.

Michael set down his glass rather abruptly and dropped his head into his hands. "Lord, give me strength," he mumbled to himself.

Jennifer stared at him. "What did you say?" she finally asked, disturbed by his actions.

He turned to face her. "Look, Jennifer, there's something we have to talk about...but I hardly know how to begin." He reached over to take her hand into his, rubbing the back of her hand with his thumb.

"You haven't fallen in love with someone else, have you?" she teased.

He ignored her question. "Sweetheart, what I'm going to tell you is one of the hardest things I've ever had to do...but I owe you the truth. I don't want you to hear it from one of your friends." He looked deep into her eyes. "Will you promise to hear me out before you interrupt or jump to any conclusions?"

"Of course I promise, but what in the world are you talking about?" she asked nervously, hearing the seriousness in Michael's voice.

"Tawana and I might have a situation that—"

"Tawana? What has Tawana got to do with this?" She suddenly remembered Tawana's telephone call while Michael was at his parents' home in Atlanta. A chill went through her.

"You promised to—"

"Okay...okay...I'll be quiet—just get on with it, please," she pleaded.

He gazed into her warm dark eyes, silently praying that she would truly understand his predicament with Tawana...or was he hoping for too much?

By the time he finished talking, her heart had sunk to the tips of her toes. She felt as if the bottom of her stomach had dropped out. *Damn her, damn her, damn her—Tawana is the consummate bitch!* She was quiet for several moments, looking at him like she really didn't believe this could be happening to him.

She ran the back of her hand over her forehead, "Oh, Michael, I don't know what to say. But don't you find it strange that Tawana wouldn't give you her doctor's name and refused to go to your doctor? Doesn't that tell you something?" She stopped for a moment. "And another thing, you mentioned the incident at her apartment happened over two or three months ago. Why is she just now telling you she's pregnant?" She was totally confused and frustrated by the whole situation.

"Tawana mentioned she has always had irregular periods or something...and she claims she just found out for sure three or four days ago." He looked as puzzled as she felt.

He slowly removed his arms from around her shoulders and stared into the crackling fire.

She reached for his hand but he wrapped both arms around his knees and turned toward her. "This whole thing has had my thinking all screwed up, Jennifer, and..." His voice trailed off.

She waited for him to continue, seeing the naked anguish on his face and the defeated stoop of his shoulders.

Oh, how I wish I could get my hands around Tawana's throat! Jennifer thought. *I could easily strangle her for causing all this anguish for Michael.*

He felt his whole world collapsing around him and he didn't know how he could handle her rejection of him.

Turning toward her, he could almost feel her struggling with the emotions flitting across her face.

He reached up and slowly ran his hand over his hair.

She twisted a strand of hers, a far-away look in her eyes.

He got up and placed another log on the fire, pulled her to her feet, then led her back to the sofa.

She didn't look at him as she reached across for the martini pitcher and poured more into their glasses.

He lifted his glass and twirled it several times, staring at the movement of the liquid.

This is it, he thought. *I've lost Jennifer...Tawana has really messed me up this time. What will I do without Jennifer?*

She remembered an expression she'd heard her mother say many times: If anything is worth having, it's worth fighting for. She made up her mind, hoping she'd never regret her decision—she wanted Michael, now and for the rest of her life! And she was ready to fight for him! To hell with Tawana!

She finally turned toward him, a sad half-smile on her face. Her voice was low and soft. "You're...you're a good, decent human being, Michael. You really want to do for Tawana what you believe is the right thing. But from the way she's been acting, don't you think something fishy is going on?" She looked down at her clenched hands, an indication of the turmoil going on inside.

A few moments later, she edged closer to him and pulled his head down to her shoulder, wrapping her arms around him and gently rubbing the back of his neck. "I've never felt like this about anyone, and I have to go with my intuition that everything will turn out in the—"

He interrupted. "But, sweetheart, I can't ask you to just ignore this—how do we know how everything will turn out? There even may be a baby to consider later, and—"

She placed her fingers across his lips. "I know exactly what I'm doing, darling, and you haven't *asked* me to do anything yet. I guess I'm hoping that if you love me as much as I love you, we can work things out together. I want to take that chance. Aren't you willing to let me —"

He interrupted her again. "Do you know what you're saying? It could be months before I can get this all straightened out, and you deserve much better than that—you mean too much to me. I want to give you the world without any deep dark valleys in it!"

She pressed her cheek tightly to his. "And I want to be your world, darling! I know now that I can deal with whatever your world is—as long as we're in it together."

Overcome by emotion, he crushed her to his chest and held her for a long time in silence. *I must have done some things right in my life to deserve someone like this!* he marveled.

She felt his mouth hot on her skin as he kissed the

hollow spot below her chin. "I love you more than you'll ever know," he murmured as he unbuttoned the top of her robe to bare her breasts. "You're one gorgeous creature," he said softly.

Tears formed behind her eyelids when she saw the tenderness in his eyes and felt his strong hands slide over her quivering body. With an effort, she muffled a groan as his lips claimed hers in a passionate kiss, knowing his passion was held in check, while he drove her almost to the point of losing control. And she knew in that instant that the happiness that welled up inside her made nothing in life more important than having and keeping his love. "Somehow we'll find a way to get through this together," she whispered against his chest.

Looking deeply into her eyes, he wanted with all his heart to believe her, and he locked his arms tightly around her and held her close to him, not wanting the moment to end, while mentally cursing the heart-breaking dilemma they were in.

They talked until almost midnight after making passionate love on the floor in front of the fireplace. Neither heard the phone ringing or a message being recorded on her answering machine in her bedroom.

On her way to bed after he left, she suddenly remembered her own problems with Dave's call which she had not mentioned to Michael. "One thing at a time," she said aloud. "Maybe by the time Michael's situation is worked out, I'll have more information about who my real parents are, and I can tell him about my real family."

While undressing, she noticed the red light blinking on her answering machine. Wondering when the call came in, she walked over and pushed the button to retrieve the message. Dave's voice came on the tape, asking her to call him.

She glanced at her watch. It was almost midnight. With shaking hands, she hung up each piece of her clothing slowly. Glancing at her watch again, she saw that only a couple of minutes had passed. She undressed and went into the bathroom to remove her makeup and moisturize her face. She stood before the long mirror for a few moments before she started her nightly ritual. The grim expression reflected in the mirror was evidence of the turmoil she was feeling inside. She took down her toothbrush and brushed her teeth for several moments before she creamed her face, removing the cleanser with tepid water. Reaching for her night cream, she slowly smoothed it on her face and neck. Those ministrations, however, did not diminish the fear building inside.

What will Dave tell me now? she wondered as she padded across her bedroom. She glanced at the number she had written on her pad and with a shaking hand nervously dialed it.

Dave picked up the receiver on the second ring. "I'm glad you're back. Can we set a time to meet?"

She swallowed a couple of times before speaking.

"How about Monday...about eleven o'clock?" She named a small restaurant near her office. "But how will I recognize you?"

"You won't have to look for me. I know what you look like." With that he hung up.

She picked up the remote and clicked through several stations, hoping to find something that would take her mind off wondering what Dave would tell her. She located an old Bette Davis movie she had seen several times but always enjoyed and settled back on her pillows to watch it again. As hard as she tried, she couldn't keep her mind on the movie. Dave's voice kept interfering. She reached for the remote and switched off the set. Maybe reading her novel would settle her down, but that didn't help either, and she resigned herself to a restless night.

か か か

Jennifer awakened late Sunday morning when the telephone jangled in her ears. She reached across to the nightstand to pick up the receiver and immediately smiled when she heard Michael's voice greeting her.

"How about a little sight-seeing today? It's a great day outside, but from the tone of your voice you're probably still in bed and don't know it."

"You've got that right, but I'm getting up now...and yes, sight-seeing sounds great."

"I was hoping you'd agree. How about picking you up in an hour or so? Will that give you enough time to throw something on? And don't eat breakfast; it's on me this morning."

Hopping out of bed, she told him she would be ready, replaced the receiver, and rushed into the bathroom, happy to do anything to take her mind off her meeting with Dave the next day.

Showering quickly, she rushed back to her closet to pull out a pair of turquoise linen pants and a matching top. Within a few minutes she was dressed and was putting on her lipstick when the door bell chimed. Picking up her purse and a sweater to throw around her shoulders, she was at the front door before he rang again.

"It hasn't been an hour since you called," she teased.

"I know, I know, but I couldn't wait any longer."

His words sent waves of happiness through her body and a flush across her face. She followed him out and locked the door. Holding hands, they hurried to the elevator and out to his car. He opened her door before going around to the driver's side. "Buckle up," he instructed, and she reached for the seat belt as he fastened his before starting the car.

"Where are we off to?" she asked.

"Do you have to know everything in advance? Just look at the scenery until we get there," he told her, a sly smile crossing his face as he headed toward the Golden Gate Bridge.

A few minutes later she recognized the Sausalito exit before he turned onto it, winding around a narrow street until he turned again to climb the hill where the Alta Mira Hotel was located. Turning his car over for valet parking, they made their way up the steps to the deck of the hotel where brunch was being served. They were immediately shown to a table which gave them a panoramic view of San Francisco Bay. While waiting to order, they watched the sailboats dipping up and down in the water. Entranced with the view, they said little until their seafood omelets were served. Both were ravenous and the omelets quickly disappeared.

Leaving the hotel, they drove down to Bridgeway, Sausalito's main street, and parked near the sailboat dock. They fed the sea gulls while gazing out over Richardson Bay to Alcatraz and the shores of San Francisco.

"Let's walk down to the wharf and check out the houseboats," Jennifer suggested, holding his hand until they reached the infamous houseboat colony.

"You mean people live in those boats all the time?"

Jennifer nodded. "Come on. Let's see some of them closer."

For the next few minutes they strolled past the converted ferries, floating domes, and housetrailers on pontoons, many of them painted like something out of a psychedelic dream. Some of the residents of the houseboat colony were lounging on their small porches reading, or listening to music, or just sitting and talking. They walked until they reached the end of the settlement before strolling back to the grassy spot of the waterfront.

"Ready to head back to the car?"

She nodded after taking a last look at the house-boats.

The sky above them was dotted with fluffy white clouds, and no sign of fog was in sight until their drive back across Golden Gate Bridge.

"It's still early. Let's stop by Ghirardelli Square," he suggested.

She readily agreed and for the next hour or so they worked their way around the ten-story maze of restaurants, theaters, boutiques of all kinds, all built around the open squares of the old structure that was once a chocolate and spice factory. They stopped to order cappuccino, and sipped it as they walked. After struggling through the crowds of tourists for a while, they bought some cookies to eat on their way back to their car, stopping a couple of times to view the work of sidewalk artists and listen to the loud music of the musicians.

On their way home they stopped in the city's Chinatown district where they walked up and down hills, stopping in whatever shops caught their fancy until both were ready to call it a day by having dinner at a small Chinese restaurant.

The streets were still crowded with tourists when they emerged from the restaurant. "I think I've had enough of playing tourist for today, sweetheart. How about you?" he asked, taking her hand and turning in the direction of the parking garage. She agreed and they headed for her apartment.

It was almost dusk when they pulled up in front of her apartment building. She got out at the curb to wait in the lobby while he hunted a parking space. As soon as he unlocked her door, she kicked off her shoes and plopped down on the sofa, exhausted but happy. He smiled down on her as he removed his jacket and walked to the fireplace to light the logs.

"It's amazing how cool San Francisco can become in just a short time," he observed while he waited for the logs to catch.

"Ummm," she murmured. "It must be the fog coming in. Would you like coffee?" Without waiting for his reply, she headed for the kitchen. She was fiddling with the coffeemaker when she felt his arms around her waist.

"Need any help?" His hands moved up to encircle her breasts.

She leaned back against him. "We'll never have coffee if you insist on standing so near to me."

He released her and moved back out of her way. "I'll get the mugs. Have any cookies?"

Together they put everything on a tray, and he carried it into the living room and deposited it on a low table in front of the sofa.

"It was really a great day, wasn't it?" she asked as she poured their coffee and took a long sip from her mug.

"We surely covered a lot in one day, but it all was big fun. I didn't know some of those places existed in Chinatown," he acknowledged, thinking about all of the things they had done.

They sipped their coffee while discussing their day, just happy to be together and enjoying the companionship they shared when they were not making love. Looking at the happiness shining through on her face, he suddenly set down his mug and drew her into his arms. The moment their lips met, both knew a kiss was not enough and they quickly discarded their clothing.

Even though she was sated from their lovemaking when she crawled into bed, her apprehension about her meeting with Dave caused her to twist and turn a long time before falling asleep.

CHAPTER 15

Jennifer rushed through the work on her desk Monday morning and walked into the restaurant at exactly eleven o'clock to meet Dave. Her dark glasses hid the apprehension she knew was mirrored in her eyes. She clasped her bag tightly to keep her hand from shaking, having no idea what Dave was going to tell her.   She glanced around the restaurant slowly but didn't spot anyone even slightly resembling the profile of the man she had seen from her bedroom window. She chose a booth and settled down nervously.

A waiter walked over and she ordered a fruit juice drink. Slowly sipping it, she saw a man approaching her booth. The same slouched hat sat atop a nondescript light brown face, a slight smile seeming a permanent part of his features. She couldn't see his eyes that were shielded by the brim of his hat. She tried to guess his age and decided he must be in his late forties or early fifties. His dark suit hung from shoulders not wide enough to fill out the coat.

For some indescribable reason the closer he got to her the more she felt an affinity towards him. It was almost as if he were drawing her to him. She had an odd sense of deja vu when their eyes met and she shivered at her reaction to him.

"Hello, Jennifer. You're as pretty as ever," he greeted her and slid into the other side of the booth, removing his hat and placing a slender hand on the table.

Blushing, she murmured, "Thank you."

The waiter approached their booth. "I'll have whatever the young lady is having."

Drawing a deep breath as soon as the waiter left, she felt herself becoming more comfortable even though butterflies still fluttered around in her stomach.

Dave waited until the waiter deposited his drink on the table and then took a long swallow.

She waited.

He took another swallow, wondering how she would take the news he was going to lay on her.

Finally, unable to bear the silence any longer, she asked, "So what do you know about my biological parents that you couldn't tell me on the phone?"

Glancing at her, he took his time to answer. "I know nothing about your father or your mother's family. What do you remember about the time you lived with your real mother?"

"I don't remember anything about my childhood, except the years I grew up with the Johnsons."

A sorrowful expression passed over his face. "Just listen, Jennifer, and you'll learn the answers to some of your questions. Marian Logan, your birth mother, is just across the bay in a hospital in Oakland. She's in pretty bad shape and I don't know how long she'll be able to hang on." He stopped talking and looked around the restaurant, a grim expression on his face.

"What do you mean she's in bad shape? What's wrong with her?" She felt as if her heart had stopped beating and she rummaged in her purse for a tissue. She leaned forward, anxious for him to continue. What was his connection with her mother, if the Marian he spoke about was truly her birth mother?

He looked over at her flushed face and a feeling of sympathy went through him. As terrible as it was, it was time that her daughter knew about her plight.

"Why didn't she keep me with her?" Her voice had risen an octave.

He dropped his head, the sad expression still on his face. He wished he could take her hand while he told her the rest. Clearing his throat a couple of times, he continued. " You'll understand better after I explain some things to you."

She leaned forward to hear him better.

Love Doesn't Come Easy

"Your mother is—or was—a nightclub singer and she traveled all over the country to find work. She always kept in touch with me, and sometimes I helped her out when she was in between gigs."

Jennifer held up her hand to stop him. Peering over at him, she asked softly, "Are you my father?"

"No, but I would have been proud to be your dad. I met your mother during a long engagement she had in Dayton, Ohio, and I fell in love with her—you were just a little tad then and I sometimes baby-sat you when she couldn't get anyone else. At the end of her work there, she left without even saying good-bye to me. I assumed she had taken you with her. A couple of days after she left, I read in the paper about a child found on the fire escape steps of Miami Valley Hospital, and I put two and two together—that child had to be Marian's. I guess she thought her life style couldn't provide the things she wanted for you, so she left you in Dayton. He stopped for a moment when he saw Jennifer's reaction.

She drew in a ragged breath, thinking how her adoptive parents had just told her she had been left at a hospital.

"Is something wrong, Jennifer?"

She shook her head—no need to involve her adoptive parents in their conversation. She waited until he lit a cigarette. "So what else do you know about my mother? Was she married?"

Dave shook his head. "No, that's the reason she left

her parents' home when she learned she was pregnant. She told me they were deeply religious and very involved in their church as well as in their small community. She didn't want to bring shame to them so she left the state and legally changed her name to Marian Logan. I never did find out what her real name was or anything else about her family. So as far as I know Marian is your only known relative."

"But how did you find me after so many years?"

"I've been keeping up with you since the Johnsons adopted you. I live near your adoptive parents. I don't know them, but we have mutual friends in the neighborhood who also have children about your age. I used to see you go to school from the time you were in the elementary grades. I've got pictures I took of you over the years, and I always sent Marian photos whenever she contacted me. Marian even knows you moved out here." She even knows you moved out here.

"Why didn't she get in touch with me?"

"Marian was always so glad you were growing up a happy child with the advantages she couldn't afford that she wanted to stay out of your life. Over and over she made me promise never to tell you about her, and I've kept that promise all these years." He thought for a few moments. "But now I need you to help me. Marian has lung cancer that's in such an advanced stage the doctors won't operate. It's only a matter of time for her, how much I don't know. The hospital out here called me in

Dayton and I caught the first plane. Marian still refuses to let me contact you, but now under the circumstances I think it would be best for both of you if you went to see her. It might bring closure to her life and, hopefully, clarity to yours."

He stared down into his drink as if deep in thought before he continued. "Yesterday Marian was so weak she could barely talk. When she tried to speak, I had difficulty understanding her. Her doctors explained they've done all they can and the rest is up to her and God."

Jennifer could no longer hold back her tears that gushed down her cheeks. She rummaged in her purse for a tissue. He reached inside his coat and handed her a neatly folded handkerchief. Several moments later she had her emotions under control. "I want to see her. Will you come with me?"

He brightened at her request, then dropped his eyes. "Jennifer, don't get your hopes up too high. I still don't know how Marian will react and I don't want you hurt because of my meddling." His eyes had a faraway look as he continued. "Life is cruel sometimes, but you've got to hang in there and ride out the storms everyone must face at one time or another. Believe it or not, there's always a rainbow when you least expect it."

She reached over for his hand. "Can we go to the hospital now?"

He nodded.

She gathered her purse and rose. "Wait here while I

call my office."

On their way across the Bay Bridge to Oakland, he explained she should know that it was possible that Marian might not be lucid enough to recognize her.

"I'd like to stop and pick up some flowers."

"Let's wait until we get to the hospital. I don't think flowers are permitted in her room, but we'll soon find out."

Her anxiety level reached its peak during their walk to the Intensive Care Unit. Her legs were rubbery when they reached her mother's room.

"Let me go in first, Jennifer. Stay out here in the hallway until I try to explain to her that you're here."

She heard Dave call Marian's name a couple of times before she heard a weak response from her mother. A few moments later he beckoned for her to come into the room.

She clapped her hand to her mouth when a gasp threatened to escape as she looked down on the emaciated woman in the bed, tubes running from all parts of her body.

Marian tried to raise her hand when she saw Jennifer but was too weak and her hand flopped back down. "I...I told Dave not...to tell you. He broke...his promise," she finally got out.

Jennifer reached for her clawlike hand and held it tightly. "I want to be here, Mother. I need to see that you really exist, not just in my mind. When you get better,

I'm taking you home with me and we can get to know each other."

Large tears ran down Marian's cheeks and Jennifer softly tissued them away.

Gasping again, Marian tried to speak. She stopped when a raspy coughing spell interrupted her voice.

A nurse rushed in and elevated her head while massaging her back for a few moments.

Jennifer and Dave stared at Marian, misery on their faces.

The nurse shooed them from the room. "You better let Miss Logan rest. She's a pretty sick lady. It's also time for her medication, and she'll be sedated for the next few hours."

They reluctantly walked out in the hallway, both disappointed their visit was so short.

Jennifer turned to Dave. "Let's go to the nurses' station. I want to leave my name and number. Maybe my mother will call me later."

He doubted that, but waited until she explained who she was to the nurse in charge.

On their way back to San Francisco, both were silent for a few miles. Dave finally spoke. "You probably won't understand this, Jennifer, but through the years I kept hoping Marian would eventually return my love and we could be together again. Wishful thinking all these years. And now there's no hope left in my heart."

His pain was so evident she could almost feel it. He

was silent for several more moments, staring out of the car window.

"Where can I drop you off, Dave?

"At the YMCA if it's not out of your way."

She pulled into a spot in front of the building and shut off her motor.

Dave reached in his pocket and took out a large envelope. Carefully opening it, he drew out some photos and passed them over to her. "Look at these. I've kept them because they're my favorites."

Jennifer took the photos and studied each, one by one. She read the inscriptions on the back of some of them: Jennifer's first birthday; Jennifer, age fifteen months; Jennifer, age twenty months. Others had been taken as she grew older and had no notations. She could see that they all were of the same little girl growing up. She studied the photos for several moments, recognizing her own features in the faces staring up at her. Tears formed behind her lids and she had difficulty keeping them from spilling over. She was filled with such emotion that for a few moments she was unable to speak.

Watching Jennifer intently while she studied the photos, Dave continued. "And over the years I was able to periodically give her some news about you—like when you graduated from college and moved out here."

She raised her head in surprise. "But how...how did you know all that?" she stammered.

"I got news from the same mutual friends I told you

about earlier. So, you see, through the years I learned a lot about you from a distance."

Jennifer stared at Dave's face, which was now almost void of expression.

He stared down at the envelope. "I wonder whether Marian might have unconsciously made her way to Oakland, knowing you were just across the bay in San Francisco even though she didn't want you to know about her. Life takes some crazy turns sometimes, Jennifer. Who knows what drives people to do what they do? I don't know what she was thinking. I'm only guessing."

"May I have these?" she asked in a tremulous voice.

"I'll give you all of them later, but not now." He reached for the photos and placed them back into the envelope.

She noticed it contained some other papers. "Do those papers belong to my mother also?"

He nodded. "These are her insurance policies I paid the premiums on for years and other papers Marian wanted me to keep for her. We can talk about them later."

She made a hasty decision. "I'm going to my office and arrange a couple of days off. I'll pick you up in the morning if you want to go back to the hospital with me."

He thought for a moment. "Maybe you better go alone. Now that Marian's met you, she may have some answers for you. I'll call you tomorrow night. Try to have a good night, Jennifer. We can't change circumstances but we don't need to beat up on ourselves by constantly thinking about them. Remember that, won't you?"

She nodded. "I'll try, Dave." She threw up her hand when he reached the sidewalk and pulled out into the traffic.

The sun was shining brightly, the fog having burned off earlier. But Jennifer didn't see the sun or the crowds on the sidewalk as she made her way back to her office. Her eyes were filled with unshed tears, and her heart felt like lead in her chest.

Later in the evening she wondered how she ever got through the afternoon without breaking down into tears while she forced herself to attend to the work in front of her.

As soon as she entered her apartment she kicked off her pumps before making her way to her bedroom to discard the rest of her clothing. Wrapping herself in a long white terrycloth robe, she went to the kitchen to put a TV dinner in the microwave. She had to eat something and she was in no mood to cook. She set the timer and by the time it went off, she had made a salad and poured iced tea into a glass. She put it all on a tray and carried it into the living room, deciding to watch the news while she ate. She located the remote and switched on the set. She had almost finished her dinner when the phone rang.

"I'm in no mood to talk with anyone, not even

Michael," she said aloud as she laid down her food and reached for the phone.

Her heart sank as she heard Michael's greeting and in a split second she prepared herself to plead a headache if he wanted to come by. She had to get through the next day at the hospital. And that was about as much as she could deal with at the moment.

"...so I've got to go to Los Angeles to do some research and—"

"What were you saying, Michael?" she interrupted.

"Is something wrong? Weren't you listening? I just said I'm leaving for L.A. but I'll be back for the benefit banquet this weekend."

"I'm sorry but my head is splitting...I guess I really wasn't listening too carefully," she apologized.

"Problems at work?"

She hesitated, wishing that her problems did concern work. They would be far easier to solve if that were the case. "Yes...yes, there are some things I have to take care of tomorrow."

"Well, okay. I'll be thinking of you every day I'm away and missing you like crazy, sweetheart."

"I'll miss you too. Call me if you have time."

"You've got it. Maybe you should get to bed early tonight. I hope you feel better tomorrow. I've got some reports to look over and some packing to do. Hugs and kisses," he said before hanging up.

She held the receiver in her hand until she became

aware of the dial tone, and then she replaced it slowly. She was now beginning to have a dull pain in the back of her head, almost as if she had caused it by thinking about it.

She felt somewhat better, however, when she realized that the problem with her mother might be solved by the time Michael returned from Los Angeles.

ॐ ॐ ॐ

Not too far away Michael was trying to get through his reports before going to L.A., but his last conversation with Tawana kept interfering. He wondered why he hadn't mentioned his meeting with Tawana to Jennifer while he was on the phone. It was in the back of his mind all during their conversation, but for some reason he couldn't bring himself to tell Jennifer about his latest encounter with Tawana.

He had reluctantly met Tawana for lunch when she called that she had to see him right away. All the time he was walking to the cafe to meet her, he wondered what she now had up her sleeve.

He slid into the booth across from her. "Hello, Tawana," he said as he sat down. "What's on your mind?"

Tawana took her time in returning his greeting while slowly sipping the drink in front of her.

"Have you ordered?" he asked.

"Of course not...I was waiting for you. You certainly took your time to get here," she added, a touch of anger in her voice.

He signaled the waiter, who approached their table and took their orders.

"So...what is so urgent, Tawana?"

She stared at him for several seconds.

He waited.

She took another sip of her drink.

He twirled his water glass around in silence, wondering why he had even bothered to see her. The ball was in her court, and he wasn't about to make anything easy for her.

She took a couple of deep breaths and raised her eyebrows. "There have been some changes in my life and you're off the hook, so you needn't concern yourself about me any longer."

"What do you mean? I...I don't understand. What are you saying?"

She squirmed in her chair. "I just told you my situation has changed—how, is my business. Just go on with your life, you don't need to worry about..." Her voice trailed off.

Totally confused by her remarks, he pressed the heels of his hands against his temples. "So...so what are you going to do now?"

"That's none of your business. Like I said, you're off the hook, so we'll both go our own ways."

Looking askance at her, he leaned back in his chair. *This woman is crazy or something! Maybe she needs some kind of therapy!*

Daringly, she stared back at him.

He had heard from several sources that many of the people they both knew were saying Tawana wasn't really pregnant, that she had put out that story just to get him to marry her. He wanted to believe it, but he just couldn't conceive that any woman would pull such a dirty trick on a man— not even Tawana.

"So is that all this meeting is about?"

"Of course. What else? I thought the least I could do was to tell you first." She looked across the room at the other diners before she continued. "So you can carry on with your little paramour without any interference from me!"

The waiter arrived with their lunch while she was talking.

Michael didn't know whether to be happy for himself or to feel sorry for Tawana. Just what kind of a woman was she, anyway? How had he allowed himself to be so fooled by her during the months they'd been friends? He had unfolded his napkin and prepared to dive into his salad when he noticed she was gathering her things to leave. "Aren't you going to have lunch?"

Throwing a venomous look in his direction, she slid from the booth. "I have better things to do at the moment than to sit here and watch you stuff yourself."

Love Doesn't Come Easy

With that said, she marched out of the cafe without another word.

Shaking his head to get that memory out of his mind, Michael proceeded to pack his bag for his early flight the next morning, still wondering what Tawana was now up to.

CHAPTER 16

On the drive across the Bay Bridge to the hospital late the next morning, Jennifer resolved to hold her emotions in check, regardless of what she might find when she got to the hospital. Her mind turned to Michael and the next hurdle she had to get over—telling him. What would he think if he knew of her activities the past few hours? Uppermost in her mind was the nagging thought of how he would react to her being adopted. Then she had to explain her birth mother's life style. How would that go down with him?

Her thoughts wandered to her parents in Ohio who were another problem. After much deliberation, she'd decided she would not tell them about Marian or Dave's part in her finding her birth mother until later when she could talk to them face to face. They would only worry

Love Doesn't Come Easy

if she phoned them. Maybe she could somehow manage to get everything settled before she talked to them. When her life was back to normal, she would share everything with them.

All her thinking led her right back to Michael. She so wanted to hear his voice, but she knew she could not hold a normal conversation with so much on her mind. She was too emotionally drained. Perhaps what she really needed was some much deserved rest. The restless nights and emotional stress were catching up with her with a vengeance and it showed in her face.

The commuter traffic had thinned out and in a short while she pulled into the parking lot of the hospital. Before locking her car, she remembered her resolve to keep her cool and took several deep breaths. She'd get through this somehow, she reassured herself.

She breathed deeply again while waiting for the elevator. Getting off the elevator, she thought her heart sounded as loud as her heels on the tiled floor of the hospital hallway as she made her way to the nurses' station. She greeted a nurse behind the counter and inquired about her mother.

"Let me call before you see her."

Jennifer drummed her nails on the counter while waiting for the nurse to complete the call.

Turning back to Jennifer after several moments, the nurse informed her the doctor was changing some of the tubes and wouldn't be finished for an hour or so. "The

220

waiting room is to your right, or if you want some coffee or tea, you can take the elevator down to the cafeteria."

She thanked the nurse and proceeded to the elevator, stepping around a maintenance man mopping the hallway. He gave her a big smile as she passed, and her spirits rose as she returned his smile. A cup of hot coffee was exactly what she needed at the moment. When she opened the double doors to the cafeteria, the aroma of fresh coffee assailed her nostrils and she hurried to get in line, picking up a Danish roll on her way to the coffee dispenser. After paying for her purchases, she found a small table near the window and sat down to enjoy her food. She looked out over the rows of tables in the cafeteria. Several weary-looking nurses were gathered at one of the long tables, evidently just getting off a long shift. White-coated doctors or interns were scattered around the room, some having lunch, others just having coffee while reading the paper. And then there were the relatives of patients, she surmised, some with sorrowful faces, others with anxious ones. She saw an older couple wiping their eyes as they leaned together, talking softly, evidently trying to console each other.

Finishing her roll and coffee, she checked her watch. Less than an hour had passed. She walked back to the nurses' station, hoping they were finished with whatever they were doing to her mother.

The nurse shook her head. "It'll be a little longer."

Disappointed she had another wait, she headed for

the waiting room. Finding a seat by a window, she fished in her purse for the novel she had shoved in at the last minute before she left home and settled down to read for a while. Some time later her reading was interrupted when a group, probably all family members she surmised, surrounded a doctor who had entered the room. His news evidently was not what they had expected. Two of the women broke into soft sobs and the others surrounded them, consoling them in their grief. The scene was too much for Jennifer and she gathered her purse, her book, and sweater and walked out into the hallway and continued to the end to look out of the window. She was surprised when, just minutes later, the nurse informed her she could go to the intensive care unit but could stay only a short time.

She steeled herself as she walked quickly down the hall toward the elevator, and once inside she leaned heavily against the back panel, her knees suddenly feeling weak. When the elevator door opened at ICU, she took another deep breath. "Well, here you go," she said aloud to herself.

A nurse was fussing with the tubes attached to her mother when she entered the room, and she stopped halfway through the door. More tubes and needles seemed to have been added. She walked as close to the bed as she could get and looked at the emaciated face on the pillow with her eyes closed, her breathing erratic.

"Your mother is still groggy," the young nurse

informed her, "so she might not make too much sense if she does say anything."

"I understand," Jennifer said before leaning closer. "Mother, can you hear me?" she called softly. "Can you open your eyes?"

Her mother turned slightly toward her voice, eyes still closed, and muttered a couple of words.

She turned to the nurse. "How long do you think it will be before she is coherent?"

The nurse consulted a chart on the foot of the bed for a few seconds.

"We're doing everything possible for her, but she was so very ill when she got here...The doctor is now trying to keep her free from pain." She saw the despondent look on Jennifer's face. "If I were you, I'd go home and not come back for a day or so. There's little you can do except look at her. She doesn't even know you're here. And you look as if you could use some rest yourself."

Jennifer thanked the nurse for her advice. "Will you please call me if there is any change in her condition?" she asked as she walked out of the room.

"Of course," the nurse answered softly. "And you can always call to check on her."

On her way out of the hospital, Jennifer stopped by the nurses's station again. "I'd like to speak to the doctor before I leave."

The nurse in charge looked at her sadly. "Let me page her doctor for you. Would you like to go into the waiting room until I can contact him?"

She had leafed through several back issues of magazines scattered around the bleak waiting room before a white-coated figure appeared in the doorway. Offering his hand, he introduced himself. "You are her daughter?" he asked, a skeptical look on his face as he took in her crisp business suit and soft leather pumps.

She nodded.

"Well," he began, "the prognosis for your mother is very bleak indeed. About all we can do now is to make her as comfortable as possible in the little time she has left. There's nothing we can do for her." He added softly, "I think you should prepare for the worst. She is merely holding on by a thread at this point."

The doctor's words uppermost in her mind, she drove slowly back over the Bay Bridge to San Francisco. She felt as if her stomach had knots tied in the bottom of it, and she wiped more tears that insisted on falling all the way home. Stopping at a deli, she picked up some Chinese food she would have for her dinner. She had every intention of going to bed early again.

Walking into her apartment, she headed for the kitchen to put her purchases in the refrigerator. She had unbuttoned her blouse by the time she reached her bedroom. The blinking light of her answering machine caught her eye, and she walked over to push the button to retrieve her messages. Sherry's strident voice came on first, asking where in hell she had been all day and to call as soon as she got in. The next message was from Michael, leaving the telephone number of his room at a hotel. Dave had also left a number for her to call.

She called Dave first. "I just got back from the hospital. The doctor changed some tubes or something and she's really out of it. She muttered a couple of words I couldn't understand, so I stayed for a short time, hoping to talk to her. But no luck. The nurse insisted there was nothing else I could do but look at her. I talked to one of her doctors and he said she's holding on by a thin thread and suggested I prepare for the worst."

Wiping tears from her eyes, she waited for Dave to speak.

The receiver was silent for several seconds.

"Dave, are you there?"

"Sorry, Jennifer, I was trying to decide whether to wait until tomorrow or to go over there now. I guess I better get over there this evening, but try to relax. I'll call you later tonight."

After talking to Dave a few more minutes, she placed a call to Michael. She was anxious to hear his voice, knowing that he could always make her feel better.

He was elated hearing her voice and almost shouted. "I was just thinking about you! And here you are, even though many miles away! How are you? Miss me?"

Unwanted tears formed in the back of her eyes as she wished he could there beside her, holding her tightly and saying everything was going to be all right.

She took a deep breath. "Yes, I'm okay, and, yes, I've really missed you. When will you be back?"

"As far as I can tell at the moment, I should be back in San Francisco Friday evening. I'll call you as soon as I get in."

For the next few minutes they commiserated about being apart for a few days and how anxious they were to see each other.

Hanging up her phone, she reached for her box of tissues to blot the stream of tears that she couldn't stop. How she wished she could tell him about the last couple of days. It took several minutes before she replaced the tissue box on her night stand. "What a mess my life is in," she said aloud on her way to the kitchen to get something to nibble on.

CHAPTER 17

Jennifer awakened with a start when the phone rang. Looking at her clock on the nightstand she saw it was three-fifteen in the morning. Disoriented, she rolled over and picked up the receiver. "Hello?"

"Is this Jennifer Johnson?"

"Yes, this is she." Her heart beat fast against her chest.

"This is Nurse Arnold, Miss Johnson. I talked with you earlier about..."

She bolted up and threw her legs over the side of the bed, her breath suddenly deserting her. Holding the receiver away from her ear with a trembling hand, she breathed deeply and exhaled slowly, waiting for the nurse to continue.

"...your mother, Miss Johnson. She's been very agi-

227

tated for the past couple of hours and keeps calling for you and Dave. I'm sorry to disturb you at this time of the night, but can you come over here as soon as possible?"

"We'll be there in about a half hour."

Wide awake now, she dialed Dave's number. The phone rang several times, and she was on the verge of hanging up when he answered.

She told him about her talk with the nurse. "Can you go over there with me now?"

"I'll be ready by the time you get here."

Dave was waiting in front of the building and hurried to her car. Since there was little traffic at that time of the morning, she sped through the city and across the Bay Bridge, reaching the hospital in a matter of minutes.

Shakily climbing out of the car, she followed him into the hospital. Approaching the bed, she sensed her mother was indeed more lucid. She took her mother's hand and felt her grasp stronger than the last time.

"I'm glad you're here, Jennifer. Did you bring Dave?"

Jennifer nodded, encouraged by the strength in her mother's voice which was now not as tremulous as yesterday's. She withdrew her hand and walked over to get a chair to sit close to Marian's bed.

"I'm here, Marian," he said as he walked over and patted her sunken cheek.

"Did you go the hotel for my luggage?"

Assured that he had, Marian turned back to Jennifer. "I have some things you...you might want to keep,

Jennifer. David, give my clothes to someone that...that needs something to wear." She stopped talking for a few moments, taking several deep breaths as if that would give her more energy.

Turning to face Jennifer, a shadow of sorrow passed over her face. "There're some things...I want to tell you. I know you can never forgive me...for what I did when you were so small. You were not quite two years old when I left you in Dayton. It broke my heart...but no way did I want to drag you from place to place. I was very young and had taken voice lessons as I had visions of eventually being an opera singer. And then I got pregnant. So after you were born, all that I knew to do was to use my singing talent...I was pretty good too, wasn't I, Dave?"

Dave nodded and squeezed her hand, happy she now had the strength to talk.

After a moment she continued. "I had...to go where my work was...and that's no life for a young child. Do...do you understand, Jennifer? Many nights I cried myself to sleep thinking about what I'd done. But now in one way I don't regret...giving you up. Thanks to Dave, I know you've had a good life...one I couldn't have given you." She again started breathing heavily and closed her eyes.

Jennifer struggled to keep her emotions under control—anger at her mother for not keeping her, yet compassion for her mother's sacrifice. She still had questions.

"What about your parents? What are their real names? Where do they live? Do you have sisters or brothers?"

Marian sighed deeply. "Mom and Dad are both dead. I was an only child they had...late in life...and I probably broke their hearts. I—" Her voice had gotten weaker and a spasm of coughing assailed her before she continued. "My real name doesn't ... matter now, just get on with your life."

Dave poured a glass of water and held it to her lips. Taking only a swallow, she waved it away.

Jennifer became alarmed seeing her mother struggle to breathe. "Shouldn't we call the nurse?"

Marian shook her head as another spasm of coughing attacked her.

Jennifer held back her tears. There was so much more she wanted to hear from her mother.

Still holding Marian's hand, Dave turned away, pain evident on his face. He reached over and rubbed Jennifer's shoulder with his free hand.

Jennifer felt a deep sorrow in her heart for the wasted woman lying in front of her. Unconsciously twisting her hair, she gazed at Marian. *She must have been pretty when she was young,* she thought as she recognized some of her own features mirrored in Marian's emaciated face.

Suddenly alarmed, they watched as Marian seemed to sink into a lethargic state. Now there was a peaceful look on her face. They looked at each other, fearful of the sudden change in her.

Charlyne Dickerson

"Shouldn't we call the doctor?" she whispered.

He shook his head slowly. "Let her go in peace, Jennifer. The end is near. She must have felt it in her soul when she insisted on seeing us. It's in God's hands now."

Contrary to Dave's instructions, she ran out and called the nurse, who came in immediately. The nurse took one look at Marian, felt her pulse, and then drew the sheet over her face. "She's gone," the nurse said gently.

A loud gasp escaped Jennifer's lips and she stared at her mother as if she couldn't believe she was actually gone.

Dave walked around the bed, put his arms around Jennifer, and took her to the waiting room. "Sit down, Jennifer. You're trembling like a leaf in a hail storm." He reached into his pocket, handed her a handkerchief, and then walked over to a window at the end of the room. His eyes teared up as he listened to the heart-rending sobs that echoed in the room.

Several minutes passed before Jennifer joined him, a question in her eyes.

"There's nothing else you can do here, Jennifer."

"But...but what about the...you know...the burial arrangements?" she asked, her voice a little hoarse from her sobbing.

"Let me talk to someone at the desk first, and then we'll decide what should be done, Jennifer," he said, drawing some papers from inside his jacket pocket. "Stay here. I'll be back in a little while."

She stared out into the darkness. Soon it would be dawn, yet the darkness would not leave her heart for a long time. She hadn't a clue as to what Dave was doing, but when he appeared at her side some time later he looked at peace with himself.

"Let's get back to San Francisco, and I'll fill you in about everything." He took her arm and held it until they were settled in the car.

While she maneuvered the car through the early morning traffic, he glanced at her several times before he spoke. "Marian always wanted to be cremated and made me promise to carry out her wishes. Do you have a problem with that?" he asked softly.

She shook her head. "If that's what she wanted, that's what we should do." Thinking for a moment, she suggested, "Maybe we could sprinkle her ashes in the bay. Somehow I think she'd approve."

"We'll do it together before I leave."

He studied the papers in his hand. "I'll take care of everything else, Jennifer. I've paid on a small insurance policy for Marian for many years, and that should take care of her expenses now."

"But—"

He held up his hand to stop her. "Listen to what I'm saying, Jennifer. I want you to go home and be comforted that the two of you got to meet, even for so short a time. I'll have Marian's ashes delivered to you and we can go out in one of those Bay cruisers. You might even want to keep a few. That way, you will at least have something to remind you that she loved you very much, had only tried to do what she thought was best for you. I'm sure she suffered every time she received a picture of you growing up."

"How can I thank you for...for everything, Dave?"

"What I did, I did for both of us, my dear."

Jennifer choked back the tears she felt forming and looked over at Dave. "You mean for all three of us, Dave. We never know what's in store for us, do we? I've never mentioned this to another living soul, but I think I've finally pieced together the reason for the hideous nightmare I've had over and over since I was very young."

"Nightmare? What do you mean?"

She explained how the same nightmare had occurred periodically over the years, and how she could never put faces to the people in her weird dream, remembering best the sound of the shrill screams at the end of the nightmare.

Listening intently, he nodded his head several times. When she finished, he looked at her with pain in his eyes. "You'll probably never remember what actually happened. And that's good. Maybe now the nightmare will go away."

She looked at him skeptically. How she wished he was right. On second thought, she remembered she hadn't been awakened by the nightmare recently.

"What are you going to do when you get everything taken care of here, Dave?" she asked, glancing over at his vulnerable face.

He didn't answer for a few miles. They were almost to the YMCA before he spoke again.

"First, every night, I'll thank whoever is upstairs that I was able to be here when Marian needed me the most. I'm going back home to my job at the post office and try to make the most of the time I have in front of me, and that's exactly what I want you to do."

She pulled up in front of the YMCA, leaving the motor running.

He leaned over and gave her a quick hug. "Call me when you get the ashes." He pushed open the car door and got out quickly, disappearing through the door of the YMCA.

She waited for a moment, looking after him, before she put her car into gear and headed home. She didn't notice the envelope on the front seat until she got home. She reached across to get it, and saw her name on it. She dropped it into her purse, knowing that Dave had meant her to have it.

As soon as she reached her apartment she opened the envelope and studied the pictures again, one by one, until she had practically memorized the features of a little girl growing up. She gasped when she reached the last two photos, one of her mother holding a microphone, the

234

other of her mother and Dave, his arms around her shoulders. Looking at them, she felt tears forming behind her eyes.

Although she was disappointed at not finding a birth certificate or any other identification, she was grateful for the pictures. Walking over to her vanity she propped the photo of her mother and Dave against her mirror, where she would see it each morning. For the first time in her life she felt she really belonged to someone. Strangely the pictures also reinforced her love for her adoptive parents.

A sense of peace spread through her until she thought of Michael. She had another mountain to climb and hoped she wouldn't slip.

Putting the rest of the pictures back into the envelope and laying it on her nightstand, she noticed the red light blinking on her answering machine and pushed the button to retrieve the message. As she expected, Sherry had called her again.

Before she could change her clothes, her door bell chimed. *Oh, Lord*, she thought, *that must be Sherry.* And it was.

She opened the door, and Sherry burst in like a whirlwind, her hands on her ample hips and an indignant expression on her face. "Where in heaven's name have you—"

Jennifer held up her hand. "Come on into the kitchen, Sherry, before you bust a gut. I'll make us some coffee."

Sherry had no choice but to follow her friend. She plopped down in a chair at the table and with a half smile watched while Jennifer slowly and carefully measured the coffee and water before turning on the coffee pot. She knew a delaying tactic when she saw it. But she was willing to wait.

Jennifer took a seat opposite Sherry and heaved a deep sigh. "I've had a hectic couple of days. I hardly know where to begin, Sherry." Her heart threatened to spill over and she certainly didn't want to break down in front of Sherry.

"How about at the beginning?" Sherry tapped her long coral nails on the place mat, her impatience clearly coming through.

Jennifer rose, opened the cabinet above the sink and took down two mugs. She poured the hot liquid into the mugs and slowly walked back to the table, depositing a mug in front of Sherry.

"Where's the sugar and cream, Jennifer?"

"Oh," Jennifer exclaimed, feeling foolish, knowing how much of each Sherry always used. She got the containers and sat back down, watching Sherry spoon an ample supply of both into her coffee. Sherry took a sip, then added more sugar. She looked over the rim of her mug. "So, what in the world have you been up to, girl-friend?"

Jennifer took a moment to collect her emotions

before she launched into the events of the past couple of days. She left out few details as she told Sherry about Dave and her biological mother. By the time she finished, Sherry was wiping her eyes with her napkin, her mouth open in disbelief.

"Oh, Jennifer, Jennifer," she finally cried. "You went through all that by yourself! Why didn't you call me? I would have gone with you, I'm your friend, remember."

Jennifer looked down at her tightly clasped hands. "I...I guess I...thought it was just something I had to take care of myself. And then Dave was there."

The friends sipped their coffee in silence for several moments.

Jennifer felt a sense of relief in telling Sherry.

Sherry was trying to put herself in Jennifer's situation, having no idea how she would have handled the whole ordeal. She finally lifted her head. "So what about Michael? Are you going to tell him when he returns?"

Tears sprang into Jennifer's eyes. She was silent for several seconds while she got her voice under control. "Of course I'll tell him. The problem is, I don't know...how he'll react. You know how much stock he and his family put into knowing a person's background. It scares me just thinking he might not want to see me again...and that would just devastate me."

Sherry leaned over and took Jennifer's hand in hers, saying softly, "If Michael is the kind of person I think he is, girlfriend, he'll want you just as you are."

"Oh, I hope you're right, Sherry. He's become a part of my world and I wouldn't know what to do without him, but still ..." Jennifer's voice trailed off and she was silent again, looking pleadingly at her friend before haltingly continuing. "I haven't told Momma and Dad about this yet. It's too fresh in my mind. I have to...to get everything together in my own mind first. I haven't had time for it all to sink in."

Sherry nodded. What Jennifer said seemed to be a good idea. "Maybe you should tell the Johnsons first and get their reaction before you tell Michael," she suggested.

"That makes a lot of sense," Jennifer agreed. Her face lost its worried look as she internalized Sherry's suggestion.

With that settled, the two friends talked a few more minutes before Sherry went back to her apartment.

Closing the door behind Sherry, she thanked her lucky stars she had a friend like Sherry, even though they had an occasional spat. "But isn't that what a true friend is for?" she said aloud on her way to her bedroom. "I can always count on Sherry to put things into perspective."

The phone interrupted her thoughts.

"Jennifer, where have you been? I've been trying to get you all day. I just found out this afternoon that I have to stop in Monterey on my way back to San Francisco, but my business won't take more than a few of hours, and I'll be back early Friday evening. How about making reservations for a late dinner?"

She brightened at his suggestion. "I'll do better than that. I'll make dinner."

"Sounds good to me if it's not too much trouble for you."

She felt a warm feeling flow through her as they talked for a few more minutes, both anticipating the time they would spend together. Some of the pieces of her life had fallen together she realized as she hung up. Now she needed to deal with the last piece, but the thought made her cringe.

"If Michael understands, my world will be complete," she said aloud.

Thinking of Michael reminded her of something else she had to do that had been in the back of her mind ever since he told her about Tawana's alleged pregnancy.

CHAPTER 18

Jennifer went to work as usual the following morning. But nothing else was the same. She was relieved now that the ordeal of the past few days was over but she was still nervous and edgy. The events of the last two or three days had been tumultuous, and it would take some time to get over the stressful situation she had faced. She still had to tell Michael and her adoptive parents about Marian as soon as she felt up to it mentally and emotionally.

It was nearly lunch time when she suddenly made up her mind to deal with something else that had troubled her ever since she learned about Tawana's pregnancy.

No way was she going to let Tawana get away with her low-down plan to snare Michael. He was hers and she intended to keep him as long as he wanted her.

What she had in mind went against her nature, but she could think of no alternative. She'd had enough of Tawana's schemes that evidently everyone else was willing to accept. Maybe they feared her wrath as the self-appointed leader in the small group of what was considered the African-American society of San Francisco. Whatever it was, she didn't care. She was going to give Tawana a piece of her mind in whatever way it took. By the time she got through with that woman, Tawana would know she had better come up with something or get out of the picture.

She pulled out her purse and dug in it until she located her lipstick, swiping it quickly across her full lips before making her way to the elevator. Once outside, she headed toward the restaurant where she knew Tawana hung out during lunch break.

She was in luck. She spotted Tawana and her groupies at a table in the back of the room.

For a moment she felt a quiver in her stomach; never before had she done what was now in her mind. Breathing deeply to rid herself of the trepidation she now felt, she walked confidently through the lunch crowd to Tawana's table. She nodded to all of the women before asking to speak to Tawana in private.

Jennifer smiled when she saw the look of astonishment on Tawana's face and the look of amusement on the faces of the other women after she made her request.

"Can't you tell me what you want right here,

Jennifer? These are my friends and we've just ordered lunch."

Not the least bit intimidated by her or her friends, Jennifer insisted, "Let's go to the lounge. What I have to say is for your ears only, Tawana."

Baffled, Tawana rose and followed Jennifer through the room, leaving the other women with smirks on their faces. Some of the women wished they could be flies on the lounge wall, while others hoped Tawana would finally get her comeuppance.

The minute the door closed, Jennifer told Tawana to sit down.

"What in heaven's name is your problem, Jennifer?" Tawana demanded as soon as both were seated on the couch facing each other. "Make it quick as I need to have lunch and get back to my office."

Jennifer drew a long breath and stared at Tawana who was now squirming in her seat. "What I've got to say won't take long, Tawana. Probably not any longer than it took you to make up your little scheme to get Michael to—"

Tawana jumped up from the couch. "What are you insinuating, Jennifer? What's between Michael and me is strictly our business and if you think—"

"That's where you're wrong. Michael is *my* business. That's why I'm here. I think you'd better sit down and listen, Tawana," Jennifer said softly. "First, I'm so sure you're not pregnant that I'd bet my life on it. Any tramp can accuse a man the way you've laid a lie on Michael. I thought you might have been above such behavior, but apparently you're not. Why do you want a man who doesn't love you—and Michael certainly doesn't. He's in love with me and has been for some time, and I have no intention—"

"Oh, can it, Jennifer. The last thing I need is a lecture from you." She picked up her purse and started to rise from the couch.

Jennifer held up her hand and continued softly, "I haven't finished, Tawana. I think you better get another story going among your so-called friends since most of them also question the truth of what you've been spreading around. In fact, many of them are laughing behind your back, saying you have gone too far this time to get a man. For my part, I couldn't care less about you or your men, just stay away from Michael and get this pregnancy business straightened out pronto. If you don't, you'll have me to deal with. And I don't take kindly to any messing around with my man. Are you clear on what I'm saying?" She rose to leave, then turned around. "By the way, I don't think you need tell Michael about this conversation." Head held high, she sauntered out of the room, leaving a stunned and irate Tawana behind.

Totally shaken up, Tawana threw her purse across the room. "Well, I'll be damned! I sure misjudged that woman. Walks around like sugar won't melt in her mouth! She's welcome to Michael." She recovered her purse and stalked out.

Little did Jennifer know that all of the women's eyes at Tawana's table followed her as she strolled out of the restaurant. Had she looked back she would have seen a couple of thumbs up in the air while others hi-fived.

All of the women were busy with their food and didn't look up when Tawana stomped back to the table and flopped into her seat.

By the time Jennifer got back to her office, her nerves were frayed, but she tackled the work piled on her desk with an elated smile on her face.

ॐ ॐ ॐ

On Friday Jennifer wrestled with the devastation of finding her mother and then losing her after only a couple of days. There was also that business of her set-to with Tawana. And now Michael was coming home, the only bright spot in her life at the moment; how long that would last, she didn't speculate. She left work early, wanting to have dinner ready when Michael stepped in the door.

Her temperature rose when she heard the door bell. He handed her one red rose when she opened the door, but she almost crushed it when she fell into his arms. They silently held each other for several moments.

"I missed you like sin, sweetheart," he said when he finally released her.

244

"And I could hardly wait for you to get back," she murmured while carefully straightening out her rose. "Dinner's ready and it will get cold if we stay out here much longer."

They soon sat down to their meal, and he told her about his work in Los Angeles while they ate.

"Did you have a good week?" he asked.

She almost dropped the forkful of food on the way to her mouth. Gathering all the composure she had, she answered him noncommittally. "Oh, we can talk about mine later," she answered, looking down at her plate.

"You can really do some food," Michael complimented as he helped her clear the table. They soon had the dishes in the dishwasher and carried their coffee into the living room where Michael had lit the logs earlier. She inserted a romantic disk into the CD before joining him on the sofa.

They silently watched the flames for several moments, just enjoying being together. He finally looked over at her and asked, "You okay, Jennifer? You seem so far away." He reached across for her hand. "And your hand feels cool. Sure you're all right?"

Startled, she brought her thoughts back to the present and withdrew her hand. Even though she was trying hard, her thoughts about the events of the week were overwhelming her. Not wanting anything to spoil their weekend though, she forced a smile to her lips and opened her eyes wide. Looking across at his handsome face with what she hoped was a happy smile, she announced, "I'm just happy being here with you."

That was all he needed to hear. He returned her smile with a dazzling one of his own. "And I feel the same way," he said, his voice husky with emotion.

His words pierced her heart. She silently vowed she would think only of him for the next few hours. *Let sleeping dogs lie for the time being,* she told herself. She would tell him everything later and pray that her news would not tear them apart when she was forced to divulge her secrets. She knew she was being devious with him as well as with herself, but that was the only way she could deal with her news at the moment.

He moved closer and pulled her against his broad chest. "I need to have you closer to me," he whispered huskily and kissed her softly. Not meeting any resistance, he scooped her up and headed for the bedroom. He threw back the comforter and sheet with one hand and lowered her onto the bed with the other. His dark eyes burned into hers. Amazed that he had controlled his passion for so long, he pelted her face with feather-like kisses, holding his own desire in check as her passion increased.

"Oh, Michael, love me...love me," she whispered, winding her legs around his firm thighs, experiencing a depth of feeling she had not known existed within her.

"Jennifer...Jennifer," he murmured hoarsely as he buried his face against the curve of her neck and shoul-

246

der. She felt the roughness of his breathing and the heat of his mouth against her skin as his hands stroked her breasts, her stomach, her thighs. He touched every curve, and she moaned as her body came alive to his touch, making her gasp, yet not wanting him to stop.

She explored him, touching the rippling muscles of his back and arms, her legs feeling the tenseness in his thighs and the hardness of his body. She felt him reach over for a small packet before he turned back to her

Her hips arched against his, driving them both to the brink of desire as he entered her. Their passion built into a raging crescendo, and they clung together until the waves of passion subsided.

It was a long time before either of them stirred.

He rolled over onto his side and she moved close to him. Her back snuggled against his stomach, and his arm lay across her waist. His breath was warm on the back of her neck. It was a silent time of tenderness and spent passion, and, huddled together, they fell asleep.

It was well after midnight when she stirred and gently removed his arm from around her waist. She rose up on one elbow and turned to gaze at his face, so handsome even in sleep, so vulnerable in the moonlight. She felt him stir as if he sensed she was looking at him.

Still half asleep, he pulled her face down and kissed her gently. "My Jennifer, my love," he murmured between kisses, and her heart sang as she heard the love in his voice and felt the passion of his kisses. She slowly turned full length toward him, and kissed his chest while he placed small fluttering kisses on the top of her head. They held each other in silence, reveling in the touch of their entwined legs.

Their passion slowly grew as they touched and fondled until their need again overwhelmed them. He gently rolled her over to her back, and their lovemaking began again, slow and tender and breathtakingly sweet, their bodies moving in perfect harmony. It was almost dawn before their passion was spent, and they fell into a deep sleep.

The bright sun streaming through the half-closed drapes slowly awakened her. She felt his warm breath on her neck and touched his hand that lay limply on her waist. Moving cautiously, she removed his hand and slipped out of bed, sighing happily as she looked down on his face, so relaxed as he soundly slept. She marveled as she thought that he was truly her dream man, her soul mate.

Resisting the urge to awaken him, she threw a robe across her shoulders and padded softly across the room into the bathroom, still wondering how she could be so lucky. She soon finished in the bathroom and headed for the kitchen. She'd just started breakfast when he walked into the kitchen.

They finished making breakfast together and ate ravenously, saying little until they finished their food. He poured more coffee for them before he spoke, a serious expression on his face. "You've become a very important part of my life in just a short time, Jennifer." He saw her face flush. "I'm very serious. You're constantly in my thoughts, no matter where I am, and I don't quite know how to handle my feelings toward you." He paused and looked at her expectantly, but she said nothing, her mind going around in circles and her heart beating too fast.

"We have a great time together. And I don't mean just in bed," he added quickly. "But I don't know how I fit into your life, and—"

She interrupted. "I think what you mean, Michael, is that we haven't talked about a future. Isn't that it?"

"Well, yes, I guess I'd like to know just where I stand with you." His voice was low and rather strained.

She carefully put down her coffee cup and reached across to take his hand. "When I'm with you, Michael, I don't think of the world out there," she said softly.

He stroked her hair, feeling a deep peace. "I'd like to wake up every morning with you beside me."

"We'll have to decide what to do about that." She sighed, feeling she would like to stay forever just the way they were at that moment.

He rose and walked around to the back of her chair, putting his arms around her shoulders. "As much as I'd like to stay here with you, I've got to get out of here. I'll call you later and maybe we can take in a movie." He pulled her to her feet and enfolded her in his arms.

She lifted her eyes to his, and her deep sigh said

more than words.

After he left, she mused that she had never allowed herself to be so vulnerable to another human being. And it scared her. Michael had control of her heart, her emotions, her trust. What would she do if he betrayed that trust when she got up enough nerve to tell him about her being adopted and the events that had occurred while he was away? The possibility of his rejection made her heart do a flip-flop. Could he turn away from her after such all-consuming experiences they'd shared? But then, she knew from experience that men can participate in and enjoy sex and still keep their hearts and minds detached. Had he really meant the words he'd whispered during the heat of their emotions?

She shook her head to dispel such depressing thoughts. She had learned early in life to avoid self-pity, and she refused to sink into that state. She knew she had to stop torturing herself about possibilities. Why not just take one day at a time and not worry about the future?

⅜ ⅜ ⅜

A couple of days later Jennifer was in the middle of returning a phone call her secretary had marked "urgent" when Greg knocked lightly on her door before walking in.

She looked up, hoping her irritation at being interrupted did not show on her face. She was in no mood for frivolous conversation. She had too much to do and too much on her mind.

"I'll be with you in a minute, Greg."

He waited at the door until she completed her call.

Hanging up her receiver, she motioned for him to come in. "So what's up, Greg?"

"Too busy to talk to an old friend?" he inquired, a crooked smile on his handsome dark face.

"Never too busy for you," she graciously replied, all the while thinking she would never finish what was in front of her by the time she had to leave. "Why am I being honored by your presence?" she asked facetiously.

He ignored her comment and flopped down on the chair beside her desk, a mischievous look on his face.

She glanced at him with raised eyebrows, wondering why he was looking so peculiar.

"So?" she asked, hoping he would get on with whatever reason he came to see her.

"I've got some hot-off-the-press gossip I think you'll be interested in." He waited until he had her full attention. "You'll never guess what everyone was talking about at Maria's get-together last night. By the way, why didn't you and Michael show up?"

She looked at him, surprise showing on her face. She'd completely forgotten about Maria's invitation. Not that she would have gone anyway, not with so much else going on in her life the past few days. But then no one knew about that, she remembered.

"Oh...oh, Michael was out of town all week and...and I've been trying to catch up with some things I needed to do."

"So that's why no one has seen you around."

"Greg, will you please stop acting like the proverbial cat that swallowed the canary and tell me what your 'hot-off-the-press' gossip is?"

He smiled, knowing he had piqued her interest. "Well, the grapevine has it that Tawana is now saying the doctor mis-diagnosed her condition!" He deliberately waited for that news to have an impact on her. Which it did.

She stared at him, trying to keep a poker face as she remembered her "talk" with Tawana.

"So say something, Jennifer."

She finally stammered, "You...you've got to be kidding! That woman is such a liar. A person doesn't know what to believe if it comes out of her mouth!"

"You've got that right. Some of her so-called friends are blackballing her. Marie didn't invite her to the party last night."

"Are you for real, Greg? You know Tawana thinks she's San Francisco's black social queen. What's she going to think if people stop including her?"

"Who cares? She's the only one who thinks she's hot stuff. A lot of people merely tolerate her. You know that, Jennifer."

"Well, that's true. But she's one pushy broad and

mark my words—she'll be out there lording it over everyone just like nothing happened. Just you wait and see.
But I kinda feel sorry for her if she got caught up in her
own machinations."

He stared at her. "I'm not so sure I feel as charitable
toward her as you do, Jennifer. That's a low-down trick
to pull on any man!" He sounded as pissed off as if it had
happened to him.

She swallowed a smile, seeing the disgusted look on
his face. "Well, I'm really more than angry at the way
Tawana tried to use Michael!" She could get upset again
just thinking about the whole messy affair, even though
it seemed that Tawana's charade was coming to an end.

The two friends exchanged a few more bits of gossip
before he announced he had to get back to his office,
leaving her with a big smile on her face for the first time
that day. She was in a better mood the rest of the afternoon, finishing the work she had to deal with before she
left her office. She smiled to herself while walking to the
elevator, thinking of one of her mother's ever ready plat-
itudes. "I guess everything that goes around really does
come around," she said out loud to the empty elevator.
"That's one more thing I won't have to worry about."

CHAPTER 19

Jennifer saw the light flashing on her answering machine when she walked into her bedroom. She pushed the button to retrieve the first message. Dave explained he was back in Dayton. He wished her well and again said he would stay in touch. Her eyes flooding with tears, she waited a few moments before continuing with the other message. Her mother's voice came through, informing her they were coming to San Francisco for a few days. They planned to arrive the following weekend. *Why have they decided to visit at this particular time?* she wondered.

Still thinking about her adoptive parents' decision, she walked across the hall to the room she used partly as an office and partly as a spare bedroom. She glanced around the room, deciding to straighten it up for her parents while she was in the mood. She cleared some papers from the desk, ran the sweeper over the area rug, and dusted each piece of furniture. After moving the convertible sofa back against the wall, she got sheets and blankets from hallway closet and made up the bed.

Famished by the time she finished, she rummaged through the refrigerator hoping to find something for her dinner. All she found was some hard cheese, a half head of wilted lettuce, and a dish of something she didn't recognize. So much for that, she thought, before going to the phone to call Sherry, who always had her refrigerator stocked since food was one of her things. After a few rings, Sherry came on the line and Jennifer told her her plight.

"Come on down, girlfriend, and we'll have ourselves a feast and catch up on some gossip. Hal won't be here until later, so we'll have some time to ourselves."

She smiled at Sherry's remark about gossip. That woman loved to talk about everything she heard and was always pumping others about what they knew. Jennifer knew she could count on Sherry to fill her in on the latest.

"I'll be there as soon as I get into some jeans." In a matter of minutes she was on her way to the elevator.

Waiting a few minutes for the elevator to get to her floor, she found it was being held on the first floor for some reason or other. She headed for an exit sign and trotted down the stairs to Sherry's apartment, calling out

Love Doesn't Come Easy

to Sherry after opening the unlocked door. Whatever Sherry was cooking smelled delicious, she thought as she closed the door.

"Come on out to the kitchen. I'm setting the table," Sherry called out, and Jennifer headed in that direction.

"Girl, you're sure looking better than the last time I saw you," Sherry observed when Jennifer entered the kitchen. "Hit the lottery or something?"

Jennifer smiled as she slid into a chair at the table. Sherry placed a salad, iced tea, and a tuna casserole on the table. She inhaled the tantalizing aroma that filled the room. "You sure can cook some good stuff, Sherry."

"That's because I like to eat good stuff, as you put it. In fact, I just like to eat, as my hips can testify," she said, patting her wide hips as she sat down. "Dig in."

They ate in silence a few minutes. Sherry finally glanced sideways at her friend. "Heard the latest about Tawana?"

Jennifer could tell Sherry was just bursting to tell her, so she pushed aside the information she had gotten from Greg and listened to Sherry's version, which was practically the same thing Greg had told her, but with a few embellishments.

"I just know that bitch wasn't pregnant in the first place, and now she makes up that weird story which no one believes," Sherry ended vehemently.

A thought ran through Jennifer's mind. *Does Michael know what's going on with Tawana?* She shook her head as if to dispel the thought and changed the subject.

"I just learned Mom and Dad are coming out for a few days. It's not the ideal time for me, but I'll be glad to see them."

"They haven't met Michael, have they?"

Jennifer shook her head. "But I've talked about him during our phone conversations, so they know something about him, and they—" She suddenly stopped speaking and looked down at her plate.

"What's wrong, Jennifer?"

"I still haven't told Michael that they're my adopted parents. What am I supposed to do now when he meets them?" she asked in a small voice.

Sherry studied her for a few seconds. "Well, if you're asking for my opinion—"

"You'd give it to me whether I asked or not," Jennifer inserted pertly.

Sherry glared at her friend. "Well, as I was about to say before you so rudely interrupted me, why not let Michael get to know them before you tell him? They're two of the nicest people I've ever met, and I'd have been proud if they'd adopted me. Being adopted is no big deal in my opinion...although you seem to make a lot out of it."

Jennifer thought about Sherry's idea. Maybe it wasn't a bad one. She could tell Michael about being adopted after her parents returned home. Not a bad idea at all, now that she thought more about it.

"You know, you may have something there, Sherry. Maybe I'll plan some things while they're here that will throw us all together two or three times, and he can get to know them." She jumped up from the table to take her plate and silverware to the dishwasher. "That's exactly what I'll do!"

Jennifer left shortly afterward, thinking her parents would really like Michael and hoped Michael would like them. Maybe she hadn't solved all the problems of the world, but she had made a good start in taking care of some of her worries.

She hurried up the stairs and as soon as she reached her apartment, she phoned Michael but only got his answering service. She left a message explaining about her parents and how she wanted him to get to know them.

ॐ ॐ ॐ

The time went by quickly for Jennifer as she anticipated her parents' visit. She talked to Michael every day or evening by phone. It was an exhausting few days for him as he was tied up with his clients and court appearances most of the week, so his long hours at the office prevented them from making plans until the weekend when her parents were due to arrive.

On Friday, she frequently glanced at her watch in between completing tasks, willing the time to pass so she could get to the airport to pick up her parents. She rushed home at the end of the day, changed into a heavy top and jeans before heading for the airport. The fog was starting to roll in when she left her apartment and the air was chilly, but as she drove south she left the fog behind. She had plenty of time to spare as she drove into the crowded airport parking garage, but by the time she finally maneuvered her car into a space several minutes had passed.

Checking the arrivals screen when she entered the terminal, she saw that her parents' plane was on time and hurried on to the gate. It seemed that everyone had de-planed before she finally saw her parents. Her eyes mist-ed when she saw them coming through the passageway, and when they reached the gate, they all hugged as if they had not seen each other in years.

"You must have been in the rear of the plane," Jennifer remarked.

Her mother smiled. "The flight was such a smooth one James went to sleep, and I had a time getting him awake when we landed."

"Not to mention having to hunt for one of your shoes," her father added, tweaking his wife's ear. Turning to Jennifer, he explained, "Elizabeth always takes off her shoes, and this time one rolled down a couple of seats in front of us. Had to have the flight attendant try to find it for her. Now that's what you call embarrassing!"

"Oh, James, you always exaggerate," Mrs. Johnson

Love Doesn't Come Easy

declared. "Let's go get our luggage."

Her parents kept up a lively conversation on their way to the baggage claim area and while waiting for their luggage to come up. Jennifer listened and smiled. She was used to their banter and realized again how well suited they were for each other. Would she have that kind of relationship when she married? She should be so lucky!

Their luggage finally arrived and they headed for the parking garage. On their way home, Jennifer pointed to Candlestick Park as they passed. "Don't you remember how cold it was one summer when you were here for one of the Giants' games, Dad?"

Mr. Johnson chuckled. "How could I forget that, baby? That's when I learned that summer here does not necessarily mean hot or even warm weather. The folks back in Ohio refused to believe how cool San Francisco weather can be in the middle of summer."

As soon as they arrived at her apartment Jennifer started coffee while her parents unpacked their luggage in the den. She could hear them teasing each other about the side of the sofa bed each would get. She shook her head. *They'll never change. I hope Michael enjoys them as much as I do.*

Both were in their robes, just as Jennifer knew they would be, when they entered the kitchen a short time later. She poured mugs of coffee for everyone and they took them into the breakfast room. A plate of warm croissants on the table caught her father's eye and he

260

smiled. "You didn't forget how I like those things." He hastened to put one on a napkin and just looked down at it. "I could really make a meal out of these," he added after taking a huge bite of one end.

Mrs. Johnson smiled at her daughter and shook her head. "I'm glad I can't make those, or he would insist on having croissants every meal." She noticed that Jennifer had been rather quiet since they had arrived at the apartment. She put her hand over her daughter's. "Is everything all right with you?" she asked softly. "You've really been on our minds the last few days."

Jennifer took a long sip of her coffee, thinking she might as well get her thoughts out in the open. "I'm really glad you're both here." She looked from one to the other. "I want you to meet Michael."

Her father and mother looked at each other and nodded.

"Well, you'll meet him tomorrow. He's joining us for brunch around eleven o'clock. So you can sleep late, and we'll just have coffee here when you get up. Does that plan meet with your approval, Dad?"

Her father faked a growl. "Only if I can have another of those croissants with my coffee."

"That's a promise," Jennifer said as she rose to gather their mugs and napkins. She saw her father trying to hide a yawn and remembered the three-hour difference in time. "You two are probably ready to turn in, so I'll see you in the morning." She gave each a kiss before they left for the den.

Returning to the kitchen, Jennifer unconsciously began humming a wordless melody while rinsing the cups and putting them in the dishwasher. She was sure her parents would approve of Michael. Her mother would probably fall in love with him. Her father would not be as demonstrative, but she thought he would probably also like Michael.

❧ ❧ ❧

It was not quite ten-thirty Saturday morning when Michael arrived at Jennifer's complex. After parking the car, he checked his hair in the mirror, a gesture that was completely foreign to him, but then it was not every day that he met the parents of a person he hoped to marry. A twinge of nervousness was still with him when he rang her doorbell.

Jennifer opened the door, gave him a quick kiss, and led him into the breakfast room. He saw a handsome brown-skinned couple smiling up at him and immediately felt at ease when he looked into their twinkling eyes.

"Mom, Dad, this is Michael," Jennifer announced, looking expectantly from one to the other.

The two men shook hands while the two women beamed at each other.

"Sit down and have some coffee, son," her father

boomed. "Jennifer has been singing your praises this morning. I can see why."

Hearing that, Michael thought maybe he had it made, but only said, "I'm sure you're aware that your daughter sometimes exaggerates about things." He was beginning to feel self-conscious as her parents studied him. Jennifer was being of no help by just sitting and smiling in his direction. Michael turned toward her. "So what have you been telling your parents, Jennifer?"

Jennifer just looked more smug. "Only the truth, Michael."

"That's what's bothering me," Michael retorted.

The Johnsons smiled at each other.

As soon as they all finished their coffee, and her father another croissant, they walked down to Michael's car and headed for Houlihan's restaurant in Sausalito. Jennifer had chosen that restaurant since she knew her parents enjoyed being near the water. They were seated within a few minutes at a table on a deck facing the Pacific Ocean. They admired the scenery while devouring their omelets. The San Francisco skyline seemed nearer than it actually was as did the white sails of the many sailboats maneuvering the choppy water of the bay. As they sat there, a ferry made its way to Alcatraz, its upper deck filled with tourists. Another ferry docked and other tourists hurried off, eager to start their browsing and buying in the myriad of shops on Bridgewater, the main street.

Love Doesn't Come Easy

Finally uttering a satisfied grunt, her father leaned back. "Now that's what I call a breakfast!"

It was early afternoon when they got up to leave. Her father suggested stopping at Fisherman's Wharf. "Jennifer, you know I won't be able to live with your mother if she doesn't get to spend some money there. Elizabeth really needs to have an empty suitcase coming out here so she can put all the junk she buys in it for the return trip," he teased as he put his arm around his wife's shoulders on their way to the car.

Since her parents had previously been to the Wharf, Jennifer suggested that they look around on their own and meet her and Michael in time for an early dinner. Her suggestion suited Michael just fine. He wanted to have Jennifer all to himself. They all checked their watches and decided to meet back at the car at five-thirty.

"Will that give you enough time, Mom?" Jennifer asked, knowing her mother's penchant for shopping.

Mr. Johnson did not wait for his wife's reply. "Elizabeth never has enough time when it comes to shopping, but I'll see that we get back here by that time." Taking his wife's hand, he said, "Come on, Elizabeth. Where do you want to go first?"

Jennifer and Michael watched until her parents were lost among the hordes of tourists who were enjoying the beautiful Saturday afternoon.

"Your parents are really something," Michael

observed. "Have they always been like that?"

She suddenly felt very sentimental toward her parents and smiled up at Michael. "Ever since I can remember," she replied. "It's funny that I notice so many things about them now that I just took for granted when I lived at home. Now that I look back, I don't remember their not being together in the evenings and on weekends, except when Mom had an emergency call she couldn't get out of. She's a registered nurse and sometimes she had to work odd hours, but most of the time she was at home with Dad and me in the evenings."

"In some ways they remind me of my parents in the way they tease each other. People their age must look at marriage a lot differently. I don't remember that many divorces among their friends. At least, not as many as occur nowadays."

She nodded her head in agreement.

They were walking toward Pier 39. "Let's hang out on the pier for a while," she suggested, taking Michael's hand.

Their hands touched and they stared at each other, each wanting to be closer. "How long will your parents be here?"

"Funny you should ask that at the very moment I was going to tell you they're leaving late Sunday evening."

"You mean tomorrow evening—not a week away?"

"I mean tomorrow, Michael. For some inexplicable reason they just had to come out to see me. Once they know that everything is all right with me, they will be fine for a few months."

"But you were just there, Jennifer."

"I know, Michael. And whatever I said—or didn't say—must have gotten them to thinking I was having a problem or something."

She didn't want to discuss the reason she went home and quickly changed the subject. "In case you're interested, Michael, my mother is enthralled with you."

He stopped in the middle of the sidewalk. "You must be kidding. How in the world do you know that?"

"Mom told me so when we went to the ladies' room this morning. I started not to tell you, I don't want you to get a big head or something."

Cautiously, he asked, "What about your father?"

"Knowing Dad, the verdict is probably still out. He usually takes much longer making up his mind about anything than my mother. But I'm sure you'll have an answer before he leaves."

That news didn't exactly make his afternoon, but he felt very comfortable in her father's company, so he assumed Mr. Johnson at least didn't dislike him. The approval of both of them was very important to him.

He had a sudden thought. "My firm usually gets tickets to the Giants' games and they're playing tomorrow. Do you think your father would like to go?"

Her eyes lit up. "Oh, he'd be too thrilled! Do you think you could get two tickets at this late date?"

He looked at his watch. "Let's find a phone and I'll call my buddy who usually uses some of their tickets, so he'd know whether there're any left."

They found a phone on the street a couple blocks down and he put the call through. She smiled when she saw him give her the thumbs-up gesture before he hung up the receiver.

"I can pick up two tickets tomorrow morning." He suddenly stopped walking again. "Our going to the game won't mess up any of your plans for tomorrow, will it?"

She shook her head. "Nothing that can't be worked out. I was going to take them out for an early dinner before they left. Now I'll just have something ready when you two get back from the game, and they'll still have plenty of time to have dinner and make their plane."

With that settled, they strolled on to Pier 39 and spent the next couple of hours holding hands while walking through the shops, just happy to be together. Before they knew it, it was time to meet her parents in the parking lot and they hurried down the stairs to the street. They had almost reached the car when they spied her parents rushing down the street toward them.

CHAPTER 20

"What in the world did you two buy?" Jennifer asked. She looked at the large shopping bags her parents carried in both hands.

Her father raised his eyebrows. "Why would you ask that, Jennifer? You know your mother!"

"You got carried away, too, James, so don't put all the blame on me," Mrs. Johnson retorted, handing him her bags to stow in Michael's trunk.

"We'd better be on our way if we're going to make our dinner reservations at Sinbad's. It's a few blocks down the Embarcadero, so we'd better drive," Jennifer informed her parents as they piled into the car.

"You've remembered all of James's favorite places, Jennifer." She reached up to the front seat and patted her daughter's shoulder as Michael maneuvered the car out of the parking lot into the line of traffic.

They were soon seated in the restaurant at a table near the window, looking out at the choppy waters under the Bay Bridge. A few brave people were still out in their sailboats, but they were keeping rather close to the shore.

"I never tire of looking at the water," Mrs. Johnson exclaimed. "I soak up all of the sights when I'm out here so I can remember the area when I'm stuck inside the house at home watching the snow pile up."

Jennifer winked and patted her mother's hand. "Mom, you'll have to work on Dad so you two can move out here when he retires."

"I wouldn't need much persuasion, especially if you're still in San Francisco." Her father looked pensive. "Yes, I think I could spend the rest of my days right here. There's enough in the whole area to keep sightseers busy the year round, it seems to me."

The waiter arrived with their menus, and the next few minutes were spent deciding what they each would have—all except Mr. Johnson. He knew he wanted the restaurant's famous bouillabaisse, so he just laid aside his menu and viewed the scenery while the others tried to choose their entrees.

While waiting for their meal, Michael brought up the Giants' game. "Mr. Johnson, I have two tickets for the game at Candlestick Park tomorrow. Would you like to go?"

Jennifer smiled when she saw her father's face light up like a Christmas tree. "You've got to be kidding!

Love Doesn't Come Easy

Would I like to go? You can bet your bottom dollar I'd like nothing better!"

Michael breathed an inaudible sigh of relief. "Great! I'll pick you up around noon. Be sure to wear something that will keep you warm. It gets real chilly out there sometimes."

They all tackled their food as soon as it arrived. The afternoon's trek had really whetted their appetites, and they said little as they devoted all of their attention to dinner. They were almost finished when Mr. Johnson suddenly laid down his silverware. "You know, Michael, we're being very selfish. Here we're going off tomorrow and leaving these ladies all by themselves. I apologize, Elizabeth. I didn't even ask if you wanted to go."

Michael held his breath. He had only two tickets! He breathed easier, however, when he heard Jennifer explain, "You know Mom doesn't really give a hoot about baseball, Dad. She usually just goes with you to keep you company. Tomorrow you'll have Michael."

"Jennifer's right, James. You two go and enjoy the game. We'll find plenty to talk about, won't we Jennifer?" Her mother winked at her.

What he heard evidently satisfied Mr. Johnson as he immediately returned to his big bowl of bouillabaisse, and the rest of the meal was eaten with little conversation as they enjoyed their food. The sun was almost to the horizon by the time they finished their dessert, and they could hear the waves from the bay slapping against the side of the restaurant. A lone sailboat was making its way to the shore, dipping up and down against the waves. They sat in silence as the sun disappeared and the lights of the Bay Bridge were reflected in the bay.

Mr. Johnson leaned back against his chair and let out a long, contented sigh. "Now all I need is a reclining chair to put up my feet."

Michael signaled for the check. "Would you like to take a short drive?" he asked.

The other three looked at each other. Jennifer knew her parents and answered for them. "I think we'll just head for home, Michael. We've had a busy day."

Michael saw them all to the door of Jennifer's apartment before saying that he would see them the next morning, knowing that Jennifer probably wanted to spend some time alone with her parents.

Jennifer walked back to the elevator with him. Looking up and down the hall, she drew Michael's head down for a long kiss. Finally breaking apart, she whispered, "We'll have some time to ourselves soon, Michael."

That was all Michael needed to hear, and he whistled all the way to his car.

Jennifer resisted the urge to hum on the way back to her apartment. But that was how she felt. Even though she wanted to be with Michael, she needed time with her parents to tell them about her birth mother, and this was probably the only opportunity she might have. She heard her parents moving around in the den when she entered the apartment and knew they were changing from their street clothes into something comfortable.

By the time they entered the living room, Jennifer had coffee waiting on the coffee table. The fire was beginning to blaze, sending a warm glow all around the room.

"It still seems odd to enjoy a fire in the middle of the summer," her father said, "but it sure takes the chill out of the air." He walked around to sit beside his wife on the sofa. Jennifer pulled up an armchair close to the coffee table and poured the coffee into mugs.

Jennifer took a sip of her coffee and then drew a deep breath. "Mom, Dad, I want to talk with you about something. I was going to call to tell you but then found out you were coming out here."

Mr. and Mrs. Johnson turned toward each other, an invisible communication passing between them. Her father nodded slightly and her mother's face flushed. "Now you see what I was talking about, James. I knew something wasn't quite right out here. I could feel it in my bones."

Jennifer looked from one to the other. "What do you mean, Mom?"

"Just what I said. For the last week or so before we came out here, I had these weird feelings that something was going on with you. I couldn't put my finger on why I felt that way and—"

272

"So she worried me to death until I agreed to come out here with her," her father added.

A chill ran down Jennifer's spine as she listened to her parents' conversation. Was there really such a thing as extra- sensory perception? She had never thought much about it, but maybe it really did exist.

Turning his attention to Jennifer, her father asked, "So what do you want to talk to us about, baby?"

Jennifer drew in a deep breath again. "To make a long story short, I found my birth mother just—"

Her mother gasped and set her mug down so hard that some coffee sloshed over the cup. Her father hurried to the kitchen to get some paper towels.

Jennifer noticed his hands were a little unsteady while wiping the coffee table. She waited until he took the wet towels to the kitchen and sat down again.

Sighing softly, Jennifer continued in a low voice. "Maybe I should mention something else first. Remember how I used to have bad dreams? Well, it was always the same nightmare that—"

"The *same* nightmare? You never told us about that, baby," her mother interrupted. She looked over at her husband. "Did you know anything about that, James?"

"No...but remember how Jennifer sometimes awakened screaming at the top of her lungs?"

Mrs. Johnson shook her head. "Yes, I do remember that. Also how I could never get her to tell us what made her wake up."

Jennifer looked sorrowfully at her parents. "I guess as I grew older I thought I'd outgrow the nightmares, but I didn't. But let me tell you how I think those bad dreams are connected with all the other things that happened the last few days."

"What in the world has been going on out here, baby"?

Jennifer was aware of the agitation in her mother's voice and she saw her father taking her mother's hand in his, rubbing the back of it with his thumb. "Just listen, Elizabeth," he said softly, and Mrs. Johnson nodded.

When Jennifer finished telling her parents about Dave's first call and all of the other events that followed, both parents looked at her with tears in their eyes. Her mother reached into the pocket of her robe for a tissue and blew her nose loudly. She handed a tissue to her husband. Neither spoke for several moments.

Jennifer knew they were suffering inside for her, and a rush of love went through her.

"And you went through all that by yourself? Why didn't you call us?"

"It was something I had to do myself, Mom. I didn't want to upset you or Dad. You two are the only parents I've ever known, and I couldn't have had better parents than you've been. Everything I am I owe to you two...I couldn't love real parents any more than I...love both of you." She drew a tissue from her pocket and wiped her eyes.

Elizabeth turned to her husband. "How many times have I told you I can always tell when something is just not going right?"

"I know...I know, Elizabeth," he answered. "Maybe one of these days I'll believe you."

For a few moments all three stared into the fire which had burned down to only embers in the grate now.

Jennifer rose. "I think it's time we all got some sleep. We've had a busy day."

"Just one more question, baby," her mother said.

Jennifer turned back to her.

"What did Michael say about all of this?"

"I haven't told him yet. He still thinks you two are my real parents," Jennifer replied, an apprehensive look on her face.

"I'm sure Jennifer will know when to tell Michael, Elizabeth. She's been handling everything pretty well up until now, it seems to me. I think she can handle this." He pulled his wife up from the couch. "Let's go to bed, Elizabeth. Jennifer will be all right."

After her parents went to their room, Jennifer took the coffee mugs to the kitchen and rinsed them before putting them in the dishwasher. Walking back to the living room, she checked the fire screen and turned out the lights before heading to her bedroom.

ॐ ॐ ॐ

Late Sunday morning Jennifer breathed a guilty sigh of relief when her father and Michael left for the game, for she couldn't deny that she was looking forward to having her mother all to herself that afternoon. Jennifer went to the kitchen to find her mother clearing the breakfast dishes, and she helped put them into the dishwasher. As soon as they finished in the kitchen, they went into Jennifer's bedroom.

"It's almost like old times, isn't it, Mom?" Jennifer observed as she dropped onto the bed while her mother took a seat on the chaise lounge. "Remember the hours you used to spend in my bedroom listening to my problems when I was in high school?"

"How could I ever forget, baby?" Mrs. Johnson smiled at the memory. "And especially when you always insisted on having catastrophes when all of your friends just had problems!"

Jennifer giggled. "Oh, I don't think I was that bad, but now that I think about it, Michael frequently says I always exaggerate about things." Her mother did not fail to notice the dreamy look in Jennifer's eyes when she mentioned Michael.

"It's really Michael you want to talk about, isn't it?" her mother asked.

"You could always read my mind, Mom. When I was small, I thought you knew every thought I had, and I was afraid to tell you a lie. So yes, you're right, I want to know what you really think about Michael." She pulled

276

her knees up to her chin and wrapped her arms around them while she waited for her mother to speak.

"I suspect you're in love with Michael, Jennifer." Her mother noticed that dreamy look come into Jennifer's eyes again, and she knew she was right on target. "And I think Michael's in love with you," she added.

Jennifer stared at her. "But, Mom, how can you say that? You don't even know him that well."

"Just watching the two of you together says a lot. Neither of you can keep your eyes off the other. Vibes, or something, seem to be in the air when you're near each other." Her mother looked up and saw a smile on Jennifer's face. "Now don't laugh at what I've just said. I'm not so old that I can't recognize love when I see it. James and I have been in love too long for me to ever forget what it can be like."

"But you still haven't said what you think about Michael," Jennifer declared.

Her mother thought for a minute. "Michael has to be right for you, or else you would not have chosen him. However, I do think he's the kind of man who would make a woman happy, if you must have my opinion. Just remember what others think is not important. You're the one who'll deal with him day-by-day."

Jennifer was satisfied with her mother's answer, which was so typical of her. And she knew in her heart that if her mother had any doubts, she would surely voice them.

Love Doesn't Come Easy

Jennifer rose from the bed. "I'm sure you're right, Mom. And, in any case, it's about time for us to get something together for dinner. The guys will be back before we know it."

They spent the rest of the afternoon interrupting each other while talking. They talked about Jennifer's job, her mother's nursing patients, and happily reminiscing. The afternoon passed so quickly that they looked at each in total surprise when the doorbell chimed, letting them know the men had returned. Before Jennifer could get to the door, her mother took her in her arms and hugged her to her breast. "I'm so glad we had this short time together, Jennifer."

Jennifer opened the door with misty eyes. Michael looked at her in surprise. "Is something wrong?"

"It's the onions," Jennifer explained, hoping he would believe her.

Her father just looked at her with lifted eyebrows. He knew his women had probably been dealing with some deep emotions.

They dawdled over dinner, and it was time to leave for the airport before they realized it. They had to make a last-minute rush in the terminal to make the plane. Laughing and hugging at the gate, with a few tears thrown in, her parents rushed down the passageway, leaving a tearful Jennifer and a somber Michael waving after them.

When they turned to leave the waiting area, Michael

reached in his pocket and handed Jennifer his handkerchief. "Don't you ever carry one of these with you?" he asked as he lovingly took her arm to make their way to the parking garage.

They said little on their drive home. He parked the car and, without asking, followed her to the elevator. He pulled her to his chest as soon as the elevator door closed, and they were still locked in each other's arms when the elevator reached her floor. Taking her key, he opened the door and without stopping in the living room, they made their way to her bedroom, their arms around each other's waist.

They were removing each other's clothes when he stopped and gently pulled her into his arms. "I love you," he murmured against her hair.

She looked up into his face and trailed her fingers across his lips. He caught the taste of tears as she placed her lips over his in a gentle but insistent kiss. "I love you, too, Michael." Her voice was husky with emotion.

They finished dropping their clothes onto the floor, their heads swirling with desire.

A low moan escaped Michael's lips as he lifted Jennifer's naked body with one arm and pulled back the covers of her bed with the other. They fell against the cool sheet, knowing the heights they could reach together. His hands trembled as he hugged her warm body to his long, lean torso. He felt her deep, shuddering breath against his neck as he fought to get his passion for her under control when he felt her thighs squeezing his leg. With infinite gentleness in his hands, he caressed her cheeks, her neck, her shoulders. He circled each breast before moving his hands down her sides to grasp her bottom.

She writhed with desire as his gentle touch sent spirals of emotion through her body. He knew exactly what she was feeling and continued caressing her stomach, her thighs, before taking a nipple in his mouth and circling each with his tongue. Nothing about her escaped his loving attention until she gasped in anticipation. Reaching back for the foil-wrapped protection, he moved over her and made her his.

Several hours later the moon shone brightly through the blinds onto their nakedness when he awakened and looked over at her. Stretched out on his back, one knee raised, he reached over to hug Jennifer. She slowly came awake. Turning over onto her stomach, she supported herself on her elbows and gazed into his eyes lovingly, a wide smile on her lips.

He returned her smile. "We had quite a night, didn't we, sweetheart?" he said, preparing to get up. "I've got to get home and change clothes. I'll probably be late getting to the office, but who cares?"

She merely nodded, too satiated with their lovemaking to carry on a conversation while he gathered his clothes.

"What about going to that movie we've been wanting to see? We could go right after work," he asked while throwing on his clothes.

"Sounds good to me. Call me where to meet you," she called out as he closed the door.

CHAPTER 21

Seeing Michael waiting in line for their tickets, Jennifer's heart skipped a beat. She walked up behind him and slipped her arms through his.

He responded with a soft kiss on her forehead. "Thought I'd been stood up," he quipped as they entered the theater and found seats. He immediately put his arm across her shoulder. She moved closer to him, feeling a surge of happiness that she hadn't felt since she last saw him. Neither saw much of what was happening on the screen; they were too involved with their own emotions.

Leaving the movie hand-in-hand, he suddenly stopped in the middle of the sidewalk and turned her to face him, his hands on her shoulders. "Why don't we go to my place and I'll make you a great grilled cheese sandwich, my specialty. I promise you'll love it."

"Okay, I'll meet you there, but your cooking better be as great as you claim it is!"

She started away but he pulled her back to him, planting a resounding kiss on her lips. "That's so you will turn up at my door, hopefully wanting more." Smiling, he released her.

By the time she reached his place she knew she wanted whatever his "more" implied. He opened the door at her first tap, and she walked into what at first sight did not appear to be just another bachelor's apartment. *He must have help,* she thought. Other than a few magazines on the floor beside a deep chair and some papers stacked on a small table, everything seemed to be in place. The furnishings were obviously expensive though not ostentatious.

She glanced around the inviting room at the long beige leather sofa and large matching chairs that faced the fireplace, a round glass-topped oak coffee table in front of the sofa. Several men's magazines were neatly stacked on the table, and a large African sculpture sat in the center. A soft brown leather love seat sat under a wide front window with matching oak tables on either side. Small pillows in autumnal colors were strewn carelessly on the sofa. The tall lamps around the room had carved wood bases, and she wondered whether he had them made. She noticed the African paintings and masks on the wall and the large plants in the corners of the front wall. The entire room radiated a coziness, one

283

that seemed to complement his personality.

"How about a martini while I make the sandwiches?" he asked as he took her jacket, throwing it across the back of a chair.

"I'd love one," she replied as she made her way to the sofa, sinking down into the soft leather and letting out a low, contented sigh.

He returned almost immediately with a pitcher and glasses on a tray and poured a small amount into her glass. "Taste. Is it okay?"

"Perfect. I couldn't have done better myself, and I make a pretty mean martini."

"Well, enjoy while I slave away in the kitchen."

She picked up a copy of *Ebony Man* and glanced through it for a few minutes while sipping her martini. She heard him whistling in the kitchen and decided to check whether he needed any help. From the doorway of the kitchen she saw him at the stove struggling with a grilled cheese sandwich he was trying to turn over with a fork. The cheese evidently had oozed out and was sticking to the grill. She stood against the door frame for a few seconds, watching his frustrations, a wide smile on her face.

"Try a spatula, Michael."

He jumped at hearing her voice, and the sandwich landed outside of the grill. He retrieved it and slowly turned around.

She sensed he was slightly embarrassed that she'd

caught him in such a predicament, especially after his bragging about his expertise in making grilled cheese sandwiches!

"How long have you been standing there, Jennifer? You might at least have tried to help me instead of laughing at the mess."

"Don't you have a spatula? You know, it's wide and has a long handle that—"

"I happen to know what a spatula is and there's one around here somewhere, but the fork was handy and I thought it would do," he informed her rather testily. He managed to get the one sandwich back on the grill and the other one turned over. He rummaged around in the bags on top of the refrigerator until he found some potato chips and then got sodas, heaping everything on a large tray and carrying it to the living room.

He filled their glasses before sitting down near her. Abruptly he rose and walked to the fireplace and lit the stacked logs. "I love the glow of flames," he remarked as he made his way back across the room. They gazed into the fire in companionable silence while eating their sandwiches.

"This is really good," she said after taking a couple of bites. She looked at him sidewise with a smile before adding, "Even if you didn't use a spatula."

He ignored her last remark.

When they finished their food, he insisted on taking their dishes to the kitchen and putting them in the dishwasher after rinsing them. He came back to the living room in a few minutes and sat down close to her. Reaching across the small space that separated them, he gently pulled her to him. There were undercurrents of passion whenever they were together. The slightest touch jarred their emotions.

His kisses were soft on her lips while his hands gently held the sides of her face to his. She sat perfectly still in his embrace, almost afraid to breathe lest the moment be disturbed. His hands slid down her neck to her shoulders, and he pulled her tightly to him. She felt his warm breath on her hair, and she let out another long sigh of contentment, knowing that this moment was what she had been waiting for all day, his soft, tender, loving touches.

In a voice husky with suppressed emotion, he whispered, "I've wanted to hold you like this all evening. You do things to me no other woman even came close to, sweetheart."

She snuggled closer to him and felt the crush of his chest against her breasts. She lifted her head and pressed her lips against his, shivering as his tongue explored the inner softness of her mouth. When his kisses stopped, she was trembling, a feeling of pure ecstasy flowing through her body.

Shifting his arms to encircle her shoulders, he felt her heart beating against his body as she pressed closer to him. Instinctively he knew that just being held close was what she wanted at the moment, even though his own fantasy was making love to her on the spot. But he could wait until she came to terms with her own desires, whatever they were. She snuggled even closer and closed her eyes while he held her as he would a child who needed comforting. Within minutes, he felt her even breathing and knew she had dozed off.

The logs had burned low before he stirred to relieve his arm. He slowly slipped his arm from around her and laid her body down, careful not to awaken her. He envied her peacefulness as he gently removed her shoes. Pulling a blanket from his bed, he gently covered her.

Thinking of how much he loved her, he walked over to his favorite chair near the fireplace and adjusted it to elevate his feet. Removing his tie and shoes, he stretched out, hoping she would soon awaken.

It was almost midnight before she sat up with a start, not knowing how long she had been asleep. She glanced over at him sound asleep in his chair. Studying his still face, she decided he was as handsome in sleep as in his waking hours. Moving stealthily, she threw off the blanket and started for the bathroom. She jumped when he reached out from his chair and pulled her down onto his lap.

"Trying to sneak away from me, huh?" he whispered. "Don't you know you can't get away from me?"

She squirmed when she felt his hardness against her thigh. "I've got to go to the bathroom." She climbed off him. "Have a washcloth? I need to really wake up before I drive home."

"Of course. I buy them by the dozen for all of my female friends," he teased.

She reached for the pillow behind his head and flattened it across his face, holding it down with her upper body. "That's what you get for making such smart remarks!" She pushed down even harder until he managed to throw her aside. As soon as she was free, she ran for the bathroom.

"The towels are in a drawer on the left side," he called after her.

While washing her face and patting her hair a bit, she decided that the world was her oyster and he was her newly discovered pearl.

ॐ ॐ ॐ

Jennifer rushed home early the evening of the benefit banquet for the United Negro College Fund, an event she always attended. She looked forward to seeing a lot of people she knew, yet hoped that Tawana's latest fiasco would not be the topic of conversation as she was sick and tire of hearing about her.

Hastily removing her office clothes, she reached into her closet for the long off-white chiffon dress with a flowing tangerine scarf she had purchased for the occasion. She carefully removed the plastic cover and hung the dress on her closet door. Rummaging in the bottom of her closet, she located gold strap sandals, which were perfect for the dress, and then took down a matching purse from a top shelf, placing both on the foot of her bed. She pulled sheer gold pantyhose and a strapless bra from her drawers and threw them on the bed with the other things.

Satisfied that she had located everything she needed, she padded to the bathroom and turned on the knobs to run a tub of hot water. Throwing in a couple of scoops of her favorite Estee Lauder bubble bath, she inhaled deeply as its scent filled the bathroom. She wrapped a towel around her hair before gingerly sliding down into the hot water.

The water was barely warm when she finally stepped out of the tub, thoroughly refreshed. She removed the towel from her head and reached for a long, fluffy towel to dry her body. Finished with that, she padded to her bedroom to apply the sparse makeup she used, mostly mascara and tangerine lipstick with just a touch of deep orange blush on her cheekbones.

Taking her time to brush her hair into the slight flip she preferred, she pulled several short strands to her fore-head. Satisfied that she had created the look she want-ed, she dabbed Estee Super Perfume behind each ear. She decided a necklace would be too much for her dress, so she selected long gold earrings with a pearl at the end and a matching bracelet before pulling the dress over her hips.

When she finished, she twirled around in front of the floor-to-ceiling mirror, satisfied that she had made the perfect purchase for the event. Glancing at the clock, she saw she was right on time. Her doorbell chimed only a few moments later, and she tensed when she heard the sound, taking several deep breaths on the way through the living room to admit Michael. Just thinking about him took her breath away.

The moment she opened the door and saw his all-too-familiar face and his fabulous suit and expensive tie, she felt her knees turn to jelly. He folded her into his arms before he crossed the threshold, and she knew that was where she belonged. He kissed her softly and tenderly for several moments, and she felt the world spin as she returned his kisses, wishing she could stay in his arms forever.

He drew back and let out a low whistle. "You're really something in that dress, girl! You look fabulous!"

She slipped out of his arms and closed the door. "We better get out of here."

He nodded. He knew what she meant.

"I've got to hold you close again—just to prove you're real," he said softly as he drew her to him again, caressing her face and shoulders before he gently pushed her from him. They held hands tightly as they hurried to the elevator and out to his car, smiling at each other as if they were very pleased with themselves.

"How's your father doing these days?" she asked when they were seated in the car.

"He's doing fine physically, but Mom is having a hard time trying to keep him at home. He's dying to get back to the office—thinks the business can't run without him. We did get him to promise to take a couple of weeks off soon and come out here for a few days, however."

By the time they got to their reserved table, the other guests were already seated, and they all greeted each other like long-lost friends. From that moment on, everyone tried to talk at the same time. The band started playing, and Michael led her to the small dance area to join a few other couples swaying to the soft music. She melted into his arms and he held her close as they moved around the floor, almost as one.

"I think it was during our first dance that I fell for you like a ton of bricks," he whispered into her ear, "and I feel the same magic tonight."

She smiled up at him tremulously as he held her tighter.

"Except it's not magic now, sweetheart, it's the real thing!" he insisted. They danced through the next three numbers before they returned to their table. During dinner they laughed and joked with their friends while their bodies ached to be close to each other. Neither paid much attention to the food they were served, even though it was much better than was served at most benefit dinners.

While several presentations were made, and then during the main speaker's speech which they heard little of, they held hands and smiled at each other. The affair lasted until midnight, typical of such gatherings. Saying hasty goodnights to their friends, they made their way to his car.

They said little while driving to her apartment. She glanced at him while in the elevator and turned quickly away when she saw the desire mounting in his dark eyes. As soon as they entered her apartment, he pulled her into his arms, and she almost dissolved as he kissed her passionately. "This has been the longest night of my life," he said softly and released her. "I could barely wait until that tiresome program was over."

"I know, I feel the same way. Would...would you like a nightcap?" she stammered, emotion spilling over in her heart.

For an answer, he guided her over to the sofa and took her in his arms. "All I want at the moment is you."

He reached for her hand and looked deep into her eyes. "Sweetheart, I've been doing a lot of thinking and—"

She put her fingers against his lips. "I've been doing some thinking and talking, too, Michael, and in some ways I've learned a lot about myself. Greg said—"

His heart contracted at the mention of Greg. "I don't want to know what Greg said right now. I want you to listen to me." He shifted slightly, still holding her hand between his. "I think I know now what you meant when you talked about two people needing to build a life together on faith and trust—and a lot of love, of course—"

"But people also need to be able to compromise when there are disagreements."

"Sure, that, also. But in our case I think—"

"Oh, Michael, you don't have to go into a lot of details. I know about Tawana's latest fiasco—"

"How did you hear that she—"

"My friends, of course, who—"

He pulled her head to his chest, muffling her voice. "Would you just please listen for a minute, Jennifer? I want you to know how I feel about you sticking by me while Tawana was acting like a fool. She called me and admitted she's not really pregnant, said the doctor ran a second test. A weight lifted from my shoulders when I learned the truth." He stopped for a moment. " She's just a little confused I think, but I wish her well."

She had her doubts about his assessment of Tawana. In her mind, Tawana was still a selfish bitch and probably always would be. At the moment, however, the last thing she wanted to talk about was Tawana. The thought that she should tell Michael about her adoption and her birth mother crossed her mind—but she ignored it. She would tell him later. She snuggled up close to him and reached up to plant a wet kiss on his chin.

Love Doesn't Come Easy

Her heart started to beat unevenly when she felt his breath feather her cheek as his mouth moved closer to hers. There was no end to their acute awareness of each other, and she sighed deeply as she relaxed in his arms, letting all thought fly from her mind.

She slid her arms up around his neck and pulled his head around to meet her searching lips. She sensed his desire as his shoulders stiffened before a moan escaped his lips. He held her to him, almost in desperation. Wordlessly, they rose and with his arm around her waist, they made their way to her bedroom, storms of emotion raging through their bodies. No time was lost as they hastily discarded their clothing, letting it fall to the floor as they made their way to the bed.

CHAPTER 22

Early Monday morning Jennifer picked up a message propped up by her phone. "Oh, no!" she cried aloud as she read it a second time. She had to leave for Austin, Texas, on the next flight—something about an emergency with her audit team there. A sense of guilt washed over her as she thought of how she had declined going with the newly-formed team because she wanted to be with Michael.

Several times she attempted to get through to Michael at his office, each time being informed that he was still in court. She tried again when she reached her apartment to hastily pack a bag while a range of emotions flooded through her—frustration, anger, disappointment, exasperation at having to leave. Calling his office again from the airport, she learned he was still out. She left word with his secretary that she would be out of town for the rest of the week and would call later to give him the number where she was staying.

Meeting with the team in Austin, she realized that Tom, the leader of the audit team, really needed her assistance with a couple of major problems. She became more disheartened during the next couple of days as the work proceeded slowly, and by Friday she was in a real tizzy. Even by working on Saturday, they would not be finished until Tuesday or Wednesday of the following week.

Phoning Michael, she learned about real frustration. He was very unhappy that she would be away so long, and by the end of the conversation she was in tears, wishing with all her heart she could fly out that night to be with him. Hanging up the receiver, she knew she had to do something about all the travel her position required if she wanted a life with him—and that she wanted!

She had brunch with Tom on Sunday to go over some details he needed help with. They had become very friendly since the audit in New York, and he sought her out on several occasions to discuss problems of the office. Having developed a healthy respect for each other, she valued his opinions. They were in the middle of a business conversation when she abruptly pushed aside the paperwork and threw down her pen, causing him to look at her in alarm.

"Tom, I'm thinking about changing positions. This

frequent travel business is really getting to me. It's been great these past few years, but now it seems I dread even looking at a piece of luggage! Have you ever felt that way?"

"Well, not really," he replied. "In fact, going to different sites every week or so is one of the perks of the job for me. Of course, if I were married, I would probably think differently, but I don't intend to enter into that state any time soon, so I'm happy to keep my bags packed." Suddenly he smiled as if he'd had a naughty thought. "By the way, are you by any chance thinking of changing your single status—or should I ask?"

She hesitated before she answered. "Nothing definite has been decided yet, but, yes, I'd like to change my 'single status,' as you put it. But that's not for publication, Tom."

He reached across the table and patted her hand in a friendly fashion. "I think you'd make some lucky guy a pretty neat wife."

"Thanks for the compliment, Tom, but I'd like to be a great wife!" she joked.

"You will be, if that's the way you want it."

"But enough about me." She leaned toward him. "Would you like my position if I decide to make a change?"

His eyes lit up. "Would I? I'd give my eye teeth to be in your spot—but you probably already know that."

"I think you'd do a bang-up job. You already get

along well with all of the staff. And it would certainly be an increase in salary. If you hold out, you may be able to top what I presently make, being a man and all that."

He raised one eyebrow. "You'd really recommend me?"

"And use my persuasive powers, if I need to, for you to get my job," she assured him as they gathered their papers to get back to work.

Her talk with Tom solidified her thinking about changing positions. She knew of a vacancy in another department which she was probably over-qualified for, but it required no travel. She called her boss and explained her interest in the job. He assured her he would speak in her behalf and to contact him as soon as she returned.

ॐ ॐ ॐ

As soon as Jennifer entered her office Wednesday afternoon she arranged an appointment with the vice president of the department that had the vacancy. Because the opening was being handled as an in-house promotion, no job vacancy was advertised. Very impressed with her record with the firm, the vice-president informed her the position was hers and she could start as soon as soon as she could arrange it.

She walked on air as she returned to her office. Dialing Michael's number, she was interrupted when

Greg walked in unannounced, a sly grin on his face. She replaced the receiver and smiled at him, but inside she was a bit put out. Her mind was on Michael.

"Hi, Greg! It's good to see you—but why are you looking so smug?"

He pulled up a chair near her desk. "I've heard some rumors, so I thought I'd come over for confirmation."

"Oh, Greg, you're always in the middle of everything. So what rumors have you heard?" she asked.

"That you're probably the first choice for the opening in the vice-president's office. True?"

"Gossip sure gets around fast. I just came from there earlier. It hasn't been officially announced, but I've accepted it."

"So we'll both be moving on."

She raised one eyebrow. "Both?"

"I've been transferred to the New York office on permanent assignment—and I can't wait to get back East!"

"That's great, Greg, if that's what you really want, but whose shoulder will I have to cry on when you leave?"

He held up his hand. "Ah, another rumor has been making its rounds. I think Michael has broad enough shoulders!"

"But nothing definite has been settled there yet either, Greg."

"Take my unsolicited advice, Jennifer—he's the man for you!"

"I think so too, but we have some things to work out

Love Doesn't Come Easy

first."

After a few more exchanges, Greg left and Jennifer quickly dialed Michael's number again, anxious to hear his voice. During their brief conversation they planned for him to stop by the deli before meeting at her apartment after work.

For both, the rest of the day was a long one.

꒷ ꒷ ꒷

While waiting for Michael later that evening, Jennifer thought of Greg's words, "He's the man for you," and knew no truer words were ever spoken.

She went into Michael's arms the moment he dumped his bags on the kitchen counter, and neither spoke as their passion with each other took over again.

"I don't believe in fate, but I thank my lucky stars for whatever it was that brought us together. You're like the other half that makes me whole," he murmured against her hair.

She pulled away slightly and smiled up at him. "Every one needs a yin and a yang," she whispered.

The food was forgotten for the moment.

They began undressing on their way to her bedroom, and by the time they reached the bed they had little to remove.

His eyes darkened as he pulled her over into the middle of the bed and leaned over her. "I love you very,

300

very much," he said softly as he caressed her hair, her cheeks, her shoulders.

Loving to touch him, she pressed her hands along his neck and over his chest, the corded muscles of his back, her heart suddenly beating like a metronome out of control.

Totally content, they lay enfolded in each other's arms for several tender, quiet moments, happy just to be so close to each other.

She felt his open mouth move down from her throat to the aching tips of her breasts, sending a sensual ache to the fork of her body. She had no control over the sensations that rioted throughout her body as he lowered his head to her stomach, planting soft kisses. A moan escaped her throat when she felt the taunting pressure of his warm tongue exploring her navel, and her body arched toward his in total surrender.

He gently eased his head down farther, leaving a trail of wet kisses, oblivious to her moans of passion. He slipped his hand under her hips, his palms cupping her bottom, and lifted her gently, planting soft kisses on her inner thighs for several moments before he moved farther up, causing an unconscious shiver up and down her spine. His warm tongue sent shock waves through her, and she cried out in ecstasy while trying to pull away from the ravages of his mouth. He pressed her back down with his head until he felt her body shudder in total submission, then pushed up to gather her tenderly to him.

The outside world did not exist for them as they reached new heights in their lovemaking.

Much later she stretched, then cuddled closer to him. She had never felt so loved, so cherished, so wanted. Tears gathered behind her lids as she looked up into his eyes. "Michael..."

"I'm listening, sweetheart. What is it?" he asked softly.

She hesitated. "I've...I've never—"

"You don't have to tell me, Jennifer. I know what you mean. All I need to know is that I made you happy." He reached over and brushed her hair back from her forehead.

Her deep sigh was all the answer he needed, and he pulled her to him, wrapping his arms around her shoulders. "Let's get some sleep," he suggested.

Hours later she awakened to the rays of the sun peeking in through the slats of the half closed blinds. Sometime during the night she had shifted in his arms and was now lying with her back to him, cuddled against him spoon fashion. She heard his even breathing as he slept with his arm thrown across her. She waited several minutes before carefully slipping his arm from her body and drawing back the blanket to pad to the bathroom. She quickly brushed her teeth and creamed her face before stepping into the glass-enclosed shower. She had almost finished soaping her body when Michael opened the shower door.

Without a word, he took the soap from her hands and made a lather in his hands. Turning her around to face him, he began rubbing her body with the palms of his hands. She breathed out a sigh of ecstasy as his hands applied sensuous, gentle strokes to her breasts, her abdomen, her thighs before he turned her around and continued on her shoulders and back. He took his time, massaging her shoulders and spine with his soapy hands. He continued down her body, cupping her bottom in his soapy hands.

Unable to bear the exquisite intimacy of his hands any longer, she murmured, "Oh, Michael, that feels—"

"Shhh," he admonished her. "Don't talk, just enjoy!" He continued his ministrations for several moments before he handed her the soap. "Now you can do me."

She took the soap and, following his lead, lathered her hands well before she started on his shoulders. Just touching him sent sensations through her, and as she proceeded down to his hard stomach and his muscular legs she knew such an acute sense of pleasure that it was difficult for her to keep her mind on what she was doing. By the time she was finished she was marveling at the heady emotions touching him produced deep within her.

He drew her to him under the cascading water, and they held each other tightly as the water cleansed the soapy suds from their bodies. Stepping out, she pulled two large fluffy towels from the shelf, and they marveled at each other's bodies as they dried off. Before she could protest, he picked her up and carried her back to the bedroom, depositing her in the middle of the bed before climbing in and claiming her lips, a reminder of the passion they had just shared and a promise of more to come.

CHAPTER 23

Except for a few days when she was out of town to bring closure to some audits before she moved into her new position, Jennifer spent all of her evenings with Michael. As if they were two halves of an inseparable whole, they needed no one else. They had fallen into a rhythm of being together that amazed them both as they continued to discover things they both liked to do—taking long walks, exploring new places, going to the movies, reading, or just sitting and talking. Even their silences were something special for them, they were so in tune with each other.

After each time they were together, she resolved that the next time she saw him she would tell him about being adopted and about her birth mother, the little she knew about her, that is. The longer she kept her secret to herself the more worried she became and the harder and harder she found it to tell him. She suspected it would end their relationship, and she didn't know what she would do without him in her life.

Late one cool evening they were sitting on large leather cushions in front of a crackling fire with after-dinner drinks in their hands, just enjoying being together. He set his drink aside and glanced over at Jennifer, who had been quiet for a very long time, longer than usual, her mind seemingly miles away. He suspected something bothered her but had no idea what it could be. Her glass was still full, evidently forgotten, and she looked so withdrawn his heart went out to her.

She turned to stare at him a moment, then glanced away, a forlorn look in her eyes. She had no idea what the future held for them once she told him, but she now knew her secret was becoming too tormenting to keep to herself...and it surely wasn't fair to him. She sucked in a ragged breath, silently crying inside for the pain she knew she would soon cause the person who had become her whole world. She had to tell him.

The loneliness and pain he detected in her dark eyes seared his soul, not knowing why she looked so vulnerable. He wanted to pull her into his arms and tell her he would try to make her world all better...if he only knew how. He simply had to find out what was bothering her. He remembered other times during the past few weeks when she appeared tense with a far-away look in her eyes, and he now had to know what was going on with her.

He tried to bring her back into his world. "Thinking about your new job, sweetheart?" he asked softly. "I'm really glad you now don't have to run around the country like you've been doing for several years. Think you can stand spending so much time with me?"

Still staring at the flames flickering in front of her, a haunting loneliness in her dark eyes, she didn't hear his soft voice.

He leaned over and touched her arm.

She jumped as if she'd forgotten he was beside her.

Alarmed by her action, he stared at her. "Didn't you hear what I just said, sweetheart? You seem so far away. What's wrong?"

She rubbed the back of her hand slowly across her forehead and turned her pain-filled dark eyes toward him. "I'm sorry...what did you say, Michael?"

"I asked how the new job is going."

"Oh...I really like it. Lot of work, but it's very interesting. Makes the work day go by mighty fast. I miss seeing Greg, though."

His eyebrows rose. He had long since stopped thinking of Greg as a competitor and had even acted more friendly toward him whenever they were thrown together. He had made up his mind that even though Greg had all the signs of being in love with Jennifer, she had no such feelings for Greg. "So why do you miss

Greg? Doesn't he stop by your new office?"

She sat up straighter. "Didn't I tell you that Greg has been transferred to the New York office? He's called back here a couple of times. Seems he's glad to be in the same city with his brother, and he likes the people he works with." She turned her attention back to the fireplace.

That news was not unwelcome to Michael; he admitted to himself he'd just as soon not have Greg around Jennifer too frequently.

"But you haven't answered my question, baby. For some time now you suddenly seem to go into a shell at times when we're together...as if you're troubled about something." Suddenly he thought of Tawana. "You're still not thinking about Tawana are you?"

She suddenly started twisting a strand of her hair, fighting to control the turbulence she felt inside.

He knew she always resorted to doing that when she was faced with some decision or when she was troubled. A habit he had noticed since their first meeting.

As hard as it was to tell him, she knew she wouldn't have any peace inside until she shared with him what she knew about her biological mother. For the past few weeks she had put off telling him for various reasons, real or imagined, when they were together. In the back of her mind she knew she was afraid he'd take her news negatively, and she just couldn't face the possibility of losing him. So she had postponed the inevitable every time she thought about telling him. But she had now reached the point when she could no longer hold her secret inside.

She drew a long, trembling breath, refusing to look at him, knowing she'd be lost if she did and would again take the easy way out.

"Uh...ah...I have to tell you something, Michael," she finally got out, her voice barely above a whisper, "and...and I don't know quite how to do it except..." Her voice trailed off into barely a whisper.

He sat up straighter, not knowing what to expect. *She is such a complex woman in some ways,* he thought. Aloud, he said, "I'm all ears, sweetheart, as long as it has nothing to do with your falling out of love with me. You do love me, don't you?"

"Oh, Michael, of course I love you. I love you so much it hurts when I think about it." Still she hesitated. She didn't know how to begin telling him about the events surrounding her adoption by the Johnsons and finding her birth mother. She drew in several deep breaths, exhaling slowly. She clasped her hands together tightly in a determined effort to remain calm in spite of the emotions raging inside. The longer she was quiet, the more her apprehension increased.

He waited, now more curious than ever as to what was going on with her. He leaned toward her and put one hand under his chin while leaning on his elbow. He stared at her tense, unreadable face. "This must be serious."

"It is," she replied. "Very serious."

His heart did a flip-flop, afraid he was losing her. What could have possibly happened to put her in such a state?

"Michael, remember the week you were in Los Angeles?"

He nodded, looking at her curiously, wondering what had taken place that particular week. *She didn't mention anything going on when I got back,* he remembered. "Whatever it is, you can tell me, sweetheart. I promise you I'll understand and try to help you any way I can." He looked over at the indecision still on her face. "Trust me, Jennifer."

Sadness permeating her entire body, she looked over at him. *Oh, I hope and pray you do understand,* she said to herself. *I don't know what I'll do if you don't.*

She steeled herself and with a lot of trepidation proceeded to tell him in sometimes halting phrases about her being adopted by the Johnsons when she was very young. "I was not quite two when they found me. They are the only parents I ever knew." She smiled at times when she recounted how happy she had been with her adoptive parents and how they had always provided her with the best they could afford, the best clothes, the best schools, and her choice of college when she decided on an accounting major.

He could sense the depth of her love for her adoptive parents as he listened, noticing some of the tenseness leaving her body.

"Who knows what might have happened to me if they hadn't taken me in?" she speculated.

"Oh...with your character and drive, you probably would have succeeded in doing whatever interested you, no matter what, sweetheart."

He reached over and rubbed her shoulder. "I had no idea they weren't your biological parents...anyone could see how they doted on you while they were out here. In fact, I kinda fell in love with them and hoped they liked me. They're quite a couple. You're lucky they chose to adopt you. Is being adopted what's been worrying you? Remember that saying about it's not where you come from that counts, it's where you're going? Someone must have had you in mind!"

She stared at him. "But...but you made such a big thing about knowing a person's background—or roots—when we first met...and that's been in my mind ever since. How could I tell you about being adopted when you made it crystal clear that a person's background is so important?"

Remembering that conversation, he suddenly felt troubled. Maybe he really had been too adamant about knowing a person's relatives. Maybe his mother had gone to extremes. Seeing now how his words had affected her made him think twice about the reality of judging where a person came from instead of where he now was. Stupid, stupid, stupid! He had to make that up to her some way; he hoped she would believe what he was going to say.

"I know exactly what I said at that time, but now I...I think I was way off base." He took her hand in his and looked deep into her eyes. "All I care about is having you. I don't care a tinker's damn about who your mother was or anything else. Does that make you feel better?"

Exhaling slowly, she nodded. "But that's not all I have to tell you, Michael."

Raising his eyebrows, he asked, "There's more?"

In a low voice, Jennifer managed to continue talking. "The next part is the hardest for me to talk about, so just listen... and I can get through it." She swallowed a couple of times before she blurted out, "I found my biological mother and—"

"What? Your mother's alive? Where is she? What about your real father?"

She reached over for his hand. "This will probably be as difficult for you to hear as it is for me to tell, but I've got to get it off my chest. You at least deserve to know the whole truth about me."

He became slightly alarmed by the sadness clearly evident on her face and the trembling in her hands. His heart went out to her, wishing he could have spared her all the heartbreak she evidently had been through.

She told him about Dave and all of the events surrounding her real mother. "And I have no idea who my real father is—not even whether I have any other relatives.

He could hardly believe his ears as he listened to her recount the ordeal she had been through in a matter of a few days. When she finished speaking, without a word he got up from his pillow and walked to the mantel, leaning one arm on it, his head lowered, an unreadable expression on his face. He stared into the fire.

She knew her world was surely crumbling around her as she watched him. Her thoughts swirled around in her head. *How repulsed he must be knowing I haven't the foggiest idea about my heritage. Have I lost him for good? I can't blame him if he now thinks differently about me.*

Her hands felt like ice in the warm room as she looked at his back, wondering what was going on in his head and wishing with all her heart she could recall her words

She thought a lifetime had passed before he slowly turned, a sadness in his eyes and a frown on his face. Her heart did a flip-flop. She shut her eyes tight when she felt tears forming.

He walked back to sink down on his pillow. Not saying a word, he reached over and pulled her to his chest. He cradled her in his arms, softly rubbing her hair, her face, her shoulders. "My poor, poor baby," he whispered softly over and over as he caressed her tenderly, aware of how difficult it must have been to share her story with him. He held her tightly to his chest for several moments until he felt some of the built-up tension slowly leaving her taut body.

He eased her from his chest and looked down into her still troubled beautiful face. "Why didn't you tell me sooner you were worried about how your news would affect me? Did you think you couldn't trust me with the truth? Don't you know that whatever troubles you also troubles me?" he asked softly. He didn't wait for her to answer. "Recently you've seemed so withdrawn at times when we've been together, and I had no idea why you were acting like that. I wracked my brain, thinking it was something I did...or something I didn't do. Not knowing has really been driving me up a wall." He still ran his soothing hands over her body as he spoke, and she felt her love for him surge through her, from the top of her head to the tip of her toes.

She finally found her voice again, stammering, "I...I didn't know just how you would...would take the news about my being adopted...and then the circumstances of my—"

He raised his hand and put his fingers across her lips. "Sssh, sssh, sweetheart. Don't say another word about any of that. I don't care about you being adopted! I fell in love with the person you now are—being adopted might have been the best thing that could have happened to you. Who knows?" He drew her closer to him, still not letting her speak. "That's all behind you now, but I want you to make me a promise. Will you do that?" He waited until she nodded her head in assent before he continued. "Promise me that whatever problems arise in the future we'll share them together regardless of what they are. Promise, sweetheart?"

She nodded again, her heart too full to speak.

He held her to him, rocking her back and forth, as if he were soothing a small child.

They were silent for several moments.

She finally turned to look up into his eyes. "I'm sorry that I didn't tell you before now, Michael, but I just couldn't bear to share it with you until I talked to my parents when they were here. Then each time I thought about telling you, I didn't want to spoil the magic we have together—I was afraid it would end. I knew from your conversations how much you and your family value where people come from—their roots, so to speak, and I couldn't bear to tell you about mine."

"Sssh, don't say another word about that. We'll start our own roots." He was quiet for a few moments. "By the way, what did your parents say when you told them?"

"I think Mom was more relieved than I that I'd finally gotten an answer about where I came from...and she asked if I'd told you which, of course, I hadn't. But Dad thought that regardless of everything that had happened you'd hang in there and take it in stride. I guess Dad had more confidence in you than I had. He was so certain that everything would all turn out all right between us."

His whole face lighted up. "I knew there was a reason I liked your father."

She couldn't remember when she'd been happier even though she felt the floodgates open behind her eyelids, but she managed to hold back many of the tears as she nestled in Michael's arms.

It was past midnight when they became aware of the time. He looked at his watch. "We'll talk more about this when you've had time to put it all into perspective, that and your nightmares. You evidently blocked out of your mind whatever happened when you were a child, just as though it never occurred. But try not to dwell on any of it, sweetheart, you'll only be hurting yourself."

She could not speak; her emotions were too near the surface. She nodded, letting him know she understood what he was saying.

"I hate like everything to have to leave you tonight, but I'm finishing up a pretty difficult case tomorrow, and I need to finish some notes before I go to court in the morning...so I better get outta here.

They held each other tightly and shared several passionate kisses before he rose to leave. She started to rise, but he pushed her back down. "Don't get up, sweetheart. I'll let myself out."

ॐ ॐ ॐ

Jennifer had just finished a cup of coffee in her office the next morning when Sherry rushed in, a big smile on her face.

Jennifer hurried around her desk to greet her friend. "Glad to see you, girl. I sure have missed you. How was your honeymoon?"

"Just stopped in to tell you we're back. Why don't we have lunch and I'll tell you all about it—at least some of the things that happened," Sherry said with a sly smile.

A few hours later, the two friends hurried to their favorite seafood restaurant, each anxious to catch up on the news of the other. They quickly ordered their lunch and then settled back in their chairs. Sherry regaled Jennifer for several minutes with some of the hilarious things that happened while she and Hal were away.

"Only those things could happen to you, Sherry. You always seem to attract mild disasters."

"That's exactly what Hal said," Sherry informed her, putting another forkful of food into her mouth. "So what's been happening with you, girlfriend?"

Jennifer felt a blush of happiness spreading across her face when she thought about the love and trust she and Michael now shared. "Life couldn't be better. I told Michael all about being adopted and about Dave and Marian and—"

"And he still loves you!"

"Right!"

"See, I knew Michael would feel like that all along. He has more going for him than just being a hunk! You just didn't have enough faith in him...or in yourself, girl-friend." Sherry hoped Jennifer could see that for herself.

Jennifer looked down at her plate. "I guess you've got that right. Maybe I'd just forgotten there really are men in the world like Michael."

"Uh-huh...that and your thinking all black men are alike!" Sherry couldn't resist throwing that in, a sly smile on her face.

"Don't even go there, Sherry. I know darn well what I've said to you in the past, but I've had a change of heart. I think what I've gone through recently has...has made me grow more tolerant of people in general. I've learned a lot in a short time." She studied her hands for a few moments. "I've been thinking that—"

"Oh, that's a bad sign."

Jennifer threw her a dirty look. "Do you want to hear this or not?"

"Guess I'll have to from the way you're looking at me."

"Okay, then just listen and stop interrupting. It's about things that have gradually dawned on me. Maybe I'm finally growing up or—"

"Huh...it's about time." Sherry could not resist zinging her friend. "So what metamorphosis has taken place now?"

"I'm very serious, Sherry. You know all those spats we've had about black men over the years? Well, as much as I hate to admit it to your face, you were right all along. I just needed to meet someone whom I was attracted to and who thought I was pretty special. I know I was being very narrow-minded in lumping all men into categories when I really had met only a few. It's...it's like white folks thinking all African Americans are alike, isn't it?"

She looked at Sherry nodding her head. "At least you're big enough to admit you were being pretty stupid sometimes. I've got to say this and then we'll get off the subject. You don't know how pissed I was every time you got on your soapbox. Now I know there's hope for all of us when *you* admit being wrong!"

Jennifer studied her hands a few moments. "Now all of my thoughts are concerned with pleasing Michael rather than feeling sorry for myself and blaming others for my own shortcomings."

Sherry looked at her friend, glad that Jennifer now seemed to be able to squarely face some of life's problems. She knew Michael probably had a lot to do with Jennifer's "change of heart" as she called it, and she was happy that Michael was in her life.

Love can help people overcome many things, Jennifer thought as she looked over at her friend.

The rest of their lunch hour was spent in Jennifer bringing Sherry up to date about happenings in their offices while Sherry was away, although Sherry had heard some of the gossip during the morning. Most of all, Sherry was happy that everything was going well with her friend, and she hoped that Jennifer and Michael were as happy as she and Hal were. She leaned across the table and told Jennifer what she was thinking. Jennifer smiled,

319

saying she was sure that life was definitely looking up for her and Michael. Finishing their lunch, they walked out of the restaurant and headed back to their offices, arm-in-arm, and still talking.

ঞ ঞ ঞ

Jennifer stuffed her purse into her desk drawer and sank down into her chair. Instead of starting her review of the audit reports in front of her, she leaned back, contemplating her conversation with Sherry and realized she had grown in ways she hadn't mentioned to her friend. Her insecurities about her adoption, which had plagued her for years, now seemed to have disappeared, or at least diminished since Michael had insisted her being adopted didn't mean a hill of beans to him. She now knew her agony of self-doubt had been wasted energy and vowed to always remember the saying that it's not where you come from that counts, it's where you're going. "Nothing could be truer in my case," she said aloud.

Before continuing with her afternoon's work, she thought about a little book she had read about "not sweating the small stuff." In some ways she decided she'd wasted too much energy on the "small stuff" she couldn't do anything about, and vowed that her focus from now on would be on the "real stuff" in her life, like her love for

Michael. If he loved her only half as much as she loved him, she would be happy.

Satisfied she now had her life back on track, she picked up the phone. She had to talk to Michael.

CHAPTER 24

After work Jennifer hurried home and changed into some light tan pants and a silk top the color of tangerines. She put on her sandals, touched up her lips, and quickly ran a comb through her hair. "I'm outta here," she said aloud and headed for the elevator, anxious to get to Michael's apartment.

He was making dinner and she wanted to be in time to help, although he'd insisted he had everything under control when she last talked with him on the phone. He seemed so secretive, he wouldn't even tell her what he was making, other than saying he wasn't going to get it from the deli—which sounded good to her since most of her meals came from a deli when she ate alone. He had also reminded her to wear jeans or something comfortable. *Maybe he's barbecuing,* she thought.

When she reached his place, she found his front door partially open. "It's me, Michael," she called out before closing the door.

"Come on back, sweetheart. You're just in time."

She walked into the kitchen, lifting her eyebrows at the disorder on the kitchen counters and the stove.

"Time for what, Michael?" She hoped he would not ask her to do anything about the mess the kitchen was in.

"Time to stop my wishing you were here to kiss you." He put down a pot holder and grabbed for her, giving her a long, crushing kiss before he steered her to a seat at a table below a window.

"Sit," he ordered. "I have everything under control. Dinner will be ready in two shakes of a lamb's tail."

He pulled out the chair for her, and there was nothing for her to do but sit down. He kissed the top of her head before returning to the stove.

"I can see we're not having grilled cheese sandwiches."

He threw a pot holder toward her. "You'll never let me live that down, will you?"

She smiled when she saw he had set the table with beautiful china and silverware, even had a small floral centerpiece flanked by two candles. *He really has gone all out,* she thought as she surveyed his work.

"The least I can do is light the candles, if you'll give me a match."

Turning around, he looked puzzled. "Oh," he said

before walking to the table and picking up one of the candles. He held it above the gas flame of the stove before going back and lighting the other candle. He noticed the smile on her face. "That's better than having to go into the living room to get one of those fireplace matches, isn't it?"

"Whatever it takes," she threw back at him, inhaling the delicious odors wafting throughout the kitchen. She wondered what he had cooked.

She didn't have long to wonder. He soon took a chicken casserole out of the oven and placed it on the table. Getting two dishes from the cabinet above the sink, he emptied steamed asparagus into one and small red potatoes into the other, two of her favorite vegetables. The crisp tossed salad he took from the refrigerator completed their dinner.

She surveyed the food in front of her. "And I didn't believe you when you said you could cook!"

He smiled slyly. "This is only the beginning."

He had just sat down when he jumped up from the table. She looked at him in alarm, wondering if something was burning on the stove. He hurried to the refrigerator and took out two frosted glasses and a bottle of chilled champagne. "I almost forgot about these," he said as he headed back to the table. "See what you do to me? Sometimes I don't know whether I'm coming or going."

"You seem to be doing very well," she observed while he filled their champagne flutes. She lifted her glass to him. "To the cook," she toasted, reaching over and clinking her glass to his. "I really could get very used to this kind of service!"

She smiled when an embarrassed look flitted across his face.

For the next few minutes all of their attention was on their food. She finally leaned back and dabbed her lips with her napkin. She raised her glass of champagne to him. "That was really good, Michael. Where did you learn to cook like this?"

"My mother made me learn when she was teaching my sisters. She always told them the way to a man's heart was through his stomach, so I decided it could work with women as well."

"You're really something else! I learn more about you every time we're together."

"Good things, I hope," he quipped.

"Very good things!"

Smiling shyly, he asked whether she wanted dessert now or later. She decided to have hers later. "I couldn't possibly eat another thing at the moment."

He reached over for her plate and stacked the other dishes.

"I'll help you with the—"

"The only thing you can do is sit there, have another glass of champagne and look beautiful until I put everything in the dishwasher. Then we'll go into the living room and listen to some romantic music and..." He stopped, a lascivious grin on his face. "So just sit tight until I've finished out here." He started whistling a tuneless melody as he rinsed and stacked the dishes in the dishwasher. In a matter of minutes, he had washed the pots and pans and put them away.

While he worked, she sipped her champagne and watched, a warm glow suffusing her whole body. Never had she felt so loved. The things he did to her were unbelievable.

Completing his chores in nothing flat, he pulled her out of her chair, and they walked hand-in-hand to the living room where logs were slowly burning in the fireplace. He stopped and stirred the fire, replacing the fire screen carefully before turning on his stereo, sending soft, romantic music throughout the room.

Removing two cushions from the leather couch, he placed them in front of the fireplace, lowering himself down onto one and motioning for her to take the other.

As soon as she sat down, he drew her into his arms and planted soft kisses on the top of her head. She melted in his arms and pressed closer to him. He leaned back a ways from her and looked into her eyes for several moments before he spoke. "Do you know I love you madly?" His voice was husky with emotion.

Looking up into his intense eyes, she whispered softly, "I love you, too, Michael."

"You're the only woman I've ever loved...I want you with me all the time, sweetheart."

The air between them was thick with emotion.

She held her breath, afraid to breathe. She bit down on her lower lip to keep it from trembling. What was he saying?

He swallowed a couple of times. How would she respond to what he was about to ask her?

Taking his head between her hands, she whispered, "No one has ever made me feel the way I feel about you."

"Will you marry me?" His heart thudded as if it might burst while he waited for her answer.

She leaned toward him, her lips slightly parted. How could she make him know he was the very air she breathed, the music she loved, the food that gave her sustenance?

"Yes, Michael, yes, I'll marry you."

He pulled her closer to him and kissed her gently, slowly increasing the pressure of his lips on hers until they both were breathless. He released her slowly and reached into his pocket, removing a small box.

Her heart skipped several beats.

He lifted her left hand and slowly slipped a large solitaire diamond ring on her finger. "I've been carrying this around with me just in case I could persuade you to marry me."

She held up her hand and gazed at the ring almost in disbelief. "Oh, Michael, it's lovely!" She felt a lump in her throat and couldn't control the tears behind her eyelids. She felt them running down her cheeks while her heart was breaking with happiness.

His eyes were bright with unshed tears as he reached in his back pocket for a handkerchief to wipe her tears away. It was a moment neither would ever forget.

They looked deep into each other's eyes, silently pledging all of their love, their hearts, their hopes and their dreams.

"I love so much," he said very softly.

She reached out to him and pulled his head down to her shoulder, rubbing the back of his neck and kissing the top of his head. "I feel the same way. You've turned my world upside down and I love it."

All of her pent-up doubts vanished and her repressed hopes rose to the surface when he lifted his head and she saw the love mirrored in his eyes. Every nerve in her body seemed to respond as she clung to him, and another burst of happiness filled her heart. She sat very still, afraid that if she moved she would shatter into a million pieces. A soft moan of need escaped from her throat, and she instinctively pressed her body closer to him. After a few moments, she felt a coolness on her cheek and realized it was her own unbidden tears coursing their way down her face again.

He looked down at her and, smiling, reached in his pocket for his handkerchief. "Will I have to put up with this very often, sweetheart?" he asked playfully as he dabbed at her tears. "If so, I'll need a new supply of handkerchiefs...or more boxes of tissues."

He held her to his chest and drew in his breath sharply as sensation after sensation raced through the lower part of his body. He held her tightly, as if he never wanted to let her go. At that moment he would have willingly drained San Francisco Bay with a cup if she asked.

Their bodies were so perfectly attuned that they both felt they were drowning in their own emotions.

His blood pressure rose and his breath caught in his throat.

Her heart soared and her eyes blazed with adoration.

He cradled her in his lap, rocking her from side to side.

She sighed happily and snuggled closer to him.

Looking down at her, Michael spoke very gently. "Just imagine having each other forever."

"I know, Michael, I know. I only hope we'll always be this happy."

They held each other tightly, not speaking for several moments. There was no need for words.

Suddenly she leaned away from him and again looked down at the ring sparkling on her finger. "You were pretty sure of yourself, weren't you, Michael?"

He shrugged. "I just couldn't imagine your saying no to such a hunk of a man—at least that's what Sherry told you I was!"

She punched him in the chest. "When did she tell you that? And I suppose you believed her!"

Smiling, he rose and pulled her to her feet. Hand-in-hand, they headed for her bedroom. They would be together the rest of their lives just as surely as the sun rises on the horizon each morning. They were in no hurry.

CHAPTER 25

A few weeks later, Jennifer slowly drifted awake and stretched languidly as she sat up on the side of her bed. Realizing that she had slept there for the last time, she looked around her all-too-familiar bedroom.

Today was her wedding day, and a deep thrill surged through her body as she thought of Michael and twisted the large diamond ring that sparkled on the finger of her left hand. Tonight she would truly belong to Michael! She rose and padded over to her window, noticing the light fog that still lingered over the city, the kind that the sun would burn off by noon.

Sighing, she turned away from the window and walked over to open her closet door to reassure herself that she hadn't forgotten anything. Everything was in order—her long, filmy white wedding gown, veil, white satin shoes at one end of her closet and her going-away clothes all together at the other end, ready to be packed as soon as their wedding reception ended.

She stood for a few moments, deep in reverie, wishing her birth mother could have shared this day with her. How proud she probably would have been knowing her daughter had made such a perfect choice. Maybe...maybe she was looking down on her now. Anything's possible, she concluded. A light tap on her door interrupted her thoughts, and she wiped moisture from her eyes.

"Are you up, baby?" Mrs. Johnson called through the door. "We've got so much to do this morning, and I don't want you to feel rushed at the last minute. The coffee is ready."

Jennifer smiled. She was sure her mother had more than coffee ready.

For the past couple of days Mrs. Johnson had literally taken over her daughter's apartment, informing her and others what they should be doing and sometimes showing them how to do it.

"I'll be there in just a few minutes, Mom." Taking a deep breath, she vowed that she would not become flustered by all the preparations that would go on for the next few hours and calmly walked into the bathroom to get started on her day.

ॐ ॐ ॐ

As Jennifer had predicted, the day turned out to be a near perfect one for their wedding. By mid-afternoon a light breeze, warmed by the soft brilliance of the sun, circulated around San Francisco Bay.

Sunlight filtered through the chapel's stained-glass windows, filling the interior with warm, colored light as ushers led guests to pews decked with multi-colored flowers and wide white satin ribbons.

Soft organ music echoed throughout the small chapel. Finally the ushers, handsome in their tuxedos and rosebud boutonnieres, escorted the bride's and groom's families to their seats. A discreet buzzing circulated among the guests as they greeted each other while waiting for the wedding ceremony to begin.

Soon the ushers stood at attention and a sudden hush fell over the guests when the minister, groom, and best man entered from a side door and stood in front of the flower-decked altar. Michael clasped his hands tightly behind his back, finally believing that in only a short time Jennifer would be totally his.

The relative tranquillity Jennifer thought she had during all the preparations for her treasured day suddenly vanished as she stood at the back of the chapel, a vision of loveliness, her hand on her father's arm. She heard the last strains of the soloist's number, and finally the swell of the organ as the sounds of the wedding march filled the chapel.

She drew in her breath sharply and her heart suddenly seemed too full when she saw Michael waiting at the end of the white carpeted aisle. Even from that distance, she saw the intensity of his look as their eyes met.

Michael caught his breath and swallowed a lump in his throat when he had his first glimpse of Jennifer standing in the doorway, slim and exquisite, seeming to float in a gown of yards and yards of white silk organza with small seed pearls sewn in the yoke and hem, and a small pearl-seeded coronet covering the top of her head, a full veil cascading from it. As he gazed at her behind the thin veil, he seemed to suddenly need more air in his lungs and his heart began thudding.. He felt he had waited a lifetime to claim his true love.

Her father felt her trembling hand on his arm and he reached across to put his hand over hers, whispering, "Smile, baby, your world is waiting for you."

His words were all the encouragement Jennifer needed. Smiling up at her father, she lifted her head high and started down the aisle on his arm to join Michael, his steady gaze drawing her toward him. Oblivious to the guests, she had eyes only for the tall, dark, handsome man standing before the altar as she floated slowly toward him, and in a never-to-be-forgotten moment, Michael stepped forward to claim her.

It was a simple but beautiful ceremony, and both of their hearts were filled with a sereneness and peacefulness neither could have foretold. They were oblivious to everything and everyone around them. They existed only for each other. The moment was truly theirs alone, and they both started as they heard the minister's voice begin the time-honored words: "Dearly Beloved, we are gathered here in the sight of God, and in the face of this company, to join this man and woman in Holy Matrimony, which is an honorable state, instituted of God in the time of man's innocence... Into this holy estate these two persons present come now to be joined..."

Her heart was full to overflowing as she glanced sideways at Michael, who looked so serene standing beside her, and she thanked her lucky stars for the choice she had made.

The minister guided them through their responses, and the ceremony was almost over before either was aware of the presence of others gathered in the chapel. They squeezed hands when the minister intoned, "I now pronounce you man and wife."

Michael heard the words, "You may kiss the bride," and he carefully lifted her veil as if he couldn't believe she was truly under it. He touched her lips very gently, almost as if he were laying his heart bare for her to see.

She felt a sentimental rush of tears behind her lids and squeezed her eyes tightly, afraid they would escape. Each silently pledged to the other all the love and passion that the sacrament of marriage offered them.

A short time later she literally floated among the

guests gathered in the large yard behind the chapel. A band and a dance floor, a marquee, beautifully decorated tables, and chairs occupied most of the space and the hundred or so guests marveled as the couple, who seemed so suited for each other, circulated among them on their way to the long table under the marquee.

For her, the delicious catered banquet was wasted—she hardly tasted the food in front of her and soon became a little light-headed from the champagne toasts that seemed to go on forever.

They toasted each other with their champagne glasses entwined before they cut the four-tiered wedding cake. Later, they heard the bridal waltz begin and he led her to the wooden dance floor. She melted into his arms as they floated around the floor, thigh to thigh, waves of pure sensation engulfing them, both wanting the day to soon end.

Their privacy was soon invaded by others wishing to dance with the bride, and it was some time later before Michael caught up with her again.

Drawing her close, he whispered, "How soon can we sneak out of here, sweetheart?"

"Give me ten minutes and I'll meet you in front of the chapel," she said softly, a lilt in her voice and stars in her eyes.

They finally eluded their guests and raced toward his car. Settling her and the voluminous wedding dress in the front seat, he walked around to the driver's side and climbed in. Gathering her close, he spoke softly. "Remind me to tell you how much I love you if I should ever forget to mention it."

No answer was necessary.

She leaned back into her seat and sighed happily before peeking around into his sparkling coal-black eyes.

"Why are you looking at me like that, sweetheart? What's going on in your devious mind?" he asked.

She reached across to clasp his hand on the steering wheel. "Let's go start our roots!" she suggested softly.

EPILOGUE

Jennifer squirmed uncomfortably in the lounge chair, shifting her body to another position. Unsuccessful at finding any relief, she heaved a deep sigh, hoping the next day or so would pass quickly as their baby was due. Slowly rubbing her swollen stomach, she knew her discomfort was worth every pain she might have. She was starting her own roots!

Tossing her novel onto the grass, she gazed out at the fog slowly descending on San Francisco Bay. The cool breeze swirling around her did little to lessen the heat inside her, and she picked up a newspaper to fan her perspiring forehead for a few minutes, hoping to get some relief.

Her mind wandered to the past couple of years and how her love for Michael had only increased as the days passed. During the last month of her pregnancy, she waited each evening for the sight of Michael's car turning into the driveway. Usually she met him at the car before he opened his door, but the weight of the baby seemed doubly heavy this evening, and she decided to remain where she was when she saw him drive up. He waved to her and parked the car, reaching back for his briefcase before closing and locking the door.

Her heart started its usual fluttering when she saw him, and she struggled to sit up a bit straighter in her chair to receive his kiss. Even after more than two years, their love for each other seemed as new as when they had repeated their marriage vows.

"Hi, sweetheart," he greeted her as he took as much of her in his arms as he could. He gazed lovingly into her eyes, thinking he could not remember what life had been like without her. He held her close to him and vowed again that he would spend the rest of his life holding her, kissing her, making love to her. "You look a little bushed this evening, sweetheart. Junior been giving you a hard time today?"

She pulled him closer to her. "You're mighty sure of yourself to insist on calling our baby junior. It could be a girl you know."

"You wouldn't dare have a girl before we have a boy! Isn't that the way we planned having a family? After that, I don't care what the rest are."

"What do you mean 'the rest'?"

Love Doesn't Come Easy

Eyebrows raised, he smiled at her. "Well, I was thinking that a half dozen would be nice."

"At the moment I feel like we may never even have the second one!" Playfully, she pulled on one of his ears.

He slowly pulled her up from the chair. "If you gain any more weight, I'm going to have to get a wheelbarrow to move you around."

She punched him in the chest once she was on her feet, and hand-in-hand they entered their dream house, as they called it. They still marveled at the way they both had agreed on that particular house during their house-hunting days. They entered the spacious living room which had been furnished with a combination of their apartment furniture, with the addition of a few other pieces they selected together.

He led her to the long sofa sitting beneath a wide expanse of glass that was shaded by a huge sprawling tree near the window. He fluffed up the pillows before helping her slowly lower her swollen body to one end.. Reaching behind her, he placed a pillow near her shoulders and pushed her back gently.

She sighed in happy relief, not only for the comfort he provided but also for his just being near her. He was the other part of her soul.

"Now don't move until I return. I'm the cook tonight."

"But, Michael," she protested, "I already have a casserole in the oven, and the salad is in the refrigerator."

340

Turning around, he winked at her. "That's what I was counting on, sweetheart. I haven't the slightest idea what I would have cooked otherwise."

"Certainly not another grilled cheese sandwich, I hope!" she called after him. "You've made enough of those recently to last us a lifetime."

In a matter of minutes he entered the living room with a tray in each hand. He pulled the glass-topped coffee table nearer and sat down beside her. Noticing she wasn't eating, he became disturbed when he saw the way she was looking at her food, a slight frown on her face.

Feeling a sharp pain, she tried unsuccessfully to shift her body to a more comfortable position.

Having no clue how to help her, he watched, feeling very useless. "Anything wrong?" He hoped his deep concern for her did not come through in his voice.

Before she could answer, she felt another sharp pain in the small of her back. Similar pains had occurred earlier in the day, but she had dismissed them, thinking she had been on her feet too long preparing their dinner. She pressed her hands on her stomach when she felt their baby move. She again shifted her body restlessly and pushed her food away.

They were so in tune with each other's wants, needs and desires that many times no communication was necessary. They could almost feel each other's pain. Marriage had revealed a passion in her which she had not been aware of—a deep primitive feeling which seemed to grow stronger each day. And she knew the love and passion they shared could only grow stronger when their baby arrived. Her thoughts were suddenly cut off by an all-consuming pain she had never experienced. She held her breath, hoping her discomfort would soon pass. It didn't.

Watching her intently, he was now certain something serious was happening and he pushed his tray aside. Taking her hand, he stroked it gently, hoping to give her some relief, his own heart beating like a small drum while he wondered what else he could do. "Maybe you should lie down for a few minutes, sweetheart. You look a little peaked."

Before she could answer, he swung her feet upon the sofa and placed a pillow beneath her head. Suddenly feeling short of breath, she gasped when another pain shot through her and she reached up to him, a pleading look on her face as if he could make the pain go away.

ॐ ॐ ॐ

Several hours later Michael glanced at his watch. It was well past midnight, but he felt he had been in the waiting room of the hospital for days. Walking to the window, he stared out, oblivious to the wailing sirens as ambulances entered the emergency entrance of the hospital. His stomach revolted when he thought of making another trip to the coffee machine.

After an eternity—or so it seemed—Michael felt an arm on his shoulder. He turned in alarm.

"Relax, Mr. Maxwell," the doctor ordered softly. "Everything went well. Congratulations, you have an eight-pound boy, and your wife is fine. She's a little groggy at the moment, but you can see them both in a few minutes."

Michael's knees suddenly felt as if they were filled with Jell-O, and he sank down into the nearest chair, heaving a sigh of relief that his waiting was at an end and Jennifer was no longer in pain, something he couldn't share with her.

He whispered a silent prayer of thanks for the past and hope for the future for the three of them as he thought of the love he and Jennifer shared. And now another phase of their lives was just beginning. Jennifer had started her roots.

Other Indigo Sensuous Love Stories
By
Charlyne Dickerson

The Missing Link
ISBN 1-58571-037-7

The moment she opens her front door electricity sparks between the divorcees, stunning them both. Shanna is speechless, expecting a woman. Against her better judgment, she shows Craig the studio for rent above her garage.

Craig's masculinity makes her senses spin and her body ache. Every time their eyes meet, her heart turns over in response. Intuitively, she knows her life will never be the same.

While they both try to deny the magnetism drawing them together, Craig's ex-wife arrives on the scene, using whatever means necessary, including her body and their son, to try to reclaim what once was hers.

One night Shanna is awakened by a noise and goes to her window to peer outside. What she sees sends waves of insecurity and doubt through her.

Will Shanna take what she sees as a sign, and cut her loses? Or fight fire with fire?